I0835772

ALSO BY NICOLE MCINNES

100 Days

Brianna on the Brink

The Jilliad

A NOVEL

Nicole McInnes

ALTITUDE PRESS

The Jilliad is a work of fiction. Other than well-known locations, people, and events featured in the narrative, all names, locations, events, and characters are used fictitiously and/or are products of the author's imagination. Any resemblance to persons living or dead, or to actual events or locations, is entirely coincidental.

Copyright © 2021 by Nicole McInnes
All Rights Reserved.

Published in the United States by Altitude Press.

ISBN: 978-1-957027-01-2
Library of Congress Control Number: 2021921897

No part of this publication may be reproduced, distributed, or transmitted in any form or by any means, including photocopying, recording, or other electronic or mechanical methods, or by any information storage and retrieval system without the prior written permission of the publisher, except in the case of very brief quotations embodied in critical reviews and certain other noncommercial uses permitted by copyright law.

Any moment might be our last. Everything is more beautiful because we're doomed. You will never be lovelier than you are now. We will never be here again.

~Homer

Take it Easy.

~Eagles

Book 1: 2009

Everything flows and nothing abides, everything gives way and nothing stays fixed.
~Heraclitus

It's the talons that stop Jillian Kensington in her tracks. Those bronze claws, splayed open at jugular level and sharpened to gleamingly lifelike points, leave her in a momentary, chilled trance—as if she's a mouse, or a rabbit, or some doomed housecat just going about its business when it's snatched and lifted without warning. Torn asunder in midair.

I need to calm down, Jillian thinks. The bright blue feathers of the duster she's holding sweep across the two words engraved at the base of the statue: *AETOS DIOS*. She's a little discombobulated at the sight of them, dizzied by how old memories have started rushing up seemingly out of nowhere lately.

"It means Eagle of Zeus." That's what Lawrence had said nearly twenty years ago as she stood in this exact spot staring up at the statue. He'd come up behind her without warning, startling her into an immediate blush—Dr. Kensington, she called him back then, her larger-than-life Intro to Mythology professor. Until that moment, Jillian, an overwhelmed college freshman, had mostly only seen him from afar as he'd stood at the front of the 500-seat lecture hall. And yet, there he was—or rather, *here* he was—standing so suddenly close that she could feel his breath on the nape of her neck simultaneously warming and chilling the skin there.

A flash of lightning followed by an ear-splitting crack jolts her from the memory. Jillian startles, nearly drops the feather duster. Then, chuckling at herself, she shakes her head. She's doing it again, daydreaming as she tidies up. It's become a regular enough thing that she's made up a word for it: *Dreamcleaning*. Moving to a narrow table to dust knick-knacks there, she gazes through the window by the front door. Thunder on the charcoal horizon is rumbling in a regular rhythm now, like childbirth contractions. In fact, it's not at all unlike late pregnancy, this feeling of expectation in the air just before the monsoon rolls in and breaks the long, dry spell of midsummer.

Jillian beholds her reflection in the mirror above the knick-knack table. Touching her cheekbone near the corner of one eye, where the crow's feet are most pronounced, she frowns. This only emphasizes the vertical lines between her eyebrows (*The Dreaded Elevens,* her aesthetician called them in a voice full of foreboding when Jillian recently went in for a Botox consult. *You're forty next year? Yeah, it's time.*). She raises the brows in exaggerated surprise, accentuating the lines running horizontally across her forehead. She hasn't quite decided on the Botox yet, but she'll at least get the caramel-colored highlights in her hair redone in a few days. Maybe she'll even have it cut into a bob. That would definitely help perk things up a bit.

A bright red Volkswagen Beetle pulls into view outside and stops near the towering Saguaro cactus at the end of the driveway. Jillian watches as the passenger side door opens and her son's long, lanky frame unfurls. Evan's girlfriend emerges from the driver's side, and the two of them meet in front of the car where they join hands and stare mournfully into each other's eyes. She's so pretty, this girl, but there's been so much drama between the two of them. It started when she—Tabitha's her name—accepted a full-ride scholarship to a small liberal arts college back East. Evan, meanwhile, had already committed to the state university down in Tucson, where they'd both originally planned to go. Cue the dramatic, late night phone calls and hours of sitting in cars hashing things out—the near break-ups and tearful reunions.

The two of them draw closer together until they're kissing in the shade of the saguaro, practically throwing off sparks. Evan holds Tabitha against his body and then lifts her into the air. The lines of their shared visage are such a perfect combination of youth, and beauty, and loss—so perfectly...procreative...that Jillian has to look away. She remembers it more clearly than she'd like to, that furious bloom of first love, the vivid reds and oranges of it.

A blinding flash of lightning rips through the dark backdrop of clouds, throwing the saguaro and the couple into sharp silhouette. Another crack of thunder follows, and Jillian flinches back from the window. She thinks of Evan at four or five years old, playing with his trucks on the flagstone patio out back. Seeing the warning flashes of lightning only a few miles away, she'd opened the sliding glass door and told him it was time to come in.

"Not afraid," he'd announced, glancing up at the sky.

Jillian's throat tightens at the memory. This is how the past comes at her lately: It lies in wait and bides its time, ambushing her when she least expects it. Another thunderclap booms, this one shaking the window and ushering in a sudden downpour of hail that sounds like bullets against the roof tiles overhead. At the end of the driveway, ice chunks pelt the young lovers, forcing them apart.

You're going to be fine, Jillian thinks at them impatiently. *Twenty years from now, you'll look back and realize this was all for the best.* She grips the feather duster more tightly as Tabitha dashes back into the safety of the Beetle. Meanwhile, Evan just stands there, solemn and drenched, a perfect human lightning rod. He knows better than to stay in the open like this during an electrical storm. "Get inside," Jillian pleads through clenched teeth.

Moments later, he jogs toward the house. Shaking hail from his hair, he stands with Jillian just inside the entry hall, watching the Beetle pull away. There's a staccato double-honk of the horn, one beep for each syllable: *Good-bye.*

Jillian reaches up and places a hand on his shoulder. "You're going to miss her," she says.

Evan rolls his eyes. "You *think*?"

Jillian removes the hand. She's almost gotten used to this new edge of his. Almost.

As if reading her mind, Evan leans down to give her an actual hug. It's a quick one, but it helps. "Sorry, Mom," he says. "It's just..." He looks back at the empty street and rakes his fingers through his hair.

"It feels impossible," she says. "I know. But it's all going to be okay."

The next morning, she's up with the sun to make breakfast—pancakes, eggs, and bacon—before he hits the road. It will be their last meal as a family until he comes home for a visit at some point. Jillian has been trying, unsuccessfully, to not think of it as the Last Supper.

"Mom," Evan says, wandering into the kitchen still groggy from sleep and wearing his pajama pants, "you don't have to go to all this trouble just for me."

She takes a deep breath, forces a smile. "Oh, you think this is for you?" Turning her head, she wipes at the corner of one eye with the back of her wrist. "Well, I've got news for you, my friend. This is a celebratory dinner for me and Dad. We can't *wait* to get you out of the house." Her voice cracks a bit, giving her away.

Evan stretches and yawns. "You're all talk, Kensington."

And then Lawrence is there, standing just inside the kitchen, dressed for the day, his silver-streaked hair newly cut and styled. Even after all these years, his presence occasionally takes Jillian's breath away. She's seen coeds at the university where he teaches still trying catch his eye despite the fact that he's in his mid-fifties.

Lawrence has an extra glow about him lately, no doubt from all the pent-up emotion surrounding this big family change. And though Evan, with his broad athletic build, stands a full three inches taller than his father, Jillian can't help but marvel at their similarities—the generous mouths, strong jaws, and piercing eyes (not unlike the eyes of the Eagle of Zeus, though Evan's have none of that cruel edge). She blinks back tears once again at the sight of her handsome men.

And then, after breakfast, the three of them stand next to Evan's Honda as it idles in the driveway, a tiny ship waiting to bear him away to semi-distant lands.

"You're sure you don't want some company for the drive?" Lawrence asks, his tone only half-joking. "I imagine your mother would be more than thrilled to ride along."

"It's true," Jillian confirms. She hugs herself close, as if it's winter in the mountains where she grew up, two hours north of here, and not already over 100 degrees in their Phoenix suburb. "I could take a shuttle back."

But Evan just shakes his head; they've already been over this. He decided last month that he'd rather say his goodbyes here in Scottsdale.

Jillian tries hard to hold herself together in the silence that suddenly descends. Wasn't it just last week that Evan was a toddler and she'd taken him to story time at the local library? Led by one of the youth services librarians, they'd recited *Five Little Monkeys* with all the other parents and toddlers, everyone holding their arms straight out in front of them like pretend jaws. *Along comes Mister Alligator,* they said in unison. *Quiet as can be. And…snap!* (a dozen sets of arm-jaws clapped closed). *Four little monkeys swinging in a tree…*

She watches as Lawrence and Evan give each other a rushed, back-slapping hug. Then it's her turn. Her arms lift away from her sides without her permission, as if they belong to someone else, as if her limbs are controlled by some unseen operator in a remote tower. She feels anesthetized, like she's received multiple Novocain injections that are only just now kicking in. Or perhaps they're more like helium injections; she's quite certain she could levitate off the concrete with very little effort. Float right down the road.

"Love you, Mom," Evan says.

Jillian has a sudden, wild urge to scoop him up in the classic football hold she used for carrying him when he was an infant. Eighteen years has not been enough time. How could she only now, at the last minute, realize this? She's nowhere near ready to let go. "I love you, too, Evan." She watches him open the driver's side door and get in. Then he's waving at them through the glass before pulling away from the curb. Jillian and Lawrence stand there in the glaring sunshine, waving back until the Honda is out of sight.

This was the job you chose, she reminds herself as they turn toward the house. This job of raising a child to leave you was your choice. And now it's done.

Once they're back inside, Lawrence heads straight to his office and closes the door.

No doubt he's processing the grief in his own way, Jillian thinks, *as men do*. She bites the inside of her lower lip, folds her arms across her chest in another self-hug, and stares out the window by the front door at the spot where the Honda idled only a minute ago. In her head, she's back in the hospital giving birth. And then she's on a mountain trail up north, with autumn leaves falling all around, as Evan takes his first steps. She's putting his third birthday hat on his head as everyone gets ready to sing, and then he's winning the seventh-grade spelling bee, leaving for summer camp, getting his driver's permit, going to his first prom, standing on the high school lawn at graduation.

She looks around to see if Lawrence has emerged from his office to come join her at the window, if he's feeling what she's feeling, the sudden, brutal inevitability of it all. But the Eagle of Zeus statue is the only other watcher in the room; it glares down at her with the usual contempt. Ignoring it as best she can, Jillian once again stares dully out the window and understands her new reality for the first time: The preparation for the empty nest is over, and just like that, it's down to husband and wife.

Two little monkeys swinging in a tree.

Book 2: 1983

I'm hunched at the kitchen table the morning after my first junior high dance, bored, playing the wires of Mom's stainless steel egg slicer like a tiny harp, when she comes rushing in all dressed for work, even though it's Saturday. She's just been promoted at the local radio station. Apparently, being promoted means you get to work during the week *and* on weekends. But whatever.

"Oh, Jill," Mom says with the same nervous laugh she uses more and more lately. "I didn't expect to see you this morning. What are you doing up so early?"

I shrug.

Her burgundy attaché case hangs from the crook of one arm as she stands next to the Mr. Coffee fastening a cubic zirconium stud through an earlobe. She smells like Jovan Musk and Cashmere Bouquet, and she's perfect, as always. Next to her, I always feel like a total Frumpelstiltskin. When she's done with the earring, she lifts the glass coffee decanter and pours herself a "cup of ambition," as she calls it. "How was the dance?" she asks me.

"It was so-so." I'm pretty sure she's not actually interested in the details. I don't tell her about how I kept waiting for

Doug Clark to ask me to dance, but he didn't at first, even though I caught him glancing in my direction more than once during the slow songs. So, I danced with my best friend Hadley Wallace instead. At one point, Veronica Delgado and the boy she was dancing with swayed into my field of vision. "Lezzies," Veronica sneered at us, ruining a perfectly good Air Supply ballad and making me feel suddenly a little less bad that people call her "V.D." behind her back.

"Bag your face," I shot back, but Hadley just laughed it off, swooping me away to the other side of the gym in a flourish of exaggerated tango steps.

Not too long after that, the DJ played "Waiting for a Girl Like You." I knew the dance was almost over, so I screwed my courage to the sticking place (we're reading *Macbeth* in English), smoothed down the front of my Laura Ashley dress (it made me feel like Laura Ingalls Wilder but foxier), and strode purposefully over to where Doug was leaning against a wall of the gym with his friends. "You wanna—" I started to say.

"Yeah," he said, cutting me off. Good grief, that crooked smile! My knees went all wobbly as we walked out to the dance floor.

Eighth grade has brought with it segregated sex ed. The boys learn about wet dreams and voice changes (from what I've overheard in the hallways) while the girls learn about our periods and how we can pretty much get pregnant by even thinking about having sex. Basically, we're ticking time bombs from the waist down. That's not exactly what our teacher, Ms. Deveaux, tells us, of course, but it's what anyone paying even half-attention figures out pretty quick.

"You all are now at the age when girls in some countries start getting married and having babies," she announced last week, peering around the dead-quiet classroom. Apparently, our eggs are like little Venus fly traps just lying in wait, all closed up and innocent looking until *BAM!* A spermatozoon flagellates a little too close, and that's all she wrote. Next thing you know, you're eating for two. Freaks me out, to be honest. Just this past week, we learned the word for the flank pain that sometimes happens when an ovary spits out an egg: *Mittelschmerz*. Now Hadley and I use it as a secret code word for just about anything interesting or unexpected. Get an extra-large helping of fries in the cafeteria on Hamburger Day? *Mittelschmerz!* Have a sub in PE who lets you do whatever you want? *Mittelschmerz!*

While I danced with Doug under the disco balls and paper streamers hanging from the gym ceiling, Hadley danced with Tony Swift, who kept trying to make out with her. She's about half a foot taller than he is, though, so it wasn't hard for her to avoid his lips. Doug wasn't trying anything like that with me, but when the guy from Foreigner sang about holding his girl tenderly and knowing that it's right deep in the night—I could feel Doug's hands suddenly sweaty on my back. That, and something hard momentarily pressed against my belly until he hunched his body away from mine for the rest of the song. When I looked up at him, he had this embarrassed smile on his face, and he was blushing. I didn't actually figure out what happened until later, when Hadley and I stood outside under the gym parking lot lights waiting for her dad to pick us up.

"Man," Hadley said, rubbing her lower abdomen. "Tony was all hands and lips. Plus, he was sporting some serious dance floor wood."

"Oh my gosh, is that what it was?"

She grinned at me. "Douggie, too?"

"I thought it was his belt buckle or something."

So, yeah. I'm definitely not sharing the details of my first boner encounter with Mom now that it's the next morning and she's practically on her way out the door. Not that she'd probably care that much, anyway; she's way too busy with all her work stuff at the radio station to care about the details of my life. But still.

"I don't think your dad's awake yet," Mom says, taking one last sip of coffee. "Tell him—"

"Tell me what?" Dad asks, suddenly standing there in the kitchen with us. He's in his terrycloth bathrobe, holding the folded Saturday funnies in one hand.

The way Mom jumps at the sound of his voice is so dramatic that she actually drops the mug she's been holding. It slips from her hand and shatters into a few big chunks and a bunch of tiny pieces, splashing coffee across the linoleum tiles. "Dammit," she mutters.

For a long moment, the three of us just stand there, staring down at the ceramic shards, which are strewn like the ruins of some ancient miniature city on our kitchen floor.

"I'll clean it up," I say, but nobody answers.

"Another working Saturday, I see." Dad's voice is flat as a pancake, and his eyes are locked on Mom as she turns from him.

"That's what I wanted Jill to tell you."

Leave me out of it, I think as I grab the whisk broom and dustpan from under the sink. I would rather be just about anywhere but here in this kitchen while my parents do this weird who-likes-the-other-person-less thing they've been doing lately. I'm pretty sure it all started with that one fight they had a few weeks ago. I obviously wasn't supposed to hear it since it was late at night and they were trying to keep their voices down. I did hear it though—some of it, at least: Mom said she was having a hard time because she never got to experience being free in her twenties after she and Dad got married so young. Then Dad asked her what he was supposed to do about that. She said she didn't know, but that something had to change. After that, their voices were muffled, but I definitely heard someone crying before I fell asleep—that and at least one of their closet doors being closed harder than it needed to be.

When I was little, I never got the sense of something being seriously wrong between my parents. As an only child, I saw them as my whole world. To me, they were gods. Even if they did occasionally start to argue back then, all I'd have to do was bring them something I'd made, like the octagonal bottom of an old, wooden planter that I repurposed when I was six. I cleaned off the octagon before painting it with some green poster paint I found in the school supplies drawer. Then I glued on baby pinecones and pictures of flowers I'd cut from an old magazine. When the weird collage—or multimedia piece, or whatever you'd call it—was done, my parents *ooh*-ed and *ahh*-ed like I'd presented a stolen treasure from the Louvre. Praising my crazy art projects was something they could agree on back then. Sometimes I envy little kid Me.

After Mom leaves for work, I look down at the coffee-soaked mess I've swept into the dustpan. It seems like a waste to just throw away those pretty fragments, so I drop them into a colander and rinse them off. If Dad notices that I'm being weird, he doesn't say anything. Instead, he shuffles back down the hall to the guest room where he's been sleeping for the past few months. When the fragments are dry, I transfer them to a small cardboard box and store them on a high shelf in my closet.

A few hours later, I make lunch for Dad. I also make sure his work clothes are washed and ironed for Monday morning. I like doing that kind of domestic stuff (which is probably a good thing, since Mom seems to be completely missing the June Cleaver gene lately).

Later that afternoon, I walk seven houses down the street to Hadley's, where her older brother, Chuck, is giving her a noogie in the dinette. "You want one, too, Jacobs?" he asks me as Hadley tries to punch him.

"Hell, no," I say.

Hadley laughs as she swings her arms wildly toward Chuck's midsection. He's holding her at bay with one hand planted firmly on her forehead now, the arm stuck straight out. When they finally knock it off, we grab a couple of ice-cold Tabs from the fridge, head to her room, and flop down onto the bed.

Hadley and I have been friends since forever. She's the one person on the planet who always seems to know what's going on in my life without me having to say a single word. It's annoying sometimes, like when I don't quite know what's going on myself, or when I *do* know what's going on but I'm not ready to talk about it yet. Her room sometimes feels more familiar than my own. This is where we argued over who got to be Princess Leia after we saw the premiere of *Star Wars* at the little Flagstaff theater, just like we always argued over who had to be Nellie Olsen when we played *Little House on the Prairie*. It's where we dressed up as Solid Gold Dancers and choreographed routines to Amii Stewart and Gloria Gaynor songs. We'd whip out those same moves at the local roller rink, twirling around as our gold lamé skate covers sparkled under the strobe lights and feather-haired girls skated around the slanted wooden floor with guys who wore their shirts unbuttoned halfway down their chests.

"*Ice Castles* is on TV tomorrow after school," Hadley says as we lie on our backs, staring up at her ceiling. She has an entire collection of Tiger Beat posters taped up there: Jodie Foster, Duran Duran, Justine Bateman, The Go-Go's.

"That movie's so corny," I scoff. "You really gonna watch it?"

"You know I wouldn't miss Robby Benson."

"Really? He kind of looks like a girl."

Hadley considers this for a second and then shrugs. "Maybe."

"I think my parents might be splitting up soon," I blurt out in response.

My best friend doesn't miss a beat. "They'll figure it out," she says. "They've been together forever, right?"

"Yeah, since, like, high school."

"And even if they do split up—which they won't—it'll still be okay. You're going to be fine."

"But what if they sell the house, and I have to *move* or something?" I'm chewing at the corner of a fingernail now, wishing I had her confidence.

"Try not to think about it," Hadley says. She rolls onto her side so she's facing me. Then she reaches up and takes my hand away from my mouth. "Seriously, Jill. Think about Monday instead."

I look at her and smile. Monday's when we're going on our class field trip to Lowell Observatory.

"You and Douggie under the old telescope, K-I-S-S-I-N-G," Hadley teases. "And don't even get me started on the bus ride there and back."

"Shush," I say, blushing. "It'll never happen. And stop calling him *Douggie.*"

But Hadley must be psychic or something. Monday afternoon, all the eighth graders gather around an observatory guide who tells us about Clyde Tombaugh and the discovery of Pluto right here in our little podunk town. Doug Clark stands next to me on the outskirts of the group. Without warning, he laces his fingers gently through mine. It only lasts a few seconds because Derek Velasquez sees what's going on and goes "*Ooooo*" loud enough for our science teacher, Mr. Russ, to look over. But then, as we're boarding the bus, Hadley says to Doug, "Wanna trade seats?" and he goes, "Sure," and so we sit together on the ten-minute drive back to school.

I haven't been sleeping all that well lately, mainly because I'm worried about my parents. After Mom got back from the radio station Saturday night, they hardly said two words to each other for the rest of the weekend. So, I'm kind of out of it. But when nobody else on the bus is paying attention to us, Doug taps me on the shoulder.

"Can I kiss you?" he whispers, and when I nod, he does. For the few blissed-out seconds that our lips are mooshed together, I don't worry about Mom or Dad. In fact, the possibility that my family might soon be as broken as Mom's coffee mug lying shattered on the kitchen floor two days ago is the farthest thing from my mind.

Book 3: 2009

...burst like a star: for here there is no place
that does not see you. You must change your life.
~Rainer Maria Rilke, *Archaic Torso of Apollo*

She's fine now, really.

It's been a week and a half since Evan left for college, and Jillian's actually amazed at how well she's held it together. Things should get even easier once schools open after Labor Day and she can get back to her job as a roving substitute aide for the district. In the meantime, busying herself with the house helps—rearranging the living room furniture, moving her fall wardrobe to the front of the closet, and scrubbing the kitchen and bathroom sinks. She's bought new dishtowels, placemats, couch pillows, and fall-scented candles with names like Pumpkin Paradise and Cranberry Soiree.

She's going to leave Evan's room untouched for now. Before he left, they'd joked about how she would probably keep it just the way it was, as a sort of shrine. But the truth is she's been thinking for the past few months how neat it would be to set up a studio. Nothing formal or permanent (it's not like she's an actual artist or anything), but a space where she could maybe start dipping her toes back into the waters of creativity. The guest room would be the most logical choice for a studio, of course, since nothing would have to be moved. Unfortunately, Lawrence has taken to sleeping there most nights lately, leaving Evan's room as the only alternative.

"These darned late work hours," he told Jillian with a resigned sigh last night when she mentioned the studio idea.

"I don't mind being woken up when you come to bed," she insisted (trying to come across as lighthearted and fun rather than whiney and manipulative, which was how she feared she sounded to him sometimes). "It's worth it to be able to sleep next to you."

But Lawrence held his ground. "I can't fully relax if I think I might be keeping you up."

Jillian kept her face as neutral as possible, but the steel gears that she sensed were inside her head at times like these began turning almost immediately. Clearly, something needed to be done.

Two days later, she stands in the kitchen naked, save for the ironically retro polka-dot apron she ordered on a whim last month. Is she wrong for wanting the two of them to seize the day, to rediscover each other as husband and wife? She doesn't think so. Surely, she can overcome their currently unsatisfactory sleeping arrangement with a little imagination and effort—a little planning. She's good at planning. She's on a planning *committee*, for goodness' sake. The sole purpose of the committee, which is made up of faculty spouses, is to orchestrate various events for the Classics department at the university—events such as tonight's faculty banquet, which will be starting in just a few hours.

Adjusting the narrow top of the apron so it covers both nipples, Jillian admires the desserts she prepared this afternoon before arranging them carefully on the china platter she and Lawrence received as a wedding gift nearly twenty years ago. She's mastered several authentic Mediterranean dishes over the years—the kinds of things actual ancient Greeks ate—and they've always been a big hit. This year, she decided to go with dates soaked in spiced red wine and walnut cake with fig jam: There's something surprisingly delightful about how the wine gently spurts when one of those plump dates is bitten, something almost seductive about the scent of dark, sweet fruit as the fig reduction sauce is poured over the cake. The very thought of it makes her flush with pleasure.

When Lawrence comes through the front door in a few minutes, she'll be there to greet him wearing the apron and nothing else. She'll lead him to the bedroom (if they make it that far—hopefully, he'll be so excited that they'll only make it to the couch, considering how long it's been since they were last intimate). Taking another sip from the nearly empty glass of Merlot on the counter, Jillian tries not to fret about her cellulite. "Courage," she whispers to herself, and then she hears the front door opening in the entry hall.

Setting down the glass, Jillian smooths the apron. "How was your day?" she calls out, but there's no answer. The sound of Lawrence's footsteps in the hallway indicates that he's making a beeline for the guest room, so that's where she goes, too, her bare feet hardly making a sound.

"I'll be out in a bit," Lawrence calls out when she knocks softly on the closed door.

"Or I can come in," she counters in a sultry voice.

There's an audible sigh just before the door opens, and then Lawrence is standing there, looking mildly annoyed. He observes Jillian's outfit, or lack thereof. "Oh," he says.

Not the reaction she was hoping for, but that's okay. "You look extra handsome tonight," she flirts, stepping toward him and reaching to undo the top button of his oxford. When she does, a boob pops out the side of the apron top. "Oops," she chirps, glancing demurely down at the escapee and then back at her husband.

"Someone's in wifely overdrive," he notes drily, one eyebrow raised.

Jillian giggles. "I just thought maybe we could, you know, mess around a little bit before the banquet..." She moves her hand down the front of his shirt, toward his belt buckle.

"These things are so tedious," he says, backing almost imperceptibly away. "In fact, you could even sit this one out if you really wanted to."

"What?" This time, Jillian's giggle is a little too high-pitched and forceful. "And miss basking in the glow of the gods and goddesses of the Classics department? Miss out on Walter Kemp's Oedipus jokes? I wouldn't dream of it."

"Kemp's a pretentious prick," Lawrence fires back, not playing along.

Chilled by the sudden darkening of the mood, Jillian nevertheless forces a winning smile onto her lips. "Oh, he's not that bad..."

"...says the woman who has *literally* no idea what she's talking about."

Jillian shrinks back. She should have known better than to bring up Lawrence's longtime rival in the department. To be honest, sometimes she wishes her husband would just let go of the fact that Walter Kemp had his book picked up by a traditional, non-academic publisher first. It happened over five years ago, for crying out loud, and it was a very small publishing house; she's not sure Walter even *knows* he's a rival. Then again, old wounds can take a long time to heal.

"He's completely oblivious to the fact that nobody's interested in whatever he blathers about on any given day," Lawrence continues. "I'm serious about my offer though. I could tell everyone that you're otherwise occupied with...I don't know, getting a root canal or recovering from Dengue fever." He laughs, but it's not quite genuine. "I just wish *I* could get out of it."

Jillian regroups. She knows her husband is also dealing with their newly empty nest in his own way, but can't he at least humor her? Still undaunted, she glides closer and takes hold of his lapels, grinning up at him like a romcom actress. "If I didn't know better, I'd think you didn't *want* me to go with you," she teases.

"Obviously, that's not the case." His voice is breezy as he disentangles his shirt from her fingers. "It's just...we both know how tedious these things are. You've been patient in attending every year when the damn thing rolls around yet again."

Jillian waggles her hips a little. "I'm on the planning committee, silly. Besides, I've already made drunken dates and a walnut cake. The cake's arranged on the platter and everything."

Lawrence sighs. "The platter. How could I have forgotten? Of course. Definitely bring your desserts." He says the last part like he's discussing crayons with a preschooler. His cell phone buzzes, and he checks the screen. "I need to take this," he says. When Jillian doesn't immediately move, he places a hand on the door in a pre-closing gesture. "And then I need to shower."

Jillian snaps to attention. She even gives him a quick little salute. "Understood," she says, wrangling her breasts to their initial position beneath the apron top as she bows out of the doorway with a hasty, exaggerated flourish. She refuses to allow the despairing sigh that's pushing against her lungs to escape. It's important to remain hopeful. After all, who knows what might happen when they get back home tonight?

Walking with Lawrence into the great hall of the Classics building an hour later, Jillian marvels, as always, at the general pomp and circumstance of the event. At the far end of the room, near the stage, long tables draped with formal bunting are laden with food. Leaving Lawrence to talk shop with his colleagues, Jillian makes her way over there to find a spot for her desserts among the charcuterie boards and breadbaskets. There are salads, too—spinach and apple, feta and salmon; kale and cranberry—followed by trays of lamb, beef, and chicken with tzatziki or avgolemono sauce drizzled over the top.

"Dark wine," a voice behind her intones. *"Dark blood, pounding sea!"* Jillian turns to see Walter Kemp approaching.

Without another word, he reaches under the plastic wrap covering the platter in her hands, grabs a wine-soaked date, and pops it into his mouth. "*Mmm,*" he hums, eyes closed as he swallows. "This is the work of a professional faculty wife. One might even say a *mythical* faculty wife." He waits half a beat, eyes twinkling. "Get it?"

Jillian forces a smile as she locates an empty spot on the table. "How could I not, Walter?" She begins to smooth the cellophane back over the dates.

"Ah, ah, ah," he says, reaching toward the platter again. "Don't wrap that up so fast (*that's what she said,* am I right?)."

He's ludicrous but harmless, and she can't help but smile for real this time. Unfortunately, it only encourages him.

"You must feel so *free,*" Walter all but bellows, "now that it's just you and Larry at home. Like a woman aboard a fabulous ship bound for exotic lands!"

"I wouldn't...exactly put it that way."

"Ouzo?" a server inquires, passing by with a tray full of small, chilled glasses.

"Sure," Jillian says. "I'll take one for my husband, too." In truth, she's never cared for this particular liqueur; she finds the licorice taste cloying, but it's tradition to drink it at this event. Holding the two glasses, she looks around the hall until she spots Lawrence mingling with a group of graduate students. Walter Kemp has grazed his way down to the opposite end of the table, so Jillian takes the opportunity to join her husband.

"Professor Kensington," one of the male students says as she approaches the group. "I thought you'd want to know that I've been reading some newer translations of Homer lately."

"Have you now," Lawrence says, looking skeptical as Jillian hands him the glass of ouzo. "And who, pray tell, are the authors in question?"

The grad student licks his lips nervously. "Uh…Stephen Mitchell, Joseph Campbell..."

"Stop right there," Lawrence says with an exaggerated roll of his eyes. "Just read the good translations. No need to bother with the new-agey fluff."

"Stick with the Lattimore or the Fagles," a husky female voice adds. "Fitzgerald, at the very least." Jillian turns to see a stunning young woman with thick, auburn hair and luminous eyes who's just joined their little group. She's one of the newer teaching assistants. Jillian remembers her from this year's Haloea, the solstice-themed party Lawrence insists on holding every January. It's grown so big over the years that it's hard to keep track of everyone, but Jillian clearly remembers this young woman sitting huddled on the living room couch with some of the other grad students. They'd laughed as Lawrence expounded on the traditions of the original celebration, the flowing wine and erotic cakes served to the women ("Sadly, I'm not able to serve those, since I'd like to keep my job…" he'd said, winking at the beautiful TA). She's a PhD candidate, if memory serves, on a Fulbright Scholarship. Noting how all the men are staring at their colleague now, Jillian remembers that brief sliver of time in her late teens and early twenties when she was able to hold a pack of males in thrall like that. Of course, she was never as curvaceous, or petite, or self-assured as this one is.

A scarf made of loosely woven gradations of purple silk hangs around the young woman's neck. "That's so lovely," Jillian says. She reaches out to touch the gossamer fabric, but the TA flinches away from her hand. "Oh, I'm so sorry," Jillian tells her. "I didn't mean to startle you." *Gosh, I can be an oaf,* she thinks to herself.

"Like something Arachne herself might have woven," Lawrence says with a small laugh, clearly embarrassed and trying to downplay the awkwardness of the moment. "How are you this evening, Penelope?" he asks. There's an odd, overly formal pitch to his voice.

Penelope ignores him. "Excuse me," she says, walking away from the group.

Lawrence watches her go until his attention is redirected to another enthusiastic grad student who seems to be under the impression that he's some sort of game show contestant.

"Arachne," the student repeats, closing his eyes and holding a finger in the air. "Okay, I've got this. It's...Ovid, right? Arachne's the girl who got into a pissing—er, *weaving* contest with Minerva, Athena, whichever you want to call her."

All eyes dart from Lawrence to the student and back again.

"Arachne wouldn't give the goddess credit for her weaving skills," the younger man continues. "And so, they had a contest. Athena was jealous of how beautiful Arachne's weaving was, so she basically turned her and all of her descendants forevermore into spiders." He turns to Lawrence like an obedient puppy. "Is that how it goes?"

"Something like that," Lawrence responds in a distracted way. The young man beams, oblivious to the dismissiveness in his professor's voice.

Before long, they're sitting at a table nibbling on hors d'oeuvres and sipping retsina. When Lawrence gets up to refill their wine glasses and doesn't come back, Jillian once again scans the hall. She sees him mingling with a different group of students, glancing around every now and then. When their eyes meet, he jumps a little, then returns to the table with her empty glass.

"I thought you were going to refill that," she says, smiling.

"Of course," he responds, clearly agitated. "What was I thinking?" This time, after he returns with the glass overly full, he excuses himself before sitting down. "I'll be back," he says. "I need to speak with a colleague for a moment."

"About?"

Lawrence gives her a stern look. "About an exam he and I are designing. We have a few things to iron out. I'll be back in a bit. Just sit tight."

While he's gone, various faculty spouses she's known forever stop by the table to chat about the same things they chatted about last year—kids, grandkids, the weather, the fact that classics curricula should be a standard element of university core requirements across the nation. At some point, Jillian realizes that the wine and ouzo have gone to her head, making her mournful and slightly dizzy. "Where's Lawrence?" she wonders out loud without meaning to.

A few of the graduate students, who have been sitting across the table gossiping amongst themselves about department politics, exchange glances. "He went to get something from…his office?" one of them volunteers.

"No," another one says firmly, giving the first a hard look. "I don't think so."

"I'm pretty sure he'll be right back," a third one offers.

Jillian gets up (somewhat unsteadily) and heads toward the corridor leading to the faculty offices. It's dim out in the hallway, no doubt to discourage tonight's partygoers from working when they should be enjoying themselves. Navigating carefully in the residual glow from the banquet hall, Jillian can't help but imagine herself as Alice falling down the rabbit hole (she really shouldn't have had that second glass of retsina). *But this is one of those things we can laugh about later,* she thinks. *This Wonderland-like adjustment to our new, more carefree life together.* That's what she wants, more than anything—to laugh with her husband once again about something, anything.

The linoleum beneath her feet, polished to within an inch of its life, makes her think of a river of ice. And now Jillian imagines that she's entranced, under a spell, an almost-ghost floating down the frigid Styx. A momentary chill passes through her, but when she rounds a corner and sees the familiar, comforting glow of warm light coming from under the door of Lawrence's office, she smiles. Maybe she'll figure out a way to get his colleague to leave before suggesting something slightly naughty as a distraction from exam designing. She can't even remember how long it's been since they've fooled around in there; back in the day, she'd visited him for special, conjugal "office hours" all the time. Oh, but they were so in love!

With as much stealth as she can muster, Jillian puts a hand on the doorknob, fixes her mouth into a beguiling smile, and gives a push. The door swings silently open on its newly oiled hinges, and the first thing she sees is the portrait that's been hanging over Lawrence's desk as long as she's known him. It's a limited-edition print of Apollo—ancient god of music, poetry, archery, and healing, known for his rampant love affairs with goddesses and mortals alike. The second thing she sees is Lawrence. He's leaning against the edge of his desk as if in conversation, his hands resting against the wood on either side of him. But no. They're not resting exactly, those hands. They're bracing. Holding his body upright as Penelope, the beautiful TA, delivers an apparently spectacular and mostly silent oration using Lawrence's penis as a microphone.

Neither notices Jillian standing there, taking in every last detail; there is, for instance, the fact that Penelope is topless, making her even more stunning than she was fully clothed—at least from the nipples up, which is all Jillian can see of her. She's like some sort of Porn Fantasy PhD Candidate Barbie: Full-lipped, full-breasted, insightful yet malleable. She looks like she could bend any which way at impossible angles without ever breaking, with nary a stretchmark or a freckle to be found—an academic aphrodisiac. Jillian feels a flash of self-loathing just looking at her.

Lawrence's head is slung back, and his eyes are closed. His mouth is open though; a low moan passes through his lips. Jillian continues to stand there, as mute with surprise as the ancient citizens of Pompeii must have been when the pyroclastic flow barreled down Mount Vesuvius at Olympian speed, consuming them before they had time to get out of the way or to even process what was happening.

When Jillian finally breathes, it's a fast, sharp intake that sucks every last bit of air from the building. The lovers freeze at the sound, realize they're not alone. Lawrence's head jerks toward the open door as Penelope sits back on her haunches, squinting calmly toward the dim light of the hallway.

At that moment, Walter Kemp rounds a corner behind Jillian without warning. He's whistling, of all things, whistling and looking everywhere but right in front of him as he approaches, his dress shoes clicking against the polished floor. "I thought," he sing-laughs to nobody in particular, "that there might be an empty loo down this…oh my!"

His footsteps, and his laughter, and his voice all cease as he comes to a halt beside Jillian. For several seconds, nobody seems willing to break the awful spell. Then Walter Kemp places a hand on her arm. "Come, my dear," he says quietly.

He attempts to lead Jillian away, but for the longest time she does not move. Instead, she remains where she is, incinerated to a pillar of gray ash, standing mute in the elongated parallelogram of sexlight cast through the office door.

Book 4: 1987

ART SAVES.

That's what I'm writing on the blackboard in huge block letters, using as many different colors of chalk as I can find. I add smiley faces and yin-yang circles all around the words. Turkeys, too, since it's November. Nobody will see it until Monday, but I like the idea of leaving something cheery on the board all weekend.

"Who's Art?"

I jump at the sound of Hadley's voice. When I turn around, she's standing in the doorway with her backpack slung over her shoulder and a wry grin on her face. She buzzed off all the hair on the right side of her head last week, and I'm still getting used to it.

"You ready to go?"

"Almost," I tell her.

"Mr. Hughes is totally cool for letting you get away with goofy stuff like this," she says, smirking at my blackboard creation.

"Yeah, I know." The truth is, Mr. Hughes is totally cool, period. I've taken so many of his drawing and painting classes since I was a freshman that he agreed to be my senior year work study sponsor. What that basically means is that I clean up after the first and second period freshman classes, and I help keep the art room organized. It's pretty much a perfect situation; for one thing, it's low stress, which I can definitely use following a hellish junior year. For another, I get credit for the work study, which might help my sagging GPA. Hanging out in the art room first thing in the morning keeps my mind off other crap, too. There's the situation between my parents, for instance (they can barely stand to be in the same room with each other for more than five seconds at this point).

"So, what are you up to this weekend?" Hadley asks as I turn out the lights and lock up the art room.

"My mom's working late again," I tell her. "Which means Dad and I will probably eat cheap pizza—again—and watch reruns of *The Love Boat* and *Fantasy Island.*" I release a deep sigh, despite trying not to. "I'm seventeen years old, and I have no life. Then again, at least I won't have to listen to my parents argue. Did I mention they've started doing that all the time lately?"

"Hey," she says, giving my shoulder a squeeze. "Your folks will work it out."

I nod, but I'm not so sure. They've been seeing a therapist on-and-off since I started high school. For a while, things seemed to be going okay. They were doing date nights, and even occasional weekends away, once I convinced them I was fine staying at home by myself (I actually loved the time alone). But then, earlier this year, things started to get not-so-okay between them again. And lately, Mom's barely home at all, which is probably just as well. I mean, I really don't even care. It's Dad I'm worried about; he's pretty much turned into a robot, his face a blank every morning as he halfheartedly eats whatever I make for breakfast. He usually ends up pushing most of it around on the plate like he's a little kid avoiding his vegetables.

"There's someone I want you to meet," Hadley's saying. He's new this year. Moved here from Durango."

"He started a new school two months into senior year? Dude, I'd totally get my GED if I was him."

"I don't know his whole story," she says, "but he skateboards downtown with my brother, and he's in my shop class. You're going to love him. He's totally your type."

"I have a type?"

Hadley shoots me a mysterious smile. "Yeah," she says. "I think you do."

There's a freshman assembly Monday morning, which means no art class for me to help with. Instead, Mr. Hughes has me clean up around the old kiln in a fenced-off area outside. There's a ton of random, multi-colored fragments left on the ground from glazed pieces that broke in the kiln or got dropped after firing. I bend down and scoop a little handful of them into my palm.

"Find something to mosaic, and those tesserae are all yours," Mr. Hughes says, leaning from the doorway of the art room in his paint-spattered apron.

Turning to him, I drop the pieces and wipe my hands on the front of my smock. "I've never mosaicked anything before."

"Nothing to it. Just find a base and figure out a design. Then, glue the tesserae down, slap some grout on there, and call it good." He scrabbles around in a scrap wood pile near the kiln and pulls out an old piece of plywood. "Start with this," he says, handing it over. "There's a tube of decent adhesive on the top shelf of the big cabinet."

"Seriously?"

"Seriously," he says. "Go crazy. But come see me when it's time to grout. I'll give you a respirator mask and some helpful tips."

I carry the plywood inside and set it on a table at the back of the classroom. Grabbing a pencil, I start by drawing a basic flower design. Then I go back outside, pick up a bunch of fragments that I think will work, and start gluing. It doesn't take me long to figure out that mosaics are messy. They're scary and exhilarating, too: You never know what might start taking shape or how it might turn out. I'm careful at first, trying to make everything perfect, but the pieces seem to do whatever they want despite my efforts. After a while, I give in and loosen up a bit. Throwing caution to the wind, I decide to just let the design take over. The end result is more abstract than I initially planned, but it's pretty anyway. Mr. Hughes helps me grout it the next day, as promised, and he gives me some tips for future projects.

"Watch the lines of your design," he suggests. "Try to get them to flow together in a logical way. Or make them work against each other if you'd rather. Either way, actively participate. Make choices. Commit."

"Uh, okay," I say, trying not to crack up at how serious he's being all of a sudden.

My teacher smiles. "You'll get it someday."

Before heading to my third period class, I find an old textbook from the 60s on one of the art room shelves. *The Wonderful World of Mosaic,* it's called, the groovy typography floating above a couple of long-haired, bell-bottomed teens. The book is covered in clay dust and old paint particles, but I blow it off and take it over to one of the big group tables. Opening to a random page, I find a list of more mosaic terminology—*smalti, millefiori, andamento*—words that are like tiny, exotic candies on my tongue when I say them out loud.

At lunchtime that day, as we're hanging out on our patch of grass by the gym, Hadley waves to a guy I've never seen before. "Yo," she calls. "Bodhi!"

Even from a distance, I can tell he's kind of cute—tall and slender with dark hair and broad shoulders beneath an oversized parka. He's carrying a beat-up skateboard covered in stickers.

"That's the guy I was telling you about," Hadley whispers as he walks toward us. "He can be kind of quiet at first." She replaces the whisper with a big, welcoming smile as the guy approaches. Once he reaches us, I can see that he's more than just kind of cute. There's something about his eyes, which are turned down at the outer corners in a slightly mournful way, and his mouth, which is turned up into an easy, relaxed smile. His longish hair curls a little at the sides of his flannel shirt collar.

"Jill Jacobs, Bodhi Paxton," Hadley says.

Bodhi raises a hand in greeting. "Hey."

"Hi," I say back.

Hadley pats the grass next to her. "Such scintillating conversationalists. Sit down and stay a while, Mr. Paxton."

Nobody says anything once he's settled in, and it's pretty clear Hadley's not willing to carry the conversation beyond basic introductions. Before long, I cave to the awkward silence. "What…brings you to Flagstaff?" It's the highest quality small talk I can muster.

"My asshole stepdad," Bodhi answers without hesitation. "Actually, correction: My awesome mom *fleeing* my asshole stepdad so we could be closer to her sister here on the mountain."

I wince. "Sorry."

"Nah, it's a good thing. The only thing that sucks about it is not getting to hang out with the friends I grew up with. So, you guys are lucky."

Hadley throws an arm around my shoulders. "Ain't we though?" Then her voice grows more serious. "Personally, I think it's amazing how cool you are with moving here at the end of high school."

"Yeah," Bodhi says. "I guess I should probably have all sorts of anger issues. Maybe I do, and they'll all come rushing to the surface one day. I'll turn all green and transform into the Hulk or something." He raises his arms in a menacing gesture. "Bust out of my clothes."

"What I wouldn't give to see that," I say, attempting to join the conversation in a more natural, socially graceful sort of way.

Hadley snorts, and my face feels like it's on fire. "I…I mean the thing about you turning into the Hulk," I stammer idiotically. "Not the busting out of your clothes thing."

Bodhi laughs. "It's okay." He has pretty teeth. They're so pretty, in fact, that I start to zone out a little staring at them.

"Jill's an art nerd like you," Hadley says, throwing me a life preserver.

"Oh, yeah?"

"Yeah," I tell him. "I love it. You should take Mr. Hughes's class."

"I tried to," he says, "but it was full. Hence, shop."

"Which is awesome," Hadley says. "Because otherwise you and I wouldn't have a class together. And you got to meet Jill anyway."

Bodhi grins at her and then at me. "Good point."

That Friday night, the three of us go see *Weird Science*. It came out last year, but movies are always slow to come to Flagstaff. Fashion, too. And music. This mountain's pretty much The Land that Time Forgot. After the movie, we head to the old downtown diner and pool our remaining change for an extra-large basket of fries.

"So, I have an art project for you," Bodhi tells me when Hadley gets up to refill her water glass. "Interested?"

"Seriously?"

"Yeah," he says. "I was telling my mom about you guys, and how you're an artist."

"I wouldn't go quite that far."

He waves the comment away. "Anyway, there's this old cinder block retaining wall in our backyard. She wants it mosaicked."

"Are you kidding? And you haven't told me about this wall of happiness before now...why?"

Bodhi holds his hands up. "I just found out about it, man. Stop browbeating me!"

This is how things have started going between us over the past few days since we first met; we fall into an easy sort of theatrical banter whenever we're hanging out. It's kind of like flirting and kind of not.

Saturday morning, I convince Hadley and Bodhi to accompany me to a local thrift store where we sort through other peoples' cast-offs in a hunt for old dishes. I find an ancient piece of embroidery—a needlepoint image of a little Dutch girl. Turning it over, I study the ugly, wrong side to see how all the knotted threads work together. I can't help but wonder about the owners of all the knick-knacks surrounding us. Did they ever imagine their treasures would end up in a place like this, pawed over by complete strangers?

Eventually, we leave the store with a random assortment of different colored and patterned dishes, mostly plates. That night, I put everything in an old pillowcase and smash it with a hammer in the backyard while Dad, looking mildly concerned, watches through the kitchen window.

On Sunday morning, I head over to Bodhi's house for the first time. I meet his mom, Evelyn, who's super nice. Standing in his bedroom, I marvel at what I see. His art is everywhere—from geographic designs painted around the mirror, to robotic-looking angels painted above the closet door, to stylized futuristic cars racing each other across the tops of the walls. There's even an abstract mobile sculpture hanging from the ceiling fan.

"Wow," I say, my head tilted back to take it all in. "Your stuff is amazing."

He doesn't respond, but when I un-tilt my head and look at him, I realize he's been watching me with those ever-so-slightly sad eyes.

At that exact moment, his mom appears in the doorway. "Ready to start?" she asks us.

"Huh?" Bodhi says, his eyes still locked on mine. "Oh! Yeah, I am."

"Me, too," I say.

We follow her out to a little shed behind the house where she reaches behind an old welder ("Pretty much the only useful thing I got from my idiot stepdad," Bodhi mutters) and hauls up a half-full bag of powdered grout they used for the bathroom tile when they moved in.

"I brought adhesive and a bunch of ceramic shards," I tell her, holding up the pillowcase. "They're all different sizes and colors and shapes, depending on the kind of design you want."

Bodhi's mom smiles. "You're the artist, my dear."

The wall she wants mosaicked isn't very big. It juts out about four feet from a corner of the garage into a patch of dirt by the side of the driveway. We decide on a basic geometric design, and I empty the shards onto a big piece of cardboard so I can start organizing them by color and size. Bodhi uses fat markers to sketch our idea onto the wall, and then we glue pieces onto it wherever they seem to work best. By the time we're done, it's getting dark and cold; hours have passed without my even noticing.

Hadley joins us the next day after school when it's time to grout. She decided last year that she wants to be a filmmaker someday, and she's brought her parents' Super 8 camera.

"Must document the process," she says in a haughty British accent. "Just promise you'll remember the little people like me when you guys are rich and famous artists snorting coke off models' bare butts at some Studio 54-like club."

I've already gathered everything we'll need—the grout, bucket, and stir stick—and I have it all set up near the water spigot by the back door. I hand Bodhi his respirator and put my own on. Before long, we're breathing like Darth Vader as I measure out the water and he stirs it into the sandy powder.

And then we're back at the wall, our gloved hands dunked into the wet mixture before spreading it across our design from yesterday. We work without speaking for several minutes, pressing grout into all the little spaces between the glued shards, smoothing it over, and then wiping off as much excess as we can without leaving gouge lines. When we're done, we rinse our hands off at the hose Bodhi's mom connected to the spigot. When the temptation gets to be too much, I point the hose toward Bodhi and squirt him with the icy water.

"Watch the camera!" Hadley warns as Bodhi grabs the hose from me and returns the favor. Eventually, the two of us end up about half-soaked, Hadley stays dry, and we're all exhausted enough to flop down onto a sparse little patch of nearby grass in a corner of Bodhi's front yard. The butt of my overalls is going to be completely covered with dirt when I get up, but I don't care. There's nowhere else I'd rather be.

Book 5: 2009

Ruin, eldest daughter of Zeus, she blinds us all,
that fatal madness...
~Homer

It's the purple silk scarf Jillian can't un-see.

Even now, three days later, the grainy celluloid film-strip of what happened in Lawrence's office won't stop un-scrolling behind her eyes as she lies in bed with a forearm slung across her face. She can't stop envisioning the scarf draped across the back of the leather executive chair she bought him two Christmases ago. Or the way Penelope, the mysterious teaching assistant, met Jillian's eyes with her own, coolly staking her claim after only a split-second of surprise at seeing Lawrence's wife standing there in the doorway. In the long seconds that followed, Penelope reached for the scarf, plucking it from the chair before arranging it casually across her magnificent breasts like some kind of pageant banner.

Lawrence, meanwhile, was practically hopping in place to get his pants pulled up, zipped, and buttoned without anyone...what? *Noticing*? Under different circumstances, Jillian might have found the entire scene absurd to the point of being hilarious.

But it wasn't hilarious. It was, in fact, like stumbling upon the scene of her own murder.

In the days and nights since, Jillian has had terrifying dreams of falling from high places, of running in quicksand. There was even one in which she was inside a lidless casket that was being carried by Evan and Lawrence, and by her own mother and father. As they'd passed through the cemetery gates, a wrought iron sign overhead read *Welcome to the Land of the Dead*.

Dehydrated, she gets out of bed and forces herself to drink some water. She feels suspended above all goings on as if by invisible hooks hanging from the sky. Back upstairs in bed, she descends into an orgy of self-loathing, dissects her hideousness, detail by detail: the 39-year-old breasts; the stretch marks from pregnancy; the crows' feet; the elevens between her eyebrows. She understands perfectly why Lawrence did what he did. Before long, her entire body is trembling the way it trembled as she stood aghast in the hallway outside his office.

She remembers looking away from Lawrence and Penelope (out of some habitual sense of decency, perhaps?) as her husband stumbled toward the open office door. Hitchcock violins shrieked so keenly in her own head at that moment—*Ree! Ree! Ree!*—that she was certain everyone else could hear them, too. After standing there, pillar-like, for the longest time (how long was it exactly? A millisecond? A day? A century?), her heart suddenly began to pound so hard that she feared it might break her chest open. One of her legs began to shake, subtly at first, and then more and more violently, until Jillian almost collapsed.

Then, Walter Kemp's hand was on her elbow in an instant, steadying her. She had forgotten that Lawrence's professional nemesis was in the hallway, too. That he had seen what she had seen.

"Damnit, Jill," Lawrence said, zipped-up now and clearly trying—too late—to fill the doorway with his silhouette so she couldn't see past him into the office. "We were just—"

Jillian held up a hand to silence him. "Don't."

"I'll drive you home," Walter said, ignoring Lawrence completely.

She doesn't remember much about the short car trip that followed (though she vaguely recalls Walter making sure she was safely inside the house before driving away). Nor does she remember going upstairs or getting into bed fully clothed, though that's clearly what happened; she woke in the middle of that first night with the sharp heel of one patent leather pump digging into the tender spot near her left ankle.

In the past 72 hours, she has dreamed of her hair and her teeth falling out, of being strapped into a chair and looking up at a dentist who turned out to be Typhon, that ancient monster from the cover of her old classics textbook, with his snake legs and snake fingers, his hundred heads of various beasts. She has imagined Lawrence and Penelope in bed together, joined like mating animals, licking each other's skin, laughing at her (how many times have they done what she saw them doing in Lawrence's office?). She has woken in a startled state over and over to find herself raw, exposed, and vulnerable, every nerve shrieking, her psyche wishing only to fall back into the restless sleep purgatory it just escaped.

Remembering the tea she got up and made at some point, in a daze, she hoists herself onto an elbow and reaches for the mug. As she brings it toward her lips, though, she glances down. Apparently, the teabag has been sitting for so long in its own juices during her visits to and from the underworld of sleep that a series of fine circular lines now stains the inside of the mug like growth rings. A drowned fruit fly floats in the brackish liquid. Disgusted, Jillian returns the mug to the nightstand, lowers her head back to the pillow, and falls into yet another harrowing dreamland. In this one, someone is knocking and knocking on a door she can't see. Jillian tries to move toward the door, but she's stuck in the pitch dark, paralyzed. *So, this is how I die,* her dream self thinks. She's surprised at the relief that realization brings as she's pulled unexpectedly back toward consciousness.

The first thing she sees when she opens her eyes again is some sort of female apparition in a tight-fitting Snoopy T-shirt silhouetted against the late afternoon light sneaking in through the blinds. She's striking, this vision, with long, black hair and high, chiseled cheekbones. A pair of incredibly toned arms is crossed over her chest, and her dark eyes are narrowed in frank disapproval. Jillian lifts her head and squints hard at the visage. "Am I dreaming?" she croaks.

In response, Hadley Wallace, Jillian's childhood best friend, places her hands on her hips. "You wake up to find a near-stranger standing in your bedroom, and that's all you have to say?"

Jillian's mouth tries to work itself into a sardonic smile, but the tiny artesian wells of blood that rush up through the cracks in her lips hurt too much. "What are you doing here?" she whispers instead, keeping her mouth as still as a ventriloquist's.

Hadley grabs the half-full glass of water from the dresser and hands it to Jillian. "You've scared everyone shitless, dumplin'."

"But I haven't seen you in—"

"More than fifteen years," Hadley says. "But who's counting?" Her voice is all business as she turns and walks out of the room with one hand holding her cell phone and the other punching numbers on the keypad. Moments later, Jillian can hear her in the living room talking to someone on the other end of the connection. Hadley's voice is too low for her to make out actual words.

"I still don't understand why you're here," she says when Hadley wanders back into the master bedroom with a fresh glass of water.

"Your mother couldn't get a hold of you, so she called Evan, who called his dad, who copped to what happened."

Jillian groans.

"Apparently, he explained the situation in the most general terms possible," Hadley clarifies. "So don't fret. Nobody knows the gory details but you and Douchebag, pardon my French. But Evan passed what he knew onto Barb, and Barb called me. Asked if I'd check on you. Said she doesn't have the numbers for any of your friends down here."

Jillian's head falls back to the pillow. A slow-building throb has started up behind her eyeballs. The last thing she needs is her mother getting more proof of her failure in life.

"Anyway," Hadley says. "This is where I get to finally say the line I worked on during the drive down here. You ready? Here it is: I'm Hadley Skywalker, and I'm here to rescue you."

Jillian lifts her head from the pillow and frowns. "Pardon?"

"Oh, yeah," Hadley says, hands back on her hips now. "I guess I left out that minor detail. The plan is for you to come hang out at my place for a little while."

The throbbing behind Jillian's eyeballs increases in tempo. "Plan?"

"Yeah. I just came up with it. Executive decision."

At this, Jillian tries to laugh, but it comes out more like a grunt. "I'm not going to Flagstaff."

Hadley is unmoved. "I would respectfully ask you to reconsider."

Now Jillian's lower jaw thrusts forward in protest. She's not going to cry. "This is my home."

"Hey," Hadley says, her voice softer now. "I get that. I do. And you don't have to explain what's going on. But considering the fact that you look like Janis Joplin coming off a week-long bender, I'm guessing you haven't been taking the best care of yourself for the past several days."

"So, what are you going to do? Commit me?"

Hadley laughs. "No, of course not. But Evan—who's apparently at college, and how completely cool is that, by the way?—just told me he's coming back here to be with you if you decide to stay."

"He can't do that." Jillian is surprised by the panic in her own voice. "He can't miss school." A few days ago, she would have loved the idea of him coming back. But not like this, not because he feels compelled to care for his emotionally invalid mother. Tears well up. She blinks them back.

"Try telling him that," Hadley says. "He doesn't want you going through whatever this is alone. And I'm pretty sure your mom's planning to move in here, too, if you refuse to come with me. But this place is big enough for the three of you, right?"

Jillian glares at her. "Fine," she says, letting out a long, defeated breath. "You win."

"Oh, goody." Hadley holds out a hand for Jillian to grasp. "My two favorite words. We'll start with the shower and work our way into the future from there, okay? Upsy-daisy."

Reluctantly, Jillian takes the hand. Her brain goes all sparkly when Hadley pulls her up to a sitting position too quickly, but she doesn't resist.

"Nice digs, by the way," Hadley says.

"I've...been meaning to invite you over." It's a stupid thing to say after all this time, but Jillian doesn't bother providing an excuse. She can't even remember why the two of them stopped talking so many years ago. All she knows is she can't handle any more shame at this particular moment.

Hadley acts like she didn't hear. "Any pets we need to load up? Dogs, cats, beta fish, coatimundi?"

Jillian shakes her head, winces at the sudden, stabbing pain in her temples. "Lawrence isn't really an animal person."

"What a shock. Sounds like he's just as peachy as I remember."

In the bathroom, Jillian pulls off her T-shirt and sweats, letting them fall to the floor. She turns on the water as hot as she thinks she'll be able to stand it but then hesitates before stepping under the spray; something tells her that once she washes off what's happened there will be no going back. She hears Hadley talking on the phone in the other room again: "I'm here with her. She'll be fine. No, don't do that. Just focus on school. I'll have her call you."

After forcing herself into the shower and standing under the hot water for a good ten minutes, Jillian puts on clean clothes. She hastily packs some essentials into an overnight bag and heads into the kitchen. Hadley is bent over a pad of paper on the counter with the tip of her tongue sticking out the side of her mouth as she writes something.

"What are you doing?"

"Penning a note to your hubby," she says, handing Jillian the yellow legal pad. "Here's what I have so far. What do you think?"

Dear Fuckface, the note begins. Jillian doesn't bother reading the rest of it. Instead, she rips the sheet from the pad, crumples it up, and throws it into the trash. Taking the pen from Hadley, she begins to write a note of her own: *Going to Flagstaff for a while. You have my cell number.* She hesitates. A few drops of water fall from her still-damp hair onto the page before she starts writing again. *I'm okay.*

"As if he cares," Hadley says, reading over her shoulder.

Jillian straightens up and turns to face her. "How would you know? He might...care." Her voice trails off.

Hadley picks up Jillian's overnight bag. "Come on. Let's go." In the truck, she hands Jillian a charging cord. "You might want to plug in your phone."

When she does, Jillian sees a string of unread messages:

Jillian, the first one reads. *it's Walter Kemp. Please call us if you need anything.* It's followed by several texts from Evan, which are followed by *This is your mother* (as if Jillian wouldn't recognize the number). *Call me.*

There are several messages from the school district, notifications of upcoming substitute aide jobs during the first week of school.

There's even a generic, encouraging text from her dad, which is surprising. Since he married his longtime girlfriend Helen a couple of years ago, the two of them have been encased in a bubble of domestic bliss from which they rarely seem to emerge. Even at Evan's graduation in June, they were cordial without being especially social. Jillian wonders who told him about her recent, unexplained departure from polite society. It had to have been either her mother or Evan.

The last message is from Hadley: *Long time no see. On my way to your place.*

Jillian puts a hand to her chest at the realization of how many people know what's happened. Letting Evan know she's okay has to be one of her first priorities, but she's also afraid of what her voice might reveal at the moment. *Will call in the morning,* she texts him instead. *Love you so much. I'm fine & in good hands. <3*

His response is almost immediate: *LU2 mom. It's going to be ok.*

Jillian looks up from the phone and stares out at the traffic through tears that have once again sprung up into her eyes. This time, she lets them spill over.

Hadley hands her a travel pack of tissues before shifting the old Ford into fifth gear. Taking the I-17 exit toward Flagstaff, she reaches for the radio knob, eventually settling on an AM country station out of Dewey. "We've got almost a three-hour drive," she says, her voice gentle. "Maybe longer with the Friday Labor Day traffic. Try to get some sleep."

Jillian pulls a tissue from its plastic wrapper and nods as she dabs at her face. Suddenly drowsy, she closes her eyes and rests her head against the seat. *Instead of a phoenix rising from the ashes,* she thinks to herself, *I am ashes rising from Phoenix.* Soon, the rocking of the truck and the hum of the wheels lull her into shallow travel-dreams as mile marker posts on the side of the interstate tick-tock a new and growing distance between the life she's always known and the void stretching out ahead of her.

Book 6: 1988

"Think of it as a canvas made of wet clay," Bodhi tells me. "Your job is to carve any design into it you want."

We're balanced on our snowboards at the top of a headwall, staring down at the steep, snow-covered slope below. Well, Bodhi's balanced; I'm clinging to him like a feral cat about to get its first bath, trying to figure out if the Sorel boots I'm wearing are strapped tightly enough onto the board I borrowed from Hadley's brother. Chuck Wallace and his friends were some of the first people in northern Arizona to get into this whole surfing-on-snow thing. Hadley assures me the equipment is top-notch and state-of-the-art. The hill we're about to tackle is supposed to be the most basic bunny slope, but from this vantage point it looks more like the side of a thousand-foot vertical glacier. Experienced skiers, eager to get in as many morning runs as possible, *whoosh* off the ledge all around us.

"You can do this," Bodhi insists, adjusting his goggles over his eyes.

Normally, I'd argue that point, but this experience is his birthday present to me, and I don't want to seem ungrateful.

Scoring a couple of early January lift tickets from a guy he knows who works up here couldn't have been easy, since the resort is always super-crowded over winter break.

"Just remember what we practiced before getting on the chair, okay?"

Taking a deep breath, I nod, and we make our way down the mountain.

We move at a snail's pace at first, Bodhi riding backward to all but carry me. I refuse to let go of him. It's been a couple of months now that we've been doing a kind of flirting/not flirting thing every time we're together; if my brain was less terror-saturated, I'd no doubt be making mental notes about the sound of his low, soothing voice so close to my ear or the feel of his upper arm muscles bulging under his navy-blue parka.

Before too long, the slope widens out, winding gently toward the bottom of the chairlift for about a quarter of a mile. Bodhi convinces me to let go of him, reminds me that I'll be fine. He's right, of course, even if my attempt at riding solo involves landing on my butt every couple of turns. It's totally humiliating, but at least it's a break from normal, humdrum life, most notably the college applications I've been slogging through for weeks.

One of them is for Bodhi's dream school, a private little art institute in the Colorado Rockies. "They're trying to promote their new industrial design program," he said when he first told me about it. "I think I might have a decent chance at a scholarship. They're pretty selective, though, so I don't know."

"You'll get in," I told him. "You're brilliant. Just wait until they see your portfolio."

He wanted me to apply, too, so we could be together. Unfortunately, unless I can get a major scholarship (not likely considering my grades for the past few years), I'll have to stay in-state.

With the snowboard whispering over fresh powder and my body starting to get the hang of things, I relax a little. Learning to surf an ocean of snow is also turning out to be a good break from the constant, ongoing crap at home between Mom and Dad.

It's gotten to the point where I find myself unable to tolerate being around either of my parents for more than thirty seconds at a time, especially Mom. *We all know you're miserable with your life here,* I want to tell her. *You married too young, and you wanted more, and now you're in the throes of a massive midlife crisis. Big whoop.* Her very presence is like a cheese grater on my last nerve, so it's probably a good thing she's never home. Then there's Dad, who's usually either at work or holed up in his room. I may be just a teenager, but even I can tell the wheels are finally coming off their marriage for real. And I'm almost okay with it.

Without warning, I'm tumbling end over end, a total yard sale strewn across the slope. My board *cathunk*s along, stubbornly attached to my feet even after I've lurched to a final resting place on my back.

Bodhi's there in seconds. He skids to a stop beside me, sending an arc of snow flying away from us. "Are you okay?"

"I suck at this," I groan up at him, squinting against the bright blue sky.

"What? You're doing great! Did you see those other snowboarders we passed just sitting on the side of the trail? You cruised right by them like a pro. You're basically…Elektra Woman and Dyna Girl rolled into one, with a dash of She-Ra thrown in."

Wincing, I raise myself onto my elbows. "You watched Elektra Woman and Dyna Girl?"

"Duh," he says, scoffing. "Who didn't?"

He helps me up, dusts me off, and then we stand there for a minute as I get my bearings before trying once more. He rides behind me as I focus on my turns, careful not to overflex or overextend my ankles. I'm flooded with relief as we near the bottom of the run. The Psychedelic Furs song blasting from the loudspeakers near the chairlift is an added bonus.

"I love this song," I call out, turning my head to see if Bodhi can hear it, too. And that's when I execute the faceplant to end all faceplants—hard and without warning—right in front of the long line of people waiting to load the chairs.

Skidding once again to a stop next to me, Bodhi drops to his knees. His brow is furrowed with worry. "Are you okay?"

"Other than feeling like a total idiot, yeah," I say, lifting my head. "I splatted wrist-first though. Feels like I landed on a bunch of needles."

"They don't call them stingers for nothing. Come on. Let's get you warmed up." He helps me sit upright so he can unstrap my boots from the board, and then he gently takes me by the elbow so I can stand without pushing off from the snow with my hands.

In the lodge, he finds a big, cushy chair for me to sit in. It's in front of the fire, which is bliss itself, but then he brings me hot chocolate. I wonder if maybe I actually died out there on the bunny slope, and this is what Heaven looks like. He unlaces my boots, pulls them off, and then examines my wrists one at a time, turning each one gently to check for swelling. "Want me to call ski patrol?" he asks. Concern still radiates from those gorgeous eyes of his as he gently supports my upturned hands in his own.

Blue veins pulse with extra intensity beneath my skin. "I'll be okay," I tell him quietly, feeling flushed and shy all of a sudden.

Our faces are just inches apart, and we stay like that for a small eternity, holding each other's gaze. Then, finally, he leans forward, closing the small gap between us, and we kiss. At the smell of his skin, the feel of his lips on mine, a tiny, molten ball of lava forms just below my solar plexus. It radiates outward in all directions until it's shooting from the tips of my fingers and toes, simultaneously illuminating and melting everything in its path.

A few weeks later, our letters from the art institute in the Rockies arrive in the mail on the same day. Bodhi shows up at my house before I have a chance to call him.

"I got into Colorado," he says before I've even opened the door all the way. "Please say you did, too." One look at my face tells him all he needs to know: My letter was a rejection.

"I'm so happy for you," I say, stepping onto the front step to wrap my arms around his neck despite the fact that I'm on the verge of tears. A lump forms in my throat, but I swallow it away and blink hard, command myself to be tough. "I did get into State though," I tell him.

Bodhi touches my face with the backs of his fingers, and my insides do the usual flip. "So, here's what I'm thinking," he says. "Plan B is that I'll do community college for a year in Phoenix to save money and then transfer to State next year. I'm sure there's some sort of scholarship I can apply for between now and then."

"You can't be serious."

"Can't I?" The playful smirk and the twinkle in his eye nearly distract me from the entire conversation.

"Bodhi, Colorado's your dream school."

"And you're my dream woman."

I take his face between my hands, kiss him, and then pull back, frowning. "There's no way I'm letting you do this."

Prom that spring is held in one of the newer hotels downtown. I'm in a dark green satin gown I found on clearance last year, and Bodhi looks dashing in his dead grandfather's three-piece suit.

During the last song, a slow one by Crowded House—I realize this is the first, and probably last, dance Bodhi and I will ever attend together. Sure, there will be dances in college, but what are the odds we'll be visiting each other's schools when those happen? The thought makes me so tired and sad that I rest my head on Bodhi's shoulder so he won't think I'm having a terrible time. The only thing I want is to be alone with him—tonight and as much as possible—to savor whatever time we have left for the next few months.

Hadley is clearly not into her date, Will Collins, a guy who's lusted after her for the entire year but who seemed to lose interest pretty quickly when he figured out he wasn't going to get anywhere with her tonight. Bodhi drove us all to Prom together, but Hadley doesn't seem at all bummed when Will ends up ditching us for a party at one of his friends' houses.

"And then there were three," she says at the end of the evening when she, Bodhi and I are back in the car. She blows her overcurled bangs out of her eyes and tugs at the neckline of her dress like she's suffocating. "Guess Will was put out that I wouldn't put out." She reaches around to unzip the bodice, breathing a massive sigh of relief as she digs around in the back seat. "Can I put this on?" she asks Bodhi, holding up one of his crumpled T-shirts.

"Sure," he says, glancing in the rearview mirror. "I mean, it's probably a little ripe, but…"

"No big. I'd rather smell like Bo's B.O. than stay trapped inside this torture device of a dress a minute longer."

We haven't made any plans for after the dance, but it would be a shame to end the night now. I'm feeling energized, and it's not like I need to be home. My parents, who are still wrapped-up in their own stuff, are used to me staying at Hadley's much of the time lately, so they aren't expecting me. I suggest we go hang out at the downtown diner or something. Bodhi stays quiet. When I turn to look at Hadley, she grins.

"Nah," she says. "You guys go. My bed's calling to me."

After we drop her off, Bodhi and I sit in silence for a while. "You okay?" I ask him, studying the strong, elegant lines of his profile.

"Yeah," he says, keeping his eyes on the road. "It's just…I kind of have a surprise for you."

We drive out of town and onto a forest service road. After we've been on it for a while, tires jouncing against the washboard dirt surface and towering pine trees rising up on either side of us, Bodhi tells me to close my eyes.

"Did Hadley know about this?"

"No peeking," he answers, ignoring my question. I can hear the smile in his voice. The car makes a sharp right, then stops, and then Bodhi cuts the engine. "Okay, you can open your eyes now."

The headlights are off, so it takes a minute for my eyes to adjust. Eventually, in the moonlight, I'm able to make out the shape of an old log cabin about twenty yards ahead of us. We get out of the car and head toward it, Bodhi keeping a hand on my elbow so I don't trip on the clumps of buffalo grass in our path. "It's a good thing I trust you," I tell him. He's holding a camping lantern he grabbed from the back seat, but he hasn't clicked it on yet; halfway to the cabin, I stop to gaze at the prairie receding into the darkness. When I look up, the ink-black sky appears swathed in layers of stars. "This is amazing," I whisper.

"It's an abandoned sheepherder cabin," Bodhi says, turning on the lantern and guiding me the rest of the way to the door. Opening it, he holds up the light to reveal my surprise: In the center of the tiny cabin, on the hard-packed dirt floor, an upturned wooden crate is covered in a lace tablecloth. On top of it, a jelly jar filled with wildflowers sits next to a bottle of champagne. Plastic flute glasses cast tall, translucent shadows that loom and sway against the pine log walls. Squinting through the shadows, I can just barely make out a couple of straw bales that have been pushed together and made up like a bed in one corner. It's covered with some heavy winter blankets and the quilt from his bedroom.

"I thought we could camp here," Bodhi says, smiling shyly. "I brought food and everything." He holds the lantern up toward the opposite corner of the cabin, where another makeshift bed has been set up, this one less fancy than the first. "I'll sleep over there."

"It's…" I start to say, but then I think better of it and stop talking altogether. Taking his hand, I pull him toward the cozier bed of bales.

I thought I knew every part of my body. I've been living in it for eighteen years, after all. I also thought I was pretty wise (intellectually, anyway) when it came to the ins and outs (so to speak) of sex. I'd heard the horror stories, of course, but nobody told me how sweet the first time could be—the feeling of someone else's heart beating right up against my own, his skin and muscle and bone and sinew so close to mine that we're more like extensions of each other than separate people. The wishful-thinking condoms he brought (just in case) make things a little awkward, mainly because it takes a few tries to get one on right, but we eventually do. Beyond that, everything is uncharted territory. I'm especially surprised by my own bold adventurousness; I didn't realize how badly I've longed for this connection with him, a connection every secret place of my body seems to know instinctually how to seek out. I suddenly understand all the horrendous analogies about first sex—the rush of desire like a dam giving way, body parts blossoming like flowers…

"I swear, we're like two ninety-year-old virgins," Bodhi says at one point.

"Ew," I say, laughing against his shoulder. "What?"

"It's just so awkward," he says, cracking up now, too.

I imagine our laughter rising up and out through the empty window frame near our heads, floating over the prairie and then up and away into the wide-open night sky filled to bursting with those overlapping stars.

"Sorry I'm not better at it," he says.

"Shh," I whisper against his lips, looking up into his beautiful eyes and panting now instead of laughing—panting because that flowery dam of pent-up desire is giving way somewhere between my navel and knees.

Afterward, lying there next to him, both of us covered in a sheen of cooling sweat and with our heartrates settling down, Bodhi leans over to turn off the lantern. When he does, something on the dirt floor catches my attention. "What's that?" I ask, and he reaches for it, holds it up. It's a perfectly formed, brilliant blue feather.

"Must be from some kind of jay," Bodhi says, turning it this way and that before setting it down and snuggling back under the quilt next to me. I lay my head against his bare chest and listen to the sound of his heart beating. Before I know it, my own pulse is keeping time with his, and then I'm asleep.

Book 7: 2009

What is a friend? A single soul dwelling in two bodies.
~Aristotle

By the time they stop for gas in Camp Verde, the saguaros of Phoenix have turned to scrub juniper and prickly pear, and the air is sage-infused. It's been a long time since Jillian's been back on the mountain—at least five years. With her mother living in Northern California now and her father living with his wife in Prescott, an hour outside Phoenix, there's been no real reason to make the trek up to the high country. She'd forgotten how quickly everything changes during the climb to 7,000 feet.

As they ascend the Mogollon Rim twenty minutes later, the distant red rocks of Sedona slide gradually into view, glowing pink in the late afternoon light. Jillian remembers a day she spent there with Hadley and Bodhi when they were high school seniors. They'd found a spot in the crowded parking lot near the trail leading to Cathedral Rock, and then they'd hiked as far away from the touristy crowds as they could. There was something undeniably magical about the sandstone rock formations and the river where the three of them ended up, which was flowing fast due to spring runoff from the San Francisco Peaks to the north.

Now, as they cross over the national forest boundary, the interstate cuts through kelly-green prairie dotted by sunflowers, lupine, and the occasional elk crossing sign. It's evening when they reach Flagstaff. Outside the passenger window, Jillian can barely make out the silhouettes of ponderosa pines, some of them just naked skeletons, long ago struck by lightning. She'd know where she was even if it was a moonless night though; there's something about the smell of red dirt roads after a monsoon rainstorm that brings her right back to her childhood and teenage years.

"Nothing like it," Hadley says. She inhales deeply through her nose as they finally pull up to a tiny A-frame set against the forest, which is only a few hundred yards away on the other side the back fence line. "I've been gradually renovating it for over a decade."

Jillian follows her along a flagstone walkway to the front door, the overnight bag slung over her shoulder. She's already decided to think of this visit as nothing more than a quick getaway, akin to a weekend camping trip in the wilderness to clear her head.

"The county's being a major pain in the ass," Hadley says as she unlocks the deadbolt and ushers Jillian inside. "I have plans for a new room and a half-bath addition already drawn up, but they keep stonewalling the approval process. Now they're saying my old septic system's not up to code, that it's not grandfathered in. So, I'm pissed." She tucks a strand of hair behind her ear, suddenly self-conscious. "As you can see, my place is way smaller than yours. But that's pretty obvious, I guess. Sorry. Anyway, here we are. I'll give you a tour."

Jillian sets her bag down on the living room couch and follows Hadley around like it's a museum, not wanting to touch anything, not wanting to leave her mark. She imagines herself a visiting ghost, here only for a brief haunting of this mountain, the scene of her life before Lawrence. At the thought of him, her heart gives a dull, aching thump. Compared to her home in Scottsdale, the slant-walled A-frame—with just one little bedroom off of the main living area, a small kitchen and even smaller bathroom—is indeed miniscule. Still, Jillian's immediately struck by how much Hadley's done with the place. It's rustic in a charming, non-cluttered way, with all sorts of funky art and furniture, everything hand-picked and lovingly tended to over the years. There's the old dresser and headboard set in Hadley's bedroom, for instance. Jillian remembers it from when they were girls and it was lime green. It's been sanded down and stained, the mattress covered with an antique quilt that was no doubt made by Hadley's grandmother. Those quilts used to be everywhere in the Wallace household.

Hadley shows her a half bath near the back door. "Use this one any time you get tired of the loo out in the Ovum," she says.

"The…Ovum?"

"The trailer where you'll be staying," Hadley clarifies. "It's a little bit of a trek in the middle of the night from out there, but the path is lit." Grabbing a flashlight from a shelf by the back door, she leads Jillian outside and down a narrow path lined with solar garden lights. At the end of the path, a tiny white travel trailer with soft light glowing from its porthole-like windows is parked next to an ancient barn.

"I see where it gets its name," Jillian says. From the outside, it does indeed look like an egg, albeit a squarish one. She falls silent. Hadley doesn't actually expect her to sleep in that tiny little container, does she?

"Total *mittelschmerz,* am I right?"

Jillian blinks as her brain processes the somehow familiar-but-unfamiliar word, juggling it back and forth like a mental beanbag until sudden memories of eighth-grade sex ed rise to the surface. "Oh," she says, a giggle escaping her. "I totally forgot about that." Her face grows solemn again, though, as she beholds the trailer. "Seriously. This is really sweet of you and everything, but I'm not sure I'm entirely comfortable with the idea of—"

"You'll be fine," Hadley says, holding open the trailer's door. The frame is just big enough for Jillian to pass through. "Mind the metal step."

Once inside, Jillian gazes around at the space. It's surprisingly less claustrophobia-inducing than she'd anticipated. "Wow," she marvels. "You got seriously...creative with this."

"Yeah," Hadley says, looking around. "I was going for old school country kitsch. If *Bonanza* knocked up *Petticoat Junction,* I like to think this is what their baby would look like."

Jillian runs her hand over another vintage quilt arranged across the narrow foam mattress.

"I stocked the kitchenette with water and snacks," Hadley's saying, "and there are a couple of trashy gossip magazines in that cupboard if you need a tabloid fix. The toilet and shower are all hooked up."

"I just…use them like normal?"

Hadley nods. "The gray water irrigates the grass outside. Toilet's hooked up to my septic system, so no worries about anything overflowing." She shows Jillian how to rearrange the bed into a couch and how to unfold a little table from the wall. "I plan to drag you into the main kitchen to eat with me most days, but this should come in handy any time you'd rather have some you-time."

Jillian bites her lip. Hadley's being so incredibly kind; Jillian doesn't have the heart to tell her she won't be here long.

"It's more comfortable than it looks," Hadley says. She sits on the bed and pats the quilt next to her. "Seriously. Try it out, will you? It's like something from a five-star Vegas hotel, just a little narrower. There's a foam mattress topper and everything."

Jillian sits. "This is one of your grandma's old quilts," she says. "Like the one on your bed."

"Yeah, she was quite the thread jockey." Hadley smiles as she traces a circle in the old fabric. "This one's a wedding ring pattern. I hope that's not a problem."

The bottom drops out of Jillian's gut.

"Too soon?" Hadley asks, winking.

Jillian's mouth is a flat line, but it takes some effort to keep from smiling at Hadley's unbridled assholery. "Too soon." A worn, stuffed dog with a felt tongue lolling out of its stitched mouth sits perched on top of the pillows. "Mr. Flarf!" Jillian cries, reaching for it. "I remember when your dad won him for you at the fair."

"1981," Hadley says.

"Boy, those were the days, weren't they?"

"They were indeed. But before you get too attached, you should know that the Flarfster's strictly out here on a loaner basis. I can't sleep without him for too many nights, but he and I worked it out. We've decided to try an open relationship."

"Not a bad idea," Jillian says, stifling a yawn. "Once I've gotten used to being single, polyamory might just become my next thing." She looks at Hadley wide-eyed, mortified. "I have no idea why I just said that."

Hadley smiles and gives her shoulder a squeeze. "See? There's the old Jill Jacobs I know and love."

That first night, she barely sleeps. She already misses her plush carpet and master bath, her laundry room and big kitchen. She feels a pang in her chest at the thought of her king-sized bed back home. She's brought so little with her, and she starts to worry about the things she needs, her bedtime routine things—electric toothbrush, special face washes and creams, that one prescription from the dermatologist, the body oil that keeps her skin from drying out in the Arizona air. She suddenly feels like a cartoon character that's sprinted unknowingly over the edge of a cliff only to find herself running in place with nothing beneath her feet.

The Ovum's little mattress *is* surprisingly comfortable though. Lying there, Jillian imagines Lawrence back inside their house, reading her note and having second thoughts, perhaps even realizing she's not the easy catch he must have assumed her to be all these years. She imagines him standing alone in the empty kitchen. What will he eat? Who will he talk to about his day? She whimpers a little at the thought. But it's going to be okay. She'll hunker down here at Hadley's for a few days, and then she'll go back home and figure out what to do next. Heaven knows they've weathered some pretty big storms together, she and Lawrence. No doubt they'll weather this one, too.

Wrapped snugly within this new fog of optimism, Jillian dozes off into a fitful sort of half-sleep, but then she's awakened by what sounds like stuttering police sirens outside. It takes her disoriented brain a full minute to remember where she is. When she does, she realizes that it's only a pack of coyotes—in a nearby canyon, from the sound of it—probably celebrating a fresh kill. Shivering at the thought and hovering once more on the verge of sleep, Jillian grips the edge of the wedding ring quilt in the dark.

The next morning, she moves the polka dot curtain away from the nearest window and peeks groggily out at the dawn sky. She reaches for the cotton Navajo blanket Hadley folded up and placed at the foot of the mattress. Wrapping it around her shoulders like a shawl, Jillian gets up and slips her feet into the flats she wore up here. When she opens the trailer door and heads outside, though, she misses the little metal step and nearly lands on her face in the dirt. Catching herself mid-stumble, she curses under her breath.

"You okay?"

Jillian looks up to see Hadley standing on the back step of the A-frame holding two mugs. "Other than nearly breaking my neck, yes," she says.

Coffee steam mingles with the smell of woodsmoke in the early morning air as Hadley hands one of the mugs to Jillian. "I figured you'd want leaded this morning."

Jillian nods and takes a long drag from the mug. The coffee's stronger that she's used to, but the bittersweet liquid makes her feel like she's getting a life force transfusion.

"Let me show you the barn," Hadley says.

Obediently, Jillian follows, taking care not to spill the coffee as she pulls the edges of the blanket more snugly closed at her chest. It's only the beginning of September, but there's already a distinct chill in the mountain air. It won't be this cold down in Scottsdale until January, if then. A big rig is parked next to the barn. Jillian gazes up at it as they pass by. "You're still driving, huh?"

Hadley nods. "Yeah, you know. Salary's not bad. Benefits are decent, yada yada. It pays the bills." Grunting, she slides open one of the barn's big wooden doors.

The first thing Jillian sees in the dim light is Hadley's old Ford Pinto from back when they were in high school. "Are you kidding me?"

"Runs like a top," Hadley says, smiling proudly. "I thought you'd be happy to know you're not completely stuck out here."

"Hadley, I really don't think—"

"You don't want to take it on any long road trips or anything, but it'll do for getting you around town."

Jill doesn't know what to say. Hanging on a nearby wall above the Pinto is a big metal sign with the words CRONE IN PROGRESS emblazoned across it. "That's depressing."

Hadley smiles. "Why?"

"Because you're only forty!"

"Call me an early adopter."

"But I'm right behind you." A hint of panic has crept into Jillian's voice. "So don't be jumping on the geriatric train just yet, okay?"

"I don't know about the whole geriatric thing," Hadley says matter-of-factly. "But crones rock. They have tons of sex, too. I mean, yeah, they might have to whack their victims—er, *part*ners—over the head with a boulder or knock them out with special herb concoctions before dragging them back to the lair, but I'm pretty sure they get some serious action either way."

Jillian raises an eyebrow. "Clearly, you've given this some thought."

"Yeah, well, I mean, look where I live. Not much else to do, right?" Hadley looks down at a tan and black pygmy goat that's come to join them in the barn. "What are you doing here, Finster?"

The goat bleats in response.

"He's so cute!" Jillian reaches down to scratch between his horns.

"Yeah, but he's a pain in the ass. I let him free roam, so don't leave anything outside that you don't want eaten. Right, Fin?"

The goat tilts his head at her for a moment before nibbling at the corner of the blanket wrapped around Jillian's shoulders.

"See what I mean?"

A few minutes later, Jillian's sitting at the kitchen table inside the A-frame watching Hadley make breakfast. She marvels once again at the great shape her friend is in. Hadley looks the same as she did all those years ago; she clearly hasn't gone soft in the ways Jillian has.

"I was thinking pancakes, eggs, and bacon," Hadley says, brandishing a spatula. "The works. Sound good?"

Jillian shrugs. "I haven't had much of an appetite lately, to be honest."

"That's pretty obvious. You're thin as a rail. But no worries. We'll fatten you up right quick."

"I wish you'd let me help," Jillian tells her.

Hadley waves the comment away. "Speaking of fattening up critters," she says. "I thought we could go check out the county fair later this morning. I might even bid on a turkey at the 4-H auction."

Jillian grimaces. "I wasn't really planning on going anywhere today." She waits for Hadley to give her some grief, to good-naturedly try to railroad her, but it doesn't happen. Jillian fiddles with a nature magazine that's on the table next to a calculator and a logbook of some kind. She considers opening it and reading one of the articles highlighted on the cover in bold font ("Get Outdoors and Out of Your Rut!") but trying to absorb even basic information feels like way too much effort. "So, what have you been up to?" she finally asks. "Other than making this place fabulous, I mean." It's an odd thing to ask of someone she used to know almost as well as she knew herself, but she doesn't have the energy right now to worry about all the implications of not keeping in touch. Besides, people change and grow apart all the time.

"Who, me?" Hadley absently flips a pancake. "Not much, other than being your average lesbian delivery truck driver. Which you already know."

"Do you like it?"

Hadley glances at her and winks. "The lesbian part or the truck driving part?"

"You know what I meant."

Hadley laughs. "Yeah, I guess. It's local deliveries, mainly, though I have some multi-day gigs coming up. Nothing too exciting. And about the other thing," she says, drawing out the words as if not totally sure how to continue. "I've just been through a breakup of my own pretty recently."

Jillian startles a little, then frowns. She wouldn't exactly call what she's going through a *breakup*, per se.

"To tell you the truth," Hadley says, "Darcy and I have been on the rocks for a while. I suppose she just finally had enough."

"I'm sorry to hear that."

"Don't be! Misery loves company, right? It's actually kind of awesome if you think about it. I've wanted to catch up with you for a while now."

Jillian raises an eyebrow.

"Seriously," Hadley insists, turning back toward the stove. "Your crisis couldn't have come at a better time for me, personally."

Now Jillian rolls her eyes and fights the smile trying to take over her face. "Screw you."

Hadley sets down the spatula and looks at her like a puppy that's just been offered a biscuit. "Oh, would you? I can't tell you how horny I've been for the past few—"

"Hadley!"

"So sorry. Is Princess shocked?"

Before she knows it, Jillian is laughing, really laughing, from her belly. She can't remember how long it's been. Until this moment, she was pretty sure her body had forgotten how. Yet here she is. Also, she didn't think she'd be able to eat anything when she woke up this morning. Fifteen minutes later, though, she finds herself cleaning her plate and shyly asking for seconds.

Back in the Ovum after helping to clean the kitchen and listening to what Hadley's parents and brother have been up to, Jillian sits on the bed and looks around. Then she grabs her phone. Before she has time to overthink it and change her mind, she sends Lawrence a text: *How are you?* It's only to check in, she tells herself as she sits there staring at the word *Sent* on the screen, her heart pounding.

To her surprise, he texts back almost immediately.

Busy. Will get back to you ASAP. And then this: *Need to talk.*

Her heart leaps in response. Suddenly anxious, she twists her plain gold wedding band around and around on her ring finger. She doesn't want to assume anything, of course, but she's pretty sure she knows what's going on with Lawrence. They've been down a similar road before, early on in their marriage. Jillian had fled to this mountain, and Lawrence had begged her to come back. Now, all these years later, she's pretty sure her show of strength has, if nothing else, at least made an impression on him once again.

Sitting there staring down at her phone is making her increasingly fidgety. What does *ASAP* mean, exactly? It's Saturday, so it's not like Lawrence has classes or meetings today. Probably, it's best not to think too much about what he's up to. Even if Penelope is out of the picture, there's still a chance she'll try to lure Lawrence back into her seductive web. Musing on this possibility transports Jillian right back to the hallway outside Lawrence's office and the purple scarf draped across the TA's bare breasts. Shaking her head quickly, she shoos the memory away. It won't do to just sit here for who knows how long, waiting and wondering—torturing herself. She sends a quick *I'm fine, don't worry about me* text to Evan and then to her mother. Barb won't buy it for a second, of course, but at least Jillian won't feel bad about not touching base. She'd send a text to her dad, too, but he and Helen don't really do modern technology, and it's not like the situation with Lawrence warrants a phone call. Likely, this is just another bump—albeit more humiliating than the ones that have come before—in the long road of their marriage.

Taking a deep breath and then blowing it out slowly, she stands up. She remembers the miniscule metal step this time as she leaves the Ovum and strides across the path toward the back door of the A-frame. Once inside, she can hear Hadley rustling around in her bedroom. The sound stops when Jillian, standing in the middle of the kitchen, calls out, "So, what time were you thinking of heading to the fair?"

Screams from the Gravitron and the Tilt-a-Whirl greet the women before they even reach the ticket booth less than an hour later. Once their hands have been stamped and they're through the gate, it's clear not a lot has changed since the last time Jillian attended this fair in high school: The rides, the displays, the animals, the smells—everything's the same, or close to it. They stroll past food vendors selling corn dogs and cotton candy, turkey legs and Navajo tacos—the local favorite concoction of ground beef, beans, cheese, and other toppings heaped onto a fat round of fry bread. At the end of the row, a Hatch green chile vendor slowly spins his wares inside a cylindrical steel roaster. Even though it hasn't been that long since breakfast, Jillian's stomach rumbles at the thought of a New Mexico-style burrito.

They head toward the floriculture barn where Hadley spots someone she knows and goes over to chat. Jillian wanders by herself past the entries—massive heirloom pumpkins stacked on shelves, groupings of broccoli, rainbow chard, and kale carefully arranged on plates next to bouquets of lovingly cultivated peonies, sunflowers, and roses, their fragrance filling the barn. She strolls past a long row of mason jars filled with honey lined up near a window. Sunlight streams in through the light-to-dark gradations of liquid amber, casting a strand of golden shadows across the wooden shelf. Jillian's breath catches in her throat. She wishes Lawrence could be here to see it all with her. The wishing makes her chest hurt, though, so she pushes those thoughts from her mind.

The 4-H animals are next. Hadley and Jillian commune with the rabbits, goats, and sheep for a while before heading to the swine barn. Hand-painted name plaques, some bejeweled and some with victory ribbons attached, hang above the stalls. "There's always a Hamlet," Hadley says knowingly. "Always a Pork Chop."

A short while later, in the funhouse, Jillian beholds herself in a series of warped, full-length mirrors. Nothing about her body is where it's supposed to be, and yet the bulbous torso, pin-sized head, and over-inflated hands somehow create the truest reflection of herself she's seen in a long time.

A local archery club has a tent outside the funhouse. About twenty yards away, straw bales with paper targets pinned to them are stacked against a concrete wall. A teen girl holds out a bow toward Hadley as she and Jillian walk past.

"Really?" Hadley asks her, teasing. "You're going to trust me with an arrow?"

"They're faux arrows," the girl responds, smiling as Hadley loads the arrow onto the bow in one deft motion. "Foam tips. The role players use them."

With elbows up and one eye closed, Hadley draws the arrow back and then lets it fly.

"Whoa," Jillian says as it hits the target almost dead center. "Where did you learn to do that?"

"Scouts," Hadley answers with a nonchalant shrug, handing the bow and arrow back to the girl.

"And that's why nobody in their right mind would mess with you," a man's voice says from behind them as they're walking away from the archery tent.

Hadley turns around and gasps. "Bo!"

Jillian turns, too, her hand going reflexively to her chest as Bodhi Paxton, her high school boyfriend, walks toward them.

"I can't believe it," he says with that smile Jillian remembers so well, a smile that could launch a thousand ships full of lovesick maidens. His arms are open wide, and before Jillian knows it, she's awkwardly returning his brief embrace. The feel of his body registers in that half-second, though it's different than she remembers; he seems taller than he used to, for one thing. Also, he's more filled out and muscular—no longer a lanky eighteen-year-old. "Jill Jacobs," he says, pulling back to gaze at her.

"Kensington," she corrects him automatically. "And it's Jillian."

Hadley elbows her in the ribs.

"Sorry," Bodhi says, holding his palms up in mock surrender. "Of course."

"Jacobs is probably better at this point," Hadley adds, hugging him. "And if this isn't a meet cute, I don't know what is."

"Except we've already met," Jillian says. She hears how catty the words sound leaving her mouth, but she feels ambushed. If Hadley arranged this "unexpected" run-in with an old flame, she crossed a serious line.

Hadley seems oblivious to her annoyance though. "What are you doing here?" she asks Bodhi. "At the fair, I mean. Obviously, I knew you were back in town."

"Got drafted to judge the school art projects," he answers. Fine lines radiate outward from the corners of his eyes when he smiles, and there are slight grooves on either side of his mouth where there used to be just dimples. Other than that, he's still looks the same.

Jillian can't help but momentarily wonder what he thinks about the changes in her own face, but she doesn't want to dwell too long on the possibilities. Seeing him so unexpectedly has thrown her into a weird, internal tizzy; her pulse is racing faster than it should, and her face feels hot. She wishes she'd spent more time—any time, really—on makeup this morning. "So, what do you do?" she asks him,

"Other than being a world-famous artist," Hadley adds.

"I don't know about that," Bodhi responds. "I may be *slightly* well known in a handful very small, very rural municipalities."

"Stop being modest," Hadley tells him.

Jillian's confused. "What does that even mean?"

Bodhi turns to her. "I do sculptures," he explains. "Corporate stuff, mainly."

"Wow." Jillian does her best to keep a polite smile on her face despite a pang of what can only be described as an old, artistic jealousy rising behind her ribs. "That's...amazing. Really." Making a concerted effort to switch gears, she slips into the kind of small talk she's grown skilled at over the past decades as a faculty wife. "So, you live in Flagstaff now?"

"It's been a few years," he says. "I originally came back to be closer to my mom, so she can stay in her house."

Jillian feels another pang as she remembers how encouraging Evelyn always was about her and Bodhi's art school dreams when they were high school seniors. "How is she doing?"

"She's good overall, but she has some mobility issues. Multiple sclerosis."

"I'm so sorry."

"No," he says, "It's okay. I mean, it's not easy for her, but between me and the caretaker who stops by, she's actually doing pretty great."

"Bodhi has a studio just outside town," Hadley tells Jillian. "Which I still haven't *seen*, by the way." She punches him playfully on the arm, and he smiles. Jillian marvels at the comradery that so clearly still exists between them.

"Well, come by, then," he says. "I've tried to get you to visit since I started renovating."

Hadley looks sheepish. "I know. I just get busy."

"Sure," he says, narrowing his eyes in mock skepticism. "Excuses, excuses. But I'm serious. Come by any time. Both of you."

Any time turns out to be a mere two days later. Hadley's waiting outside the Ovum with the usual cups of coffee Monday morning when Jillian emerges. "Look who's bright-eyed and bushy-tailed," she chirps. "Ready for another holiday weekend adventure?"

Still groggy, Jillian doesn't respond right away. Instead, she takes the mug Hadley's holding out and sips, wincing a little. She's still trying to get used to the strength of the French press brew.

"I called Bodhi and told him I have today off," Hadley continues. "I'm dying to see his studio. Aren't you?"

"I'm pretty wiped," Jillian says. What she doesn't say is that she was up half the night, still waiting for Lawrence to call or text back after his cryptic *We need to talk* message.

"Anyway," Hadley says, ignoring Jillian's barely-there protest. "Why don't you throw on some clothes? We'll head out in about ten minutes." She turns to go back inside the A-frame, but Jillian puts a hand on her shoulder to stop her.

"This may sound weird, but you're not thinking about…trying to set me and Bodhi up or anything, are you?"

Hadley pauses before responding, clearly trying to choose her words carefully. "Um, I don't know if you know this, hon," she says finally, "but you're pretty much the hottest of hot messes right now. And by *hottest,* I don't mean sexy or beautiful. I mean overcooked. Charred. Flambéed…just a complete pile of wreckage."

Jillian stares.

"Seriously," Hadley continues. "I wouldn't do that to Bodhi. I do love you though."

Jillian blinks. "Gee, thanks. Is that how you charm the pants off all the ladies?"

"I'm just saying."

"You sure you know where you're going?" she asks Hadley about half an hour later as they turn off the pavement and onto a dirt road at the edge of town.

"Yeah," Hadley says. "Bodhi gave me directions over the phone."

A weird sort of déjà vu comes over Jillian as the truck jounces along. The road seems familiar, but she can't figure out why. She's quite sure she never spent time out here growing up. It's beautiful though. Oak leaves on either side of the road have turned a deep, burnished gold so that they practically glow against the dark green pine boughs and the bright blue sky.

"We're a little early," Hadley says as they pull into a gravel driveway and get out of the truck. They approach a modern-looking structure surrounded by professional landscaping. Metal sculptures, most of them abstract and at least ten feet tall, have been placed at various intervals on either side of the flagstone walkway. Jillian pauses to admire one. She'd love to study all of them, but instead she catches up with Hadley, who's already knocking on the front door of the building. When nobody answers, Hadley pulls the door open to reveal an enormous one-room art studio with vaulted ceilings and massive, multi-paned windows.

A guy with his back to them is working at one end of the studio. He's way too large to be Bodhi. From a split-second glance at the big Harley-Davidson patch on the back of his black leather vest and the wallet chain hanging from his hip, Jillian gathers he's a biker. He's wearing a welding mask and working on a long piece of metal with some sort of welder or torch, oblivious to their presence.

In contrast to the biker dude, and looking like some sort of celestial vision, a young woman wearing a bandeau top sits on a stool in the dead center of the studio. She's illuminated by cloud-mottled light falling in through the windows, and she raises a hand in greeting to the women standing in the doorway.

Porcelain skin? Jillian thinks, not returning the wave. *Check. Thick hair piled atop her head? Check. Long neck curving down into a flawless décolletage? Check-a-rooni.* The woman looks like something Michelangelo would have chiseled from a hunk of marble. "Freakin' perfection," Jillian mutters to herself, the words leaving her mouth in a bitter rush before she can stop them. She can't help it. The sight of this young woman has brought her, once again, right back to the Classics department hallway outside Lawrence's office. She feels sick, cold, and enraged all at once—and also crazy, now that she thinks about it, since there's no logical reason for her to have such a reaction.

Hadley, meanwhile, just stares at the woman in awe. "Holy—" she whispers finally.

The welding biker stops what he's doing. He stands up, raises his mask, and turns around to face them. "Looking for Bodhi?" he asks in a gruff voice.

"No," Jillian answers, turning on her heel. "We were just leaving."

Moments later, Hadley jogs to keep up with her as she speed-walks toward the truck, head down and eyes focused straight ahead. "Do I even want to ask what that was about?" she wonders out loud a minute after that as they're backing out of the gravel drive. She looks both concerned and amused.

Jillian, sitting in the passenger seat with her arms crossed over her chest, just shakes her head.

"Onto plan B, I guess." Hadley drives them to Walnut Canyon, a national monument just east of Flagstaff. After paying their admission in the visitor center, they descend hundreds of concrete steps leading to a surreal looking, raised geological island rising up from the river-carved chasm below. They don't say much as they hike the perimeter trail, exploring the ancient dwellings built into the sides of the cliffs by those who lived here thousands of years earlier. Clouds are stacked high overhead, glowing bright orange as if lit on fire by the September afternoon sun. At the end of the hike, as they're making their way back up the stairs (Jillian panting hard to get enough air into her burning lungs), her phone buzzes. When she pulls it out of her pocket and glances at the screen, her already-pounding heart breaks into a flat-out gallop.

Hearing the footsteps behind her stop, Hadley turns around and frowns. "What is it?"

"Lawrence," Jillian whispers. For a moment, she debates whether or not to answer. What if he wants her back? What will she say? (Well, she knows what she'll say, but *how* would she say it exactly? She doesn't want him thinking he can just toy with her emotions willy-nilly any time he feels like it. He needs to know she's serious about maintaining her dignity in this marriage. That she's serious about respecting herself and being respected by her husband). Knowing that the phone's insistent vibrations will soon stop, she answers before the call disconnects. "Hello," she says, keeping her voice as level as possible.

"Jillian."

There's something…off…about Lawrence's voice. He sounds hesitant—nervous even—which is unusual; normally, he sounds completely sure of himself. Then again, it can't be easy reaching out after what he did.

"Yes, Lawrence," she says. She wonders if he can hear the encouragement in her voice, the longing. "I'm here."

"That's good to know." Lawrence releases a long exhalation.

Could it be he's feeling the same relief at this reconnection that she's feeling? Could it be he wants her to come home, that he's ready to start again but just doesn't know how to phrase it? "What can I—" she starts to say, but Lawrence cuts her off.

"Penelope's pregnant."

Book 8: 1988-1989

As usual, it's art that saves me.

I'm only allowed to take one art class in the blur that is my first semester at college. It's Painting I, and it's pretty basic. The professor is amazing though. Madame Imre. She's this crazily joyful Hungarian woman in her sixties who (as she informed us during the first minutes of the first class) fled Budapest during the Hungarian revolution in the mid-1950's. If I was casting the role of a university art instructor for a movie, she'd definitely be my first pick. With her white-blonde hair and old school, Zsa Zsa Gabor makeup, complete with a penciled-in mole next to her mouth, she's something to behold. Then there's her vast collection of rings and bracelets—gold and silver, diamonds and turquoise—everything clinking together when she uses her arms and hands to emphasize a point she's trying to get across.

"You have," she tells me in her heavy accent during the second class, "a *zertain zomezing*." We've just started to work on our initial self-portraits, based on photos we took of ourselves the first day. We're also allowed to have mirrors near our easels.

Madame Imre watches me work for a while, observing my technique as I sketch out the shape of my face on the canvas. "Now, why you do this thing?" she asks, imitating the small, incremental brush stroke-type marks I use, even with a pencil. "This thing where you move the hand like so?"

"I honestly have no idea," I tell her. I've started feeling a little defeated by all the stuff I realize I don't know about art or about myself as an artist.

But Madame Imre doesn't seem fazed by my inexperience. "I see," she says with an encouraging smile. "Well, you have very good instincts. But they are young and still delicate. You are...how do these Arizona cowboys say it... *green*, yes?"

"Okay," I tell her, trying to act like I know where she's headed with this when I am, in fact, clueless.

"Begin by experimenting with longer, bolder lines," she tells me. "I think you will find it is good!"

That night, back in the dorm, I crouch on the carpet below the pay phone at the end of the hall, the flexible metal handset cord pulled taut.

It's been a few weeks since Bodhi and I went our separate ways—he to Colorado and me down here to Tempe—but the last time we saw each other is still too fresh, too raw, to talk about.

I'll call and write every day, one of us had said, standing out there by the car he'd bought over the summer, a mini-Chevy pickup truck.

I'll miss you, the other one of us said.

We'd both said *I love you* at the same time.

And then his mom Evelyn was there, too, handing him snacks for the road. It was time to say goodbye. When Bodhi drove away, his mom and I stood there waving. As soon as he was out of sight, we basically collapsed into each other's arms.

Now, crouched at the end of the dorm hallway, I tell him in a low voice how much I want to kiss his mouth and taste his neck, his chest, his belly, his hipbones, the clean muskiness of the juncture where his torso meets his thighs...and then I have to stop talking because Bodhi, panting at the other end of the line, tells me he can't take anymore, that he'll have to call me back when he can find a more private phone somewhere. Which works out just fine because another girl is standing a few yards away from me now, arms folded across her chest. No doubt she wants to talk to a boyfriend back home, too.

"Have you found your community here?" Madame Imre asks me one day near the end of class. In the month-plus that I've been at college, I've figured out that this is just something she does, this sneaking up to my easel out of the blue to ask random questions.

"I'm not sure I understand," I tell her, setting my brush down.

"The people you surround yourself with," she explains. "Other artists."

"I...guess so?" I think of my roommate, Natalie Edelmann, who's not an artist but who's sweet and enthusiastic about pretty much everything here at college—especially the guys (her older brother goes here too. He's a junior, so Natalie has access to his friend group). Half the time when I go back to my dorm room, the plaid necktie she uses as a privacy flag is hanging from the doorknob. I get along with Natalie and her friends just fine, but there's something keeping me from fully giving in to the zany social life all around me.

"I sense a loneliness in you," my teacher continues gently. "And this concerns me. It is hard enough being an artist as it is, yes?"

"Well," I tell her with a smile, "I have you."

"Pah," she says, tossing a hand in the air. Her bracelets and rings glint in the desert light coming in through the studio windows. "I am an old woman. I can share wisdom, but you need other young people. Other artists."

I think about Hadley and Bo. Since college started, I feel like I have one foot here in the present and one still back in a time when it seemed like the three of us were together more often than not. Without them, I feel lost, adrift. I feel like everyone here at the university (even my professors, apparently) can see that I'm just half a person. I keep waiting for that feeling to pass.

"So, tell me," Mademe Imre says, changing the subject. "Who are your favorite artists?"

"Georgia O'Keeffe," I tell her without hesitation. "Also, Gustav Klimt and Frida Kahlo."

"Ah, Frida." Madame Imre's voice is wistful. "Do you know what André Breton once said about her art?"

I shake my head.

"He said it was 'a ribbon around a bomb.'" My teacher's expression becomes stern. "Jill," she says. "Being an artist is like going to war. A pursuit not to be entered into lightly. You see?"

I nod, even though, as usual, I don't really know what she's talking about.

"You must reach deep down inside and bring whatever's there up to the surface and into your work," she continues. "Otherwise, what is the point? Think about it over the holiday, okay?"

"I will," I promise her.

I take a Greyhound bus home for Thanksgiving, even though it's going to completely suck not seeing Bodhi, who's saving up his money to fly out for Christmas.

"I hate that you're not going to be there," I told him on the phone last night.

"I know," he said, his voice mopey. "But at least you and Hadley will get a chance to hang out like you used to without me tagging along the whole time."

And then there's the stuff between my parents. They don't tell me as much when we talk on the phone, but I know they're still not doing well. I don't even want to think about how weird they're going to be around each other during the four days I'll be home. Still, I'm kind of looking forward to sleeping in my own bed again.

Dad hugs me when I come through the door. He looks thinner and grayer than when I last saw him, but I don't say anything. Instead, I look around at the half-empty house, frowning. It takes me a second to realize what's different. "Where's Mom's stuff?"

Dad sighs and rubs a hand down his face. "She moved out last week."

My head swivels toward him. "What? Where to?"

"To the place she's staying," he says wearily. "It was a pretty sudden decision. I told her she could stay here, and I'd go somewhere for the time being, but she said she just wanted out."

"Wow," I say, trying unsuccessfully to hide my shock. Apparently, a lot more has happened in the three months I've been gone than I realized. I figured life would more or less stand still back here at home. Wrong again. "And you're...okay with that?"

He shrugs. "Not much I can do about it, is there?"

Mom calls the house that evening. "I probably should have told you about my move," she says.

"You think?" I've had a few hours to stew, I'm tired from the trip up here, and I make no effort to temper the sarcasm in my voice.

Mom ignores my tone. "Would you consider having Thanksgiving dessert with me? I'm sure your dad's planning to take you out for the actual meal."

A hard nugget of laughter escapes me. "What is this? *Kramer vs. Kramer*?"

"Your father and I are trying to be respectful of each other, Jill."

"Yeah," I say with a bitter laugh. "That might have been a good idea about a decade ago." I know it's a bitchy thing to say, but I guess I'm still reeling from how fast everything's going to hell all of a sudden. True, for the past ten years their marriage has pretty much been circling the drain, but I guess I still wasn't prepared for the final gurgle to happen all at once like this.

My mother is silent at the other end of the line as I pinch the bridge of my nose between a thumb and forefinger. "I'll come for dessert," I tell her.

Dad and I have an early Thanksgiving meal at Big Dee's Buffet. I always liked coming here as a kid, but now the plastic upholstery in the booths combined with the discolored sneeze shield over the buffet give off a dismal vibe. Our waitress starts out nice enough until she starts flirting with my dad, who's not wearing his wedding ring. To my surprise, he flirts back. I roll my eyes and shake my head to let them both know how completely gross it is. I don't care how immature I'm being. When the food comes, I take a few bites before pushing my plate away, resisting the small talk Dad keeps trying to make with me. When he finally pays the check and we're able to leave, I drop him off at home before driving his car over to Mom's new place.

It's a mother-in-law unit just yards from the main house, which is owned by a woman she knows from the radio station. Mom tells me she's renting it on a short-term basis, just until one of the out-of-state jobs she's applied for comes through. The space looks barely lived in. At one end, there's a bed and a dresser. At the other, there's a tiny kitchen with a mini fridge, a microwave, and a little dining nook where we each eat a small slice of the pumpkin pie she picked up at the grocery store. I'm hungrier than I let on due to hardly eating anything at the restaurant, but I don't ask for seconds.

"I probably won't be here at Christmas time," Mom tells me as we sit at the little table.

Big shock, I think.

"But I want you to know something," she continues. "I want you to know that this stuff between your dad and me isn't about you. Sometimes a woman just needs to find her own way. Maybe someday you'll understand that for yourself."

I put down my fork next to the half-eaten slice of pie on my plate. Dab my mouth with a paper towel. "Can I go now?"

Once I'm back behind the wheel of Dad's car, I don't feel like going home, so I head over to Hadley's house instead. We're supposed to get together tomorrow, but what the hell—who doesn't like a surprise? Standing on her front porch, I knock on the door, but nobody answers. Her parents' car is gone, which means they're probably watching the football game at Hadley's uncle's house west of town like they usually do on Thanksgiving. Hadley's Pinto is in the driveway, though, so I know she's probably just in her room listening to her Walkman or something. Opening the front door, I step into the Wallace's entry hall, just like I've done since we were little kids. "Hello?" I call out.

There's no answer, just some thumps from Hadley's room followed by laughter.

"Yo," I holler, making my way down the hall to her room and pushing the door open a little.

That's when I see Hadley Wallace—my best friend, the girl who's always danced the slow songs with me when no boys were asking, who French braided my hair and spooned me whenever I freaked out over stuff between my parents—in bed with another girl. They're kissing, they're in their underwear, and they have no idea I'm standing there. I try to back away, but the heel of my tennis shoe catches on a wrinkle in the hallway rug, and I fall backward, arms windmilling until I land on my ass. Loudly.

The girl in Hadley's bed sits up, clutching a blanket to her chest. She has coppery skin that's a little darker than Hadley's and a full face surrounded by a halo of thick, brown hair. "What was that?" she asks, alarmed.

Seeing me through the slightly opened door, Hadley gets up from the bed. She doesn't bother to cover herself, and I don't wait around to see what happens next. Instead, I scramble to my feet and get the hell out of there. Driving home, I try to get my thoughts to fit together in some sort of way that makes sense, but it's like trying to solve a Rubik's Cube with all the stickers peeled off: How could I have not known this Very Basic Thing about my best friend? Why did she feel like she had to keep it from me? Have I known all along and somehow just didn't *know* that I knew? Do I maybe like girls and just don't know that yet, either? I think back to junior high, hear the voice of our nemesis, Veronica Delgado, in my head: *Lezzies.*

Hadley knocks on the front door about an hour later.

At first, I don't answer, but she keeps knocking. Dad's in his room. I don't want him getting involved.

"We're going to have to talk about this eventually," she says when I open the door enough to stick my face through. "Might as well be now."

I let her in and walk to the living room couch. She follows. We sit at opposite ends, arms folded across our chests.

"So, is this a thing?" I ask quietly after an eternity of silence. "Like, a *real* thing, or are you just, you know, experimenting?"

Hadley looks me in the eye. "It's a thing," she says. "It's always been a thing. I'm just starting to figure that out myself, I guess."

"You could have told me."

"I was going to," she says, looking down at her hands, which are folded in her lap now. "I just didn't know how. I definitely didn't want you to find out this way."

More silence. I won't look at her. I look at the ceiling, the floor, the walls, instead. "Who was that girl, anyway?" I finally ask.

"She's a freshman at the university. We met downtown just after you and Bodhi left."

I don't say anything.

"So, are we good?" It sounds like she wants this conversation to be over as much as I do.

And that's when I decide to store the whole situation in a back corner of my brain, in a cubby next to the one where I've already stuffed my parents' split, which is next to the cubby holding my physical separation from Bodhi. I'll figure out how I feel about it all later. "Sure," I tell Hadley. "We're good. It's not like it's a big deal or anything."

Back on campus, I work hard for the last couple of weeks before winter break. Final Exams kick my ass, but it's okay; studying for them has helped pass the time until I'll see Bodhi again. With the holiday so close, we haven't been talking on the phone or sending letters as much recently. I ache for him.

My last final is for Painting. It's a Kandinsky-inspired mood piece in blues, and I'm proud of it. When Madame Imre approaches my work area to give her critique, I mention how excited I am to be taking her Painting II class in the spring.

"You don't belong in that class," she tells me, her voice matter-of-fact.

"Excuse me?" I must look totally crestfallen because Madame Imre places a hand on my forearm.

"Frankly," she says, "you're too good."

"Oh." I'm blushing now. "That's very kind of you to say."

"I plan to approve you for my upper-division studio classes as soon as possible, but I cannot do that until all your core classes are done. This university is strict with me that way."

"Oh," I say again, feeling my shoulders slump.

My teacher takes a long look at me. "Jill," she says. "I will get you back into a good class. Come see me in the fall, after you have finished these others. How do you say it here in America? *Hang in there*. Like the little kitten, yes?"

I force a smile.

"Take Professor Xenakis's mythology seminar when you return from your holidays," she says finally. "This will satisfy the Humanities requirement."

I pull a notebook from my backpack so I can write down the name. "Professor Zeh…?"

"Xenakis," she repeats, gazing heavenward now. "Wonderful man, vibrant…*sexy*." Refocusing her eyes on mine, she adjusts her posture. "Well, perhaps not to *you* he won't be. He is in his late seventies, after all."

"Yeah," I tell her. "I'm not really into older guys."

Being back on the mountain for Christmas vacation is like stepping out of the technicolor world of campus and into an old black-and-white movie. It's only been a few weeks since I was here for Thanksgiving, but it hadn't snowed yet then. Now it's a winter wonderland outside, everything covered in a blanket of snow from the storm that rolled in last week. The sky is a rich palette of gray tones.

Mom ended up moving to the Bay Area when her dream job producing a radio show in San Jose came through right after Thanksgiving, so it's just going to be me and Dad over the break.

"The house looks better," I tell him after setting my duffel bag down and taking off my parka.

Oddly enough, he blushes a little at the compliment. "I've been doing some…entertaining for the past week or so," he says. When he doesn't say anything more for several seconds, it finally dawns on me what he's getting at.

"Oh! You mean you're…dating?"

He nods.

"Wow," I say, trying to act happy for him. "Good for you, Dad." I don't want a repeat of Thanksgiving (in hindsight, I'd acted pretty bratty about him and that waitress flirting at Big Dee's). But the truth is this new information is just one more thing I'll need to file away and think about later, when my mind is clear. I check my watch. Bodhi's connection flight from Phoenix is due to land at the tiny Flagstaff airport in just a few minutes. "See you later," I tell my dad, giving him a hug before putting my parka back on and heading for the front door.

"Want a ride?"

"No," I tell him. "The exercise will do me good."

Walking the half mile to Bodhi's house, I can hardly focus on anything except putting one foot in front of the other. When I get there, he and his mom haven't arrived yet, so I stand on their front porch, shifting my weight from side to side to stay warm. And then—finally, finally—his mom's car rolls into view down the road. It doesn't even come to a complete stop before Bodhi's out and running toward me, slipping on random patches of ice but somehow managing not to fall.

I meet him halfway and jump into his arms, immediately affixing my face to his. Everything blends together—the scent of his balsam shampoo, the warmth of his skin, the Peaches n' Herb song from fifth grade that suddenly won't leave my head. Bodhi's mom gives my shoulder a quick squeeze as she passes us on her way into the house. And still I stay there, my legs wrapped around his waist. I'm only slightly worried that he's noticing the dreaded freshman fifteen I'm well on my way to gaining, thanks to the endless vats of spaghetti, and mashed potatoes, and apple strudel, and Cap'n Crunch in the university dining hall.

The next several days pass in a blur of being together as much as possible, talking on the phone when we can't, sneaking into my bed when my dad's not home (which is most of the time, it turns out), and trying to catch up on all the stuff we've missed in each other's lives since August.

In his room, with crisp December daylight falling in through the blinds and Cocteau Twins playing in the background, I sit for him, nude, with just a sheet draped over my legs so I don't totally freeze to death as he sketches me.

At one point, Bodhi stops and lets his hand fall to the paper. "I love you, Jill," he says.

"I know," I tell him. "I love you, too."

Not too long after that, I start to get bored sitting there, so I get up and straddle him instead, wrapping the sheet around both of us.

And everything else in the world disappears.

But still. Even though rediscovering Bodhi is a dream come true, my stomach stays clenched in a perpetual knot, a knot that gets tighter with each day that passes, knowing that it's one less day we have together before we'll have to go our separate ways again.

It's not just me; Bodhi seems preoccupied, too. I discover him staring, studying me at random times when he doesn't think I notice. We don't talk about the hours slipping away because what's the point? Best to just enjoy the time we have together, even though that's easier said than done.

For Christmas, he gives me a garnet infinity pendant on a sterling silver chain. I give him my final project from Madame Imre's class, the study in blues.

"It's not as good as your stuff," I tell him.

"Are you kidding me?" He holds up the canvas and then sets it on the windowsill of his bedroom so he can step back and view it from a different angle. "It's unbelievable."

I tell him all about Madame Imre, trying to copy her accent and gestures. I end up sounding more like Dr. Ruth, though, which cracks us both up until I notice a little furrow of concern between Bodhi's eyebrows.

"And the guys in the art classes?" he asks. "I'm sure they're all head-over-heels in love with you."

"I wouldn't know," I say, reaching for him. "And I wouldn't care." It's true. I stare right into his eyes when I say it, so he'll know how serious I am. But Bodhi seems more than just a little preoccupied now; he seems almost panicked.

On New Years' Eve, we're supposed to go downtown where Hadley and a bunch of other people we sort of knew in high school are going to watch the big pinecone descend from the roof of one of the historic hotels—Flagstaff's version of Times Square. But we don't go.

We don't go because Bodhi lets it slip that he—kind of, sort of—kissed another girl last month at his school. Theresa is her name. She's a graphic artist. They met on the first day and have been friends ever since. "She actually kissed me," he's saying in a hurried voice. "And it was completely awkward and out of the blue, but I still didn't stop her as fast as I should have."

The confession blindsides me. It smashes me upside the head like a snowball with a big rock inside.

"It shouldn't have happened at all," Bodhi says when I just stare at him silently, mouth agape. "I'm not even interested in her that way. But I was drunk, and that's no excuse and…I am a complete asshole. I guess that's all there is to say. I wanted to tell you right after it happened, but I was afraid you'd break up with me over the phone and never talk to me again."

Wires spark, transformers explode. "This can't be happening," I whisper.

"I take responsibility for not stopping the kiss," he says, his voice a plea now. "But I *did* stop it, Jill. I'm not interested in her. I'm interested in you. I *love* you. You know that. It was stupid of me to not stop it sooner, but it only lasted for about three seconds..."

Imagining those three seconds, my heart drops through my ribcage and falls to the ground. *The wheels are coming off this thing,* is all I can think. *Just like they came off Mom and Dad's marriage.* I've been trying to shove all the stuff I haven't known how to deal with into cubbies at the back of my brain—Mom moving out of the house, my long-distance relationship with Bodhi, seeing Hadley with that girl in her bed. But I can't deny the truth anymore. We're all breaking apart and flying off in different directions like the shards of Mom's ceramic mug dropped on the kitchen floor all those years ago, never to be put back together in the same way again. Until hearing this new information about Bodhi kissing another girl, I haven't realized how overfull that place at the back of my brain has gotten, how close it was to exploding. But now here we are, Bodhi and I, the first casualties of the blast.

"Everything is just changing so much," I tell him, wiping tears from my eyes with the back of a sleeve. "We're changing, you and me."

"Don't say that," Bodhi says, shaking his head and staring into my eyes. "I'll leave later, start school a few days late, so we can talk. We can work this out, Jill. I'll transfer to State so we can be together." He reaches for me, but I pull away.

Bodhi seems to understand that there's no point in trying to talk to me anymore tonight. "I'll be back in the morning," he says with quiet resignation in his voice. He tries to meet my eyes. "I love you. You know that, right?"

I nod, but I don't say anything more as he walks backward for a few paces before turning and heading toward the front door with his head down and his shoulders hunched. A minute later, I stand in the doorway watching his tail lights as the old pickup slides sideways before fishtailing around the icy turn at the end of my street.

I wake up at four-thirty the next morning, so I'll have enough time to make the six o'clock bus departure. After getting dressed and throwing my stuff into the duffel bag, I tiptoe down the hall toward the kitchen. Dad's bedroom door is open, though, and he's not in there. The bed is still made, which means he never came home last night. While coffee's brewing, I write a note for him. "Must've been some party," I mumble against my coffee cup before bundling myself up in a parka. I pull on gloves and snow boots before closing the door of my childhood home behind me. Then I follow the trail of streetlights toward the bus station downtown, my breath pluming out in front of me as I stumble every few steps on the frozen road.

Book 9: 2009

Eros, again now, the loosener of limbs troubles me,
Bittersweet, sly, uncontrollable creature….
~Sappho

W*hhh…*

That's the sound that escapes her—the beginning of *What?* followed by stunned silence, her mouth frozen in an elongated O. Something inside Jillian vaporizes itself in that millisecond, leaving an infinite, icy nothingness in its place. Standing on a concrete step overlooking Walnut Canyon, she feels like she's floating above the ancient cliff dwellings like a long-dead former tenant. Or like one of the ravens presently circling the air above the chasm below. She'd been struggling for breath as she and Hadley climbed back up the stairs toward the visitor center. Now, with just two simple words—*Penelope's pregnant*—Lawrence has completely taken that breath away.

Hadley, standing a few stairs above, watches with her head cocked inquisitively to one side. Then her eyes grow wide, and she hops down a few steps to steady Jillian, who's suddenly reaching for the steel handrail.

At the other end of the call, Lawrence sighs. "I should also mention that I'm going to be on a more…limited income now that the baby's coming," he says.

With Hadley's assistance, Jillian sits down on the step, certain she's going to start hyperventilating. She bends forward so she's doubled over. "What are you saying?" Her voice is a hoarse whisper.

Lawrence sighs again (*as if all of this is terribly taxing for him,* a distant part of Jillian's brain observes). "You do recall that we had an…agreement…at the time we decided to…when we got married."

"Prenup," she manages to say. She's vaguely aware of Hadley's face transforming into a scowl in the periphery of her vision now.

"The prenuptial agreement," Lawrence confirms. "Exactly."

Jillian tries to remember how to keep her heart from stopping as Lawrence proceeds to explain the tight spot he and Penelope have found themselves in. "There's no way we can stay in Penelope's apartment," he says. "Not even short-term, as we originally planned."

Planned? Jillian wants to scream. *How long has this planning been going on?*

"I know this may be hard for you to hear," Lawrence continues. "But we need to move into the house in time to get the nursery ready."

"The nursery?" She's going to throw up. She's sure of it. "Please tell me you're not going to use Evan's room."

"We're going to convert the guest room," he says. "That way, Evan will still have his room to come home to."

Home. At the sound of that word, the nausea changes to something else—white hot rage poured into a huge, bubbling cauldron of sorrow. "What about me?" she demands. "Are you kicking me out?"

"Let's be honest," Lawrence says, clearly not appreciating the new edge in her voice. "It's pretty obvious you're not committed to staying here."

"I've been gone *three days*." She's practically gasping now. "Also, *I'm* not committed to staying? Are you kidding?" She manages to call up a hard, bitter nugget of laughter from some dark place within. When she glances up, Hadley is still watching her.

"Apparently you've found a place to stay."

A thread of terror worms its way up Jillian's spine. She can already feel the rage dissipating and dissolving as it's replaced by something so much worse—the same pulseless void that kept her in bed for an entire week, the bottomless pit of despair she's only now starting to climb out of. She feels dizzy all of a sudden, unbalanced, as dark sparkles seem to float into her brain.

"...don't know how to put this," Lawrence is saying from some faraway place. "I need to know when you're going to come gather your belongings...including your car...We need the driveway space..."

Which is when the phone falls from Jillian's hand and rattles down the stairs below.

And everything fades to black.

"We had a life together!" Jillian wails once they're back at Hadley's.

The fainting spell hadn't been too serious. Hadley had steadied Jillian, managing to keep her from falling down the concrete stairs as she'd come back to full consciousness. They'd sat for a long while before slowly climbing the rest of the way up toward the parking lot, pausing frequently so Jillian could sip water and breathe. The phone was a little banged up, but even it was okay. She'd been more or less catatonic on the drive home; now she can hardly speak through the tears. "We have a son! How could Lawrence do this?"

"I know," Hadley says, rubbing Jillian's shoulder. "I know. It's going to be okay."

After a while, when her breathing has leveled out yet again and she's downed two cups of chamomile tea, Jillian heads to the Ovum to lie down. Once she's in there, though, she has no clue what to do. If she was back home in Scottsdale, she'd likely go straight into *wifely overdrive,* as Lawrence calls it. She'd get right to work cleaning the house, or baking a batch of chocolate chip zucchini bread, or booking that Botox appointment with her aesthetician—anything to take her mind off what she'd ultimately convince herself was nothing more than an unpleasant event. Their long marriage had survived some pretty major bumps and potholes in the road over the years, she'd tell herself. And like those others, this one would surely, eventually pass.

But the domestic distractions she's become used to are in short supply up here on the mountain, in the relative middle of nowhere. Which means her choices are to curl up in the Ovum and cry until dawn or...or what? Once again, Jillian can feel herself descending involuntarily back down into the pit she's only recently started to claw her way out of. It feels like she's being forcibly *pulled* downward in an inevitable spiral, with no choice in the matter. But then she remembers the moment she heard Lawrence utter the word *pregnant*—the instantaneous oblivion she felt blooming within. She thinks of how she let herself languish in bed after catching Lawrence and Penelope in his office. How she was willing to give up at the drop of a hat. Well, if she could decide to waste away, then she can decide to the opposite, too, can't she? She can choose how she's going to feel from this point forward, right? And if that's the case, then there's no way she's choosing to go back down into that pit. Mind over matter. The thought is an adrenaline-fueled revelation.

"You know what?" she calls out minutes later, letting the back door of the A-frame bang closed behind her as she rushes into Hadley's kitchen. "You're right."

Hadley appears from the tiny living room, clearly surprised to see Jillian standing there. "I am?"

"One-hundred percent!"

"Jill," Hadley says, her tone that of someone trying to coax a coworker back into the office from the thirty-ninth story window ledge. "What's going on?"

"I think I'm having a breakthrough. That's what."

"You're having some kind of break," Hadley mutters under her breath.

"Seriously, Hads. It sounds silly, I know, but when the going gets tough, the tough get going, right? You win some, you lose some. Nothing ventured, nothing—"

"I get it," Hadley says, fingers at her temples. "You're a life coach now. Where the hell are you going with all this?"

Jillian takes a deep breath. "I'm pretty sure I need to just get back out there, get back on that horse, hitch my wagon to a—"

"Jill."

"I want to go out somewhere and flirt it up a bit!" Jillian can feel herself growing more manic by the second, but she doesn't care. Any kind of energy feels better than despair. Any kind of forward momentum feels better than entropy.

"Flirt it up?" Hadley repeats, shaking her head. "Seriously?"

"I'm a free woman now, right? No more ball and chain. And, hey, you know what we hetero women say—"

Hadley sighs. "Honestly, I'm afraid to even ask."

"The best way to get over a guy is to get under another." Jillian's laughing now. Her eyes are watering a little, too. Can a person laugh and cry at the same time? If a heart shatters into a million pieces and nobody's there to hear it, does it make a sound? "Hey, can I borrow a beer?"

"Crikey," Hadley says, heading toward the fridge. "I've created a monster." She grabs a couple of beers and hands one to Jillian, who twists off the cap and takes a deep swig in one fluid motion. Then she belches.

"Is that place on Route 66 still open?"

Hadley's eyes narrow to slits. "The Zoo?"

"Yes!"

Cautiously, Hadley nods.

"We have to go. Tell me you have some clothes I can borrow. Like, like…" She snaps her fingers. "A western hat and some boots."

"Are you kidding me right now? Have you ever even *been* to the Zoo?"

Jillian shakes her head.

"Yeah," Hadley says. "I'm thinking it's a better idea for you to just rest here for a while. You've had a pretty rough day."

"Pah!" Jillian swipes a hand through the air the way her old Hungarian art professor used to do. "It's fine. I'm *fine*!"

Hadley opens her mouth as if to keep arguing, but then she closes it. "This is all against my better judgement," she says as she disappears into the bedroom. When she emerges a few minutes later, it's with a black felt Stetson hat balanced upside-down on her open palm. Draped over her arm is a pair of jeans with rhinestone-encrusted pockets. "Try these on. There's a full-length mirror on the back of my door."

Ten minutes and two beers later, Jillian emerges from the bathroom where—while deliberately NOT thinking about Lawrence—she'd gotten dressed, ratted her hair and then sprayed it using an old can of Aqua Net from under the sink. She did her best to emulate the "smoky eye" she's seen in magazines lately, using the one eyeshadow palette and the one liquid eyeliner she brought up from Scottsdale. She used a little extra blush, too, since bars are usually dark. "How do I look?" she asks, posing dramatically in the doorway.

Hadley looks up from the couch where she's been waiting. "Like you're headed to a *Hee Haw* casting call."

"Hmm," Jillian says, chewing at a fingernail. "I was really going more for *Urban Cowboy* Debra Winger."

Sighing, Hadley heaves herself up. "Come on, Sissy," she says, leading Jillian back into the bathroom. "Let me see what I can do."

They pull into the dirt lot in front of the famous old Route 66 honky-tonk just after sunset. Hadley rolls down the driver's side window of her truck so an attendant on horseback can tell them where to park. "I cannot believe I let you talk me into this," she says a minute later, as they're walking toward the massive, shellacked tree trunks framing the entrance.

"What's wrong with this place?"

"Nothing's wrong with it," Hadley snaps. "Darcy and I used to come here all the time. I just think it's a bad idea to bring *you* here at the moment."

"Relax," Jillian says, feeling only a little buzzed from the beers now. "You look totally hot, by the way." It sounds like she's kissing up, but it's true; with the booty-hugging Wranglers and tank top she changed into, combined with her toned arms, and her long, shiny hair, Hadley's breathtaking. "It must be so nice to be gay."

Hadley shoots her a *Don't test me* look, and they go inside.

A Garth Brooks song fills the dimly lit building. Squinting, Jillian can make out the roughhewn timber support beams and general western décor—old saddles and spurs, vintage posters advertising John Wayne movies, walls adorned with antlers and the taxidermied heads of miscellaneous wildlife. They find two unoccupied stools at the bar, and Hadley orders a couple more beers. Jillian beholds the rows of whiskeys, tequilas, and rums lined up in immaculate rows behind the vest-wearing, handlebar-mustachioed bartender who looks like he just stepped out of a spaghetti western. Nearby, resin balls clack and thump on a felt pool table.

They haven't been sitting there for more than two minutes when a cowboy approaches. "Get lost on your way home?" he asks Jillian, tipping his hat.

She glances quickly behind herself and then at Hadley, who's rolling her eyes. "Uh, no," she says, feeling the confusion registering on her face. "Why?"

The cowboy looks amused. "Because Heaven is a long way from here."

Next to her, Hadley makes a disgusted sound. "Give me a freakin' break," she mutters.

The cowboy turns his attention to her. "Well, if it isn't the raven-haired Hadley Wallace."

"Pound sand, Herman."

"Aw, c'mon," he says, drawing back a little as if she hurt his feelings. "You don't mean that."

Hadley levels a death glare at him. "I do, actually."

A wide grin spreads across the cowboy's face. "Who's your friend?"

Hadley holds up a middle finger. "You mean this friend?"

"Spicy," he says with an unhurried wink. "As always." Settling onto the stool next to Jillian's, he sits there, right at the edge of her personal space. "I mean this one, actually."

Jillian leans away instinctively, but she's intrigued: Is this the sort of thing people actually *do* in places like this? She shakes her head a little, amazed by all the basic things a person can miss by getting pregnant and married at nineteen years old.

"Go away," Hadley tells him.

To Jillian's surprise, the cowboy stands back up and touches the brim of his hat once again. "You lovely ladies have a good evening."

Watching him go, Jillian notes the area just below the back pockets of his jeans where the denim is extra faded, no doubt from riding the range. "He's so *handsome,*" she hisses, turning toward Hadley with a stupefied expression on her face.

"Yeah," Hadley agrees, rolling her eyes. "I guess he is. If you're into man whores."

Jillian laughs. "Get out."

"I'm serious. He used to drive for the company I work for. He'll bang anything with tits and a pulse."

"That's...colorful."

At that moment, someone flips a switch. The polished wooden dance floor on the other side of the bar is suddenly awash in rotating blue lights that make Jillian a little dizzy when she looks at them for too long.

The opening slide guitar notes of a country song from the nineties fill the air, and Hadley raises a fist. "Oh, *hell* yeah," she calls out. "Bring on the Tippin!"

Jillian's confused. "The what?"

Hadley turns toward her. "Aaron Tippin," she says. "'My Blue Angel' is a bonafide two-step anthem. Hearing this almost makes me glad you talked me into coming here."

"So, you wanna dance to it?" a sultry voice behind them asks. "Or are you in the middle of a date?"

Jillian swivels on her barstool to see a gorgeous redhead with cherry-red lips and a low-cut tank top similar to Hadley's staring them down. She's busty as a pinup, this woman.

She cuts her eyes at Jillian, maintaining a cold stare for a full five seconds.

"What's up?" Hadley asks her. Jillian can tell she's trying to play it cool, but the little quaver in her friend's voice tells a different tale.

"Not much," the pinup answers, still staring.

"This is Jill," Hadley says. "My friend from way back when. Jill, this is Darcy."

Jillian, trying to appear as neutrally ignorant as possible, extends a hand. *So, this is the heartbreaker*, she thinks but does not say.

Rather than shaking her hand, Darcy holds the tips of Jill's fingers for the briefest moment. She smells like the inside of a Victoria's Secret store. "Oh," she says, recognition dawning. "*That* Jill." She returns her focus back to Hadley. "So, are we dancing, or what?"

Clearly entranced and with an *I can't believe this is happening* expression spreading across her face, Hadley turns to Jillian. "Is it okay with you if Darcy and I....?" She motions with her head toward the dance floor.

"Oh," Jillian says. "Of course! Go. Have fun. I'll be...here. Obviously." As the two women disappear in a small sea of slow-dancing couples, she tries to appear less awkward than she feels. Looking around the bar, she sees cowboys standing in the shadows with their thumbs hooked into the front pockets of their jeans, hands nonchalantly framing their crotches. Girls with overly processed hair and too-tight jeans mill about, transmitting casually available vibes from under the brims of their western hats. On the flat-screen TV above the bar right in front of her, horses gallop, slide, and spin on a repeating loop.

"They get penalties for every little mistake," a man's deep voice says at her left shoulder. "Like an overspin, or a sliding stop that falls a little short of the traffic cone."

Jillian turns to see that Herman has appeared at her side again. "Sorry?"

"The horses," he says, lifting his chin toward the television as if she's the one interrupting his involuntary alone time and not the other way around. "Reining horses are fine-tuned athletes. It's serious competition."

Jillian isn't sure a response is warranted, but she also doesn't want to be rude. Plus, it's not like this guy's trying to get into her pants or anything, right? "So," she says after some inner deliberation during which she wonders how to best imitate Debra Winger talking to John Travolta. "You're a real cowboy?"

Herman smirks. Calmly levels his eyes at her. "You were thinking I wasn't?"

"I...I didn't know," she stammers, feeling ridiculous all of a sudden.

"Buy you a drink?"

"No, that's okay," Jillian says. "Thanks though. I'm just really, um, here with Hadley."

Herman's jaw goes slack. "Oh, I get it. You two ladies are *together* together."

"What? Oh, no, it's not like that. We're just really good friends."

"I bet," he says with a wink.

"Seriously. We've known each other since we were little kids."

"Forgive me for saying this," Herman says, settling down on the barstool Hadley vacated when she got up to dance with Darcy. "But I have a hard time imagining Hadley Wallace as a youngun. She strikes me as someone who was born a full-fledged adult—ready to kick ass and take names."

Jillian laughs, and they both glance over at the dance floor, where Hadley and Darcy are swaying inside the curtain of blue light. "Yeah, she's always been pretty tough, I guess," she says. "The best friend you could ever imagine though."

Herman nods. "I believe it. Hey, seriously, let me buy you that drink." There's something cheesily charming about the gesture; he flashes a smile, and Jillian half expects an accompanying *ding* from his sparkly teeth. "Double RCs, Jerry," he tells the bartender, who nods with his back to them and starts fixing the drinks.

"RCs?"

Herman smiles and winks at her again. "Reverse Cowgirls."

Jillian feels her cheeks get hot, but she tries to act natural. "What's in them?"

"Oh, you know. Fruit juice, fizzy water, girly stuff like that." The bartender picks up a bottle of Jose Cuervo. Seeing her notice this, Herman holds his index finger and thumb a millimeter apart. "Plus, the *teensiest* splash of tequila."

Jillian glances instinctively at the dance floor again. Hadley and Darcy are still doing their thing, completely wrapped up in each other now.

"If you don't mind my saying so," he says, "you look like someone who's recently changed course in life."

"Is it that obvious?"

Herman nods. "It is to me. So, what happened?"

"It's a long story," she says. "Long but typical, I guess."

"I got all night."

"My husband..."

Herman waits for her to say more. When she doesn't, he gives a sober nod.

Choosing to see it as encouragement, Jillian takes a long, deep breath and then lets it out. "He left me for another woman," she says, giving voice to the simple fact of her new reality for the very first time. "I think," she continues, feeling emboldened now, "that I might actually be getting dismembered." She claps a hand over her mouth. "I can't believe I just said that. Di*vorced*. I think I might be getting divorced."

Herman's lips curve into a grin. "Is there a difference?"

Jillian, sighing again, takes a sip of the colorful drink the bartender slid in front of her while she was talking. "Doesn't feel like there is, now that you mention it."

"Well, that almost-*ex*-husband of yours sounds like a jerk *and* a stone-cold fool to boot."

"He's kind of a genius, actually," Jillian says, her voice glum. "He's a professor."

One of Herman's eyebrows goes up. "Oh yeah? What does he teach—how to lose a beautiful woman in ten easy steps?"

Jillian smiles and shakes her head. "Classics. Mythology, mainly. Ancient Greek history."

"Ah," Herman says. "I see. And are you an expert, too?"

"I was never much of a scholar, especially when it came to mythology."

"Could be you're just better at living it than studying it. Ever thought about that?"

"No," Jillian says, slightly taken aback. "I haven't, actually."

"Well, anyway," Herman says, raising his drink. "To new beginnings."

"New beginnings," Jillian echoes, absently clinking her glass against his. She can't help but wonder what Lawrence would think if he walked into this honky-tonk and saw her flirting like this. He'd probably be embarrassed for her, but she's not going to think about that right now. Instead, she squints at Herman over the rim of the glass as she sips, allows herself to notice that he's more than just a little handsome. He has one of those old-school, Virgil Earp mustaches, which is something she's never been into. It works on him though. Goes with his dark hair and those dark eyes, soulful as a mustang's. Taking another gulp of her Reverse Cowgirl, she wonders, fleetingly, if she should maybe slow down a bit. Then again, there's probably not that much alcohol in it; she doesn't feel tipsy in the slightest. When her glass is drained, she looks down at Herman's. "You've tarely buttch'd yours," she observes.

"I have a secret," Herman says, sliding the glass towards her. He bumps her shoulder lightly with his own. "It's for you. I'm too nervous to drink anything."

Jillian frowns. "Why nervous?"

Herman gives a little laugh and shakes his head. "Girl, have you even looked in the mirror tonight? 'Cause you are one heck of a stunner. I'd try another clever pickup line, but looking at you made me forget all of them."

"Oh," she says, suddenly unsure of where to put her hands or how to arrange her face, which feels, now that she thinks about it, just a tad bit numb. "Well, that…is very kind of you."

"I'm not being kind, sweetheart. Just telling the gods' honest truth."

Jillian doesn't know what to say to that, so she starts in on Herman's drink instead.

"You two-step?" he asks her.

"I…I'm not really much of a—"

"Dance with me," he says, leaning well into her space bubble for several drawn-out seconds before getting to his feet and holding out a hand. "It's easy. Just follow my lead."

Jillian takes the hand, but she's hit by a wave of wooziness the moment she gets to her feet. Herman waits for it to pass, then leads her to the dance floor where couples are slowly circling around to an old Bellamy Brothers song now. It turns out he's the kind of dancer who makes a woman look good even if she has no idea what she's doing. With one hand on her waist and the other holding her hand slightly out to the side, he guides her expertly in their own little circle on the floor. "So, if I said it, would you?" he murmurs close to her ear.

"If you said what?"

"That you have a beautiful body. Would you hold that body against me?"

It takes Jillian a long moment to realize what he's referring to. "Oh!" she says. "The song. Dumb me." Holy smokes, to dance this close to a man again. The moves never change. When she closes her eyes, it's almost like she's nineteen once more, dancing with Lawrence the night they first went out together, back in that brief, pre-pregnancy window of time when he still made her feel like she was the only person in the—but no. She'll have none of that. This time—with the music, and the alcohol, and this cowboy's hot breath on the side of her neck, right above where it meets her collarbone—kicking thoughts of Lawrence out of her mind isn't as hard as she expected.

"So," Herman says, his voice sultry now. "Here's another line: What's a beautiful girl like you doing on a mountain like this?"

"Grew up here," Jillian murmurs, closing her eyes. "Hadley's kind of...helping me get a break from all the stuff with my husband. My ex."

"Ah, I get it now," he murmurs. "It's a *querencia* thing."

"A what?" Jillian opens her eyes and lets her head loll back a little so she can get a better look at him in this light, her neck muscles loose and relaxed for the first time in recent memory.

"*Querencia,*" he repeats. "Ever do groundwork with a green horse in a round pen?"

"I have no idea what you're talking about right now."

Herman squints at her for a moment, then spins her slowly around. "See, a wild-minded horse will almost always try to claim a patch of dirt wherever it is you're working him," he explains. "It might happen near the gate, or it might be somewhere else. He'll stop and linger there as long as he can before you chase him away from it."

"Interesting. I'm still not following."

"Well, bear with me a minute. Here's the deal: Whatever spot that horse picks is where he feels safe, where he'll still be able to hold onto some power as he's being trained to submit. And he'll kind of stick to that spot if you let him get away with it."

"I did not know that."

Herman's smiling down at her now, pressing his hand against her lower back ever so slightly to bring them closer together. "Can't blame a scared critter for wanting safety, I suppose," he says. "Anyway, I'm thinking maybe that's why you're here on the mountain. Maybe it's your *querencia*. Your safe spot while life's working you over a bit."

"*Querencia,*" she says, tasting the sound of those muzzy syllables. "I like it."

Herman brings his lips close to her ear again. "It also means *desire*."

Electricity shoots straight down to the base of Jillian's spine, zinging her in the same reptilian spot that used to get a jolt when Evan would trip as a toddler or fall off the bottom of the metal slide at the park. This particular zing isn't unpleasant though. It pulses outward, warming her entire pelvis as she sways under those revolving lights with this absurdly handsome cowboy. His face is even closer now, and there's a little extra movement in his hips, which she can feel because he's drawn her close enough for the button flys of their jeans to rub against each other.

"Damn, you're beautiful." Lust-soaked words against her collarbone.

Hadley and Darcy drift into her line of sight, and for a moment, the two couples dance parallel to each other. Jillian, time-warped unexpectedly back to junior high and Doug Clark's boner poking her in the belly, lets out a small cackle; she'd forgotten how fun this could be—so much more fun than walking around brokenhearted and uptight all the time.

But Hadley's glaring. She catches Jillian's eye and shakes her head. The disapproval written across her face reminds Jillian of how Lawrence would look at her if he was here—like she was pathetic and desperate. *This sort of thing doesn't come naturally to you, Jillian,* he'd no doubt scold. *And it shows.*

Well, screw you, Lawrence, she thinks to herself. She closes her eyes again to try to make the image of his frown disappear. When she opens them, Herman moves his hand farther up her back as if to steady her. "You okay, darlin'?"

"Mm hm," she hums, focusing on his lips. It takes a little more effort than she expected, but it's worth it; he really is a handsome devil. "You smell good," she tells him. "Like alfalfa and...danger."

Herman laughs, showing off those pearly whites again. "As do you," he murmurs. "Smell good, I mean. Want to get out of here?"

This time, Jillian looks right into his eyes and holds his gaze for a long, drawn-out moment while nodding emphatically.

"This is me," he says a few minutes later, leading her across the dirt parking lot toward a restored vintage king-cab pickup with a *Goat Ropers Need Love, Too* sticker in the rear window. When they get there, Herman reaches for the driver's side door handle, but Jillian pins him against the quarter panel without warning, smooshing her lips—sloppily at first—against his as the wide, stiff brims of their hats bump together.

"Whoa," Herman says. "Easy there. You sure about this?"

Jillian nods. "I'm sure," she says.

At which point Herman nestles his face into her hair, right behind her ear. The faint rake of his mustache across the edge of her earlobe nearly does her in. And then the door is open, and she lets herself fall backward in slow motion onto a Naugahyde bench seat that smells like Brut aftershave and pipe tobacco. She's never had a one-night stand before. Turns out that in the right light and with the right amount of alcohol it's almost like falling in love. She's not lingering on thoughts of Lawrence, or Penelope, or their baby on the way as she pulls Herman into the cab with her. She's also not dwelling on the beautiful young woman she saw in Bodhi's studio earlier today, right before Lawrence called. It's such a tired stereotype, the way men Jillian's age seem to have no problem attracting hot young things. She doesn't think about how many of those hot young things Herman has probably canoodled with inside this very truck. She doesn't care about any of it. All that matters is how it feels to be pinned beneath this cowboy, the two of them moving now like they're on a choppy, open sea. All that matters is that she's a woman desired by a man, her body feeling things it hasn't felt in way too long. Soon, the cab of the truck is filled with the hot-from-the-oven smell of a torn hunk of bread with butter slicked across its soft insides.

Herman moves his face downward until Jillian feels like she might stroke out from the intensity of hot breath and mustache and tongue, first on her nipples, and then moving down her torso. The sensation makes her eyes roll back in her head. Between the two of them, they get each other's jeans undone. His face moves a little lower still until his mustache is grazing the tender skin on the inside of her left hipbone. And it is exquisite. Every moment of it. This man smells good, tastes good, and feels good in a way she hasn't experienced in a long, long time, and she can't imagine ever regretting any of it. What could possibly be wrong with what they're doing? Nothing, that's what. Noth—

A violent pounding on the window makes both of them freeze. "Herman, you son of a bitch," a muffled voice shouts. "I know you're in there."

Jillian freezes. "Who is that?"

"Probably my wife."

She starts to sit up, alarmed. "Your *wife*?"

"It's a long story," he says. "Like yours." Drawing himself quickly away from her, he squints up at the window, but it's too steamed up to see anything out there.

"Jill? Jill, honey? Are you okay?" A thread of panic is woven through the voice outside the truck now, a voice Herman and Jillian both recognize at the same time.

"Shit, strike that," Herman says. "It's worse than my wife. It's Hadley. Let's get you buttoned up."

"I've been buttoned up my entire adult life," Jillian responds, trying not to giggle as she glances up at the looming, blurred silhouette on the other side of the window. "She'll be fine," she adds with a dismissive wave of her hand.

"I'm warning you, Herman," Hadley hollers as if in response. "I've assisted cattle ranchers at castration time. I'm not above putting those skills to use again."

Jillian's laughing now. "Or not."

"Aw, hell," Herman says. "Get up." There's a new edge of panic in his voice as he cracks open the driver's side door. "Just give us—" he starts to say, but Hadley reaches through the crack, grabs the front of his shirt, and hauls him out of the truck and off to the side before he can get another word out. Thusly tossed and stumbling to remain upright, Herman keeps himself at a safe distance while Hadley retrieves Jillian and helps her get her clothes tugged back into place.

"I should have known better than to leave you alone," she grumbles, guiding Jillian across the parking lot.

In response, Jillian (who's been craning her neck back toward Herman, trying to wave bye-bye as she stumbles along), lets her head flop sideways until it finally comes to rest against her best friend's shoulder. "I don't feel so good," she says as the Reverse Cowgirls—her newest besties up until this moment—turn on her without warning. The earth isn't turning slowly anymore; instead, it's in a dead spin, like those reining horses on the flat-screen TV above the bar, spinning first in one direction and then in the other, the penalties adding up with each revolution. She lurches toward a nearby bush to throw up.

You never could hold your liquor, Lawrence used to say, and something else wells up in her at the sound of his voice in her head. Something like hatred. Something like murderous rage.

She finds herself yelling at him between heaves: "Shut up, Lawrence!" *Belch.* "Screw you for stealing the best years of my life!" *Hork.* "I was loyal!" *Blat.* "And all you could ever do was put me down!" She's crying for real now—sobbing, and puking, and spitting, and crying. It's the worst she's ever felt in her entire life.

And then, after a while, it's over. Hadley stays right there, rubbing Jillian's back with one hand and holding her hair with the other. After a few minutes, she asks, "You ready to head home, hon?"

Jillian manages a weak nod. On the way back to Hadley's, the road beneath the Ford's tires feels unnaturally tilted. Jillian can't seem to raise herself to a proper sitting position. Instead, she's slumped against the passenger side door. "God, I hate him," she groans.

"Yeah," Hadley says. "I know."

Overly aggressive sunbeams of happiness shove their way through a gap in the living room curtains and across Jillian's sleeping face the next morning. Cracking open one eye, she squints against the accusatory glare. Apparently, she never made it out to the Ovum last night. "What the hell was I thinking?" she groans, slinging a forearm across her eyes.

Hadley appears from the A-frame's kitchen with a glass of water and a plate of plain toast. "Dunno," she says. "Pretty sure you weren't doing much thinking at all. Unless you were using your crotch brain."

Jillian starts to lift her head in protest, but her neck is killing her. Gingerly, she brings it back to rest on the antimacassar protecting the arm of the velvet couch. "Did you seriously just say *crotch brain*?"

"You know," Hadley continues. "Lady loins logic. Muff mind. Call it what you will." She sets the water and toast down on the coffee table and settles onto the loveseat across from Jillian.

"What the hell's wrong with me, Hads?"

"Nothing's wrong. You're coming apart at the seams a little. It happens."

"Not to me," Jillian groans. "I'm the one who holds it together, remember? And a cowboy? In a honky-tonk? That's so not my thing. I've never even been to the rodeo."

"You have now, sweetheart." Hadley drops an Alka-Seltzer into the glass of water and hands it over. "Okay, so maybe it wasn't the best idea to let you talk me into taking you out in public just yet, but you're fine. Seriously. Just think of it like this: Maybe you needed that kind of adventure. Maybe you needed to try walking on the wild side for a change."

Jillian flings the arm back over her eyes. "I don't feel adventurous or wild. I just feel like a drunk, dumbass loser."

"Dude."

"Seriously, I don't even recognize myself. I mean, who even am I right now? What's happening to me? I think I need a psychiatrist. Or maybe I should just skip that and go for shock therapy and a lobotomy."

Hadley laughs. "For pete's sake, woman. You made out with a cowboy in his truck. I hardly think it's time to check you into the cuckoo's nest."

The arm comes back down. "Herman and I did a little more than just *make out*. We went to, like, third base."

Hadley holds both hands up, palms toward Jillian. "Whoa—easy there, Judy Blume. Seriously, don't get too worked up about it. In this town, odds are good that the first guy a woman'll boink after a breakup will be a cowboy."

Jillian sits up. "Boink? *Really*?"

"Okay, okay. *Almost* boink, in your case. That or a snowboard instructor on food stamps who, nevertheless, has a very impressive collection of goose down vests. I'm just saying."

Jillian slumps back against the couch. "I can't believe this is my life."

"Now, lesbians in this town are a different story," Hadley continues.

"Yeah, what happened with you and Darcy last night, anyway?" Jillian's more than happy to change the subject. "I saw you two dancing. Are you back together?"

Hadley laughs. "No way. This is just how she does. She likes to torture her exes a little bit here and there after she breaks things off."

"Cat and mouse."

Hadley nods. "Hey, what can I say? I like my women unavailable. The last gal she was with actually tried to warn me about it when Darcy and I first got together, but at the time I thought she was just jealous. I need to call her up and offer a *mea culpa*. Anyway. Women. I tell ya."

"But why'd you guys break up in the first place? What was the final straw?"

Hadley blows an errant strand of hair out of her eyes. "Hell, I don't know. Or maybe I do. I signed up for a bunch of multi-day delivery runs because the money was good. Darcy said she was sick of me being gone all the time. Got lonely. Which, now that *she's* gone, I totally get. But live and learn, right?" Then she grins. "It was nice seeing her a little jealous when she first saw you and me together though."

"Well, good. Apparently, being a wing woman is one thing I don't totally suck at."

"Hey," Hadley says, nudging the plate of toast toward Jillian. "Cut yourself some slack."

"That's not really my forte."

"Well, it's a skill worth developing. Let me tell you."

"Okay, doctor," Jillian says. "But how?"

Hadley thinks about it for a second. "I don't know. Maybe just swim as hard as you can in the general direction of okayness."

Jillian nibbles at a corner of the toast.

"Before I forget," Hadley says. "Bodhi's coming over later. The water pump's been acting up, and he's going to check it for me. I need to show you where the main shut-off valve to the house is so you can show him, okay?"

The sudden shift in the conversation catches Jillian off guard; she looks up, alarmed. Bodhi's one of the last people she wants to see right now; no doubt his supermodel girlfriend told him all about how Jillian left his studio in a huff at the sight of her. "You know how to fix that kind of stuff, don't you?"

"I do," Hadley says, "but it's an old pump, and I don't have the right wrench. He said he'd come have a look at it himself, and I accepted the offer. Unless *you* want to fix it, of course."

Jillian says nothing.

"That's what I thought. So, keep an eye out for him, okay?"

Once Hadley's gone, Jillian goes out to the Ovum to lie down for a while, but she's restless. When, she wonders, did her life start to resemble a Salvador Dali painting—everything surreal, contorting, melting down?

About an hour later, she hears what she assumes is Bodhi's truck pulling up in the driveway. A quick glance out the window confirms the assumption. Reluctantly, she gets up, runs a brush through her hair and checks the mirror before emerging from the Ovum to go meet him.

"Rough night?" he says as she approaches.

"Thanks a lot."

Bodhi smiles as he reaches into the back of his truck and pulls out a toolbox. "Just messing with you."

"Whatever." Jillian hears the peevishness in her voice, but she doesn't bother trying to temper it. "Congrats on the hot teenager, by the way. I'm sure she never looks like she had a rough night."

Bodhi blinks in surprise. "What? Oh, you must be talking about Rita. She said you guys showed up at the studio while I was out in my supply shed. How come you split without even saying hello?"

Jillian ignores the question. "Honestly, I don't know how you middle-aged men do it." She knows she should probably stop talking, but her mouth seems to be operating without her consent at this point. "Then again, I guess I fell for a guy way older than me at that age, too."

Bodhi clears his throat and then just stands there, as if wanting to make sure Jillian's done. "Rita's the daughter of an old friend of mine who teaches at the community college," he says finally. "She's sitting for some sketches I'm doing in prep for an upcoming project."

"Oh."

"There was absolutely nothing inappropriate going on," Bodhi continues, his voice quiet but insistent. "In fact, her mother and her aunt were there that day. They never let her do sittings with any artist unsupervised. The three of us were out in the shed when you and Hadley arrived, trying to find a box of old oil pastels." He laughs and shakes his head. "I mean, for crying out loud, I know you had at least one figure drawing class in college, right?"

"Actually, no," Jillian says. "I didn't get that far."

"Well, anyway. I wish you'd stayed. I wanted to give you guys a tour."

"I'm sorry," Jillian says, shaking her head. "It was totally inappropriate of me to assume anything about your life. Honestly, I should probably just go hydrate and lie back down. De-harpify myself. But first, can I start over, please?"

"Of course," Bodhi says. He grabs one more tool from the back of his truck, and they walk together toward the A-frame. Before they go inside, she shows him the location of the shut-off valve per Hadley's instructions.

"So," Jillian says, focusing on being as socially capable as possible as he sets his tools on the floor near the water pump by the back door. "Tell me about this project you're working on."

Bodhi hesitates for a moment as he checks the pressure gauge. "It was commissioned by the Chamber of Commerce of this burb in Colorado," he says. "They wanted a sculpture for their town square. It's going to be abstract but based on human form—hence Rita and also another model who's been sitting for me, an old timer here in town. The finished piece is going to be pretty massive when it's done. They're going to have to transport it in sections."

Jillian's trying to listen as objectively as possible, but she's envious of his obvious enthusiasm for his work; she vaguely remembers being so excited by a new creative project that she could barely contain herself. But that was a long time ago—before Lawrence, before motherhood, before all the voluntary and involuntary letting go of all the pieces of who she used to be.

"Are you still doing art?"

Jillian shakes her head.

"You should start again," he says, reaching for a wrench. "I remember clearly how good your work was. When I first met you, you had this…inner fire. And yes, I know how corny that sounds, but I can't think of a better way to describe it. Not everyone has that gift."

Jillian rolls her eyes. "Yeah, right. It's a gift I haven't taken out of the box and actually used in almost twenty years."

"So, make something. You did it before."

"Life was a lot simpler back then," she fires back, her hackles rising once again.

"True," he says, grunting a little as he works a fitting loose. "But I still can't help but wonder where that fire went. I mean, I've definitely wallowed in self-pity a few times in my life, but—"

"I'm not wallowing," Jillian says, cutting him off, her jaw thrust forward in defiance.

Bodhi stops what he's doing and looks at her.

"I'm…processing."

He smiles. "My mistake."

A few minutes later, as Jillian stands in the living room staring out the window at nothing in particular, she hears Bodhi packing up his tools. And not too long after that, he's standing beside her.

"Pump should be good to go," he says, wiping his hands on a blue shop rag. "And if you're willing to come out to the studio again, I'll show you some of the stuff I'm working on. Maybe it'll jump start your muse."

Jillian tries not to scoff too audibly. "You make it sound like I have a muse to jump start."

"Oh, she's in there," Bodhi says with a grin—the same one that used to liquefy her knees back in the day. "Mark my words."

Book 10: 1989

Bodhi needs u to call him back.

That's just one of the handwritten notes I find on the whiteboard next to my dorm room door when I return to school early after Christmas vacation. Another one reads *JILL: Haley (?) called. Wants to know what the hell ur thinking.*

I wipe the messages away with my fingers. A clean break. That's what this situation calls for. Who knew I'd be even better than my mother at cutting ties?

When my roommate Natalie gets back to campus the next day and learns what happened, she does her best to cheer me up. "You're almost nineteen!"

"Not for another couple of weeks," I tell her.

"Happy early birthday anyway!" Unpacking the bag of groceries she brought with her, she hands me a four-pack of wine coolers and then does a little curtsy. "I insist her ladyship accompanies me to a party some of my friends are throwing across campus tonight."

A Love and Rockets song is playing too loud when we get there, the bass track thumping inside my chest. Natalie and I shout small talk with her friends for a while. One of the guys,

Jeff, is pretty cute. He looks even cuter after I've had one of the wine coolers and we're sitting on a ratty couch talking about what we're studying. He asks me what it's like being an artist.

"I don't really consider myself an artist," I tell him. "What's it like being an engineering major?"

Jeff laughs. "It's left-brained," he says. "Which means I don't consider myself an artist, either."

After that, we kiss—simple as that, no formalities. It's not great. His mouth doesn't taste right, and his skin doesn't smell right, and nothing happens in my heart or my gut the way it always did with Bodhi. I think about our first kiss at this time last year, warmed by the fire in the ski resort lodge. Then I push the memory from my mind before pulling away from Jeff. "Excuse me," I tell him, as I get up from the couch. Grabbing my coat from a nearby chair, I signal to Natalie that I'm leaving, and then I'm out the door.

The first day of my Intro to Myth class, all I can think about is getting enough core requirements out of the way so I can finally get back to art. The class is held in one of the big 500-seat lecture halls; the din of voices is deafening until a tiny, gray-haired man in a three-piece suit approaches the lectern. "Hello?" he says into the microphone.

Somehow, that one word is enough to quiet the hall almost immediately as he clears his throat and dives right in.

"Please call me Professor X," he says. He tells us briefly about growing up on the island of Hydra, how he'd learned about all the ancient Greek myths right in the land where they'd supposedly happened. And then, when he was a teenager, he came to America with his family. "All around me," Professor X says, "I saw the gods and goddesses of this new country: John Wayne. Greta Garbo. And Wall Street was Mount Olympus. The reason myth resonates with people to this day is that we can see ourselves in the characters—mortals and immortals alike."

Madame Imre was right; Professor X *is* vibrant. I can even see how he could be considered sexy (for an old guy, I mean). There's something about the kindness emanating from him, the warmth blended with his obvious intelligence. I am laser-focused on everything Professor Xenakis teaches us during that class and the one that follows—Psyche holding a lamp up to her husband's face even though it was forbidden; Athena being birthed, fully formed, from the forehead of her father Zeus; Persephone snatched from a field of wildflowers into the underworld (where she was forced to remain for half of every year after being duped by Hades into eating six pomegranate seeds). The characters and myths form a pleasantly jumbled, panoramic mural in my imagination: All that intrigue! The sex and the jealousy, gods betraying mortals, and vice versa! I have no doubt it's exactly the kind of stuff that gets housewives addicted to soap operas.

Somehow, the way Professor Xenakis teaches myth starts to bring me out of the deep funk I've been in since returning from the winter break. I'm pretty sure it has something to do with the associations my mind makes between the stories he tells and things I've experienced in my own life. When he teaches us about Callisto, for instance—the hunting companion of Artemis, who was seduced by Zeus, turned into a bear, and eventually became a star in the night sky—I think of my mother, how growing up with her was in some ways like living with a trapped animal. I think of a field trip my fifth-grade class took to a wild animal park. When I asked the guide about a female black bear pacing, zombie-like, back and forth in a groove she'd worn into the earth near the enclosure entrance, he said only, "They do that at this time of year." But even back then, I knew this was bullshit. I knew on a gut level what that pacing meant. Now, thanks to the myth of Callisto, I understand where that intuition came from: I'd grown up with my mother, after all, a she-bear who wanted one thing and one thing only; she wanted OUT. She wanted to be somewhere, anywhere other than where she was being held captive as a wife and a mother by invisible forces. I've never thought about her in quite this way before. Making the connection is startling, but it's also a relief. That's what kind of a gift this class is to me. The other core classes I have to take before moving into upper division art—Composition II, History of World Religions, Astronomy—pale in comparison.

When Professor Xenakis is late for the third class, the volume of chatter in the lecture hall starts to gradually increase until it's a wall of sound that makes me want to clamp my hands over my ears. I keep my eyes on the front of the hall where another man, one I've never seen before, finally steps up to the lectern and taps hard on the microphone to get our attention. The speakers screech, and everyone jumps.

"My name is Professor Kensington," the man announces. He's not nearly as old as Professor X—in his late thirties, I'm guessing. "And I'm sorry to inform you all," he continues, "that Professor Xenakis was admitted to the hospital last night with pneumonia."

We all gasp in unison.

"But never fear," Professor Kensington continues. "I've agreed to step in until Professor Xenakis returns or a more permanent replacement for this course can be assigned. And despite the fact that I haven't taught this introductory class for several years, I'm a classics professor in the graduate program as well. In fact, most of your TAs are also my students." He sweeps his hand out in a theatrical arc, and several of the TAs raise their hands in acknowledgement. "So, let's get started, shall we?"

He starts to lose me about five minutes into that first lecture, when it quickly becomes clear that his teaching style is super technical and dry—the exact opposite of Professor X's. He's droning on about the typical structure of epic poems, which involved things like dactylic hexameter and trochees (*tro-key*, he writes across the whiteboard), and the fact that epic poems translated into English were generally not written in dactylic pentameter because it didn't tend to work well in English, so, instead, they were written in iambic pentameter, and how Homer's *Iliad* consists of twenty-four books, with 15,693 lines of dactylic hexameter verse, and *blah, blah, blah*.

People all around me appear to be dozing in their seats. After a while, Professor Kensington switches gears and starts lecturing about the worthy versus unworthy translations of the ancient Greek texts.

"Dude, we get it," a guy sitting a few seats away from me says under his breath. "You're a freakin' expert."

To keep from slipping into a coma, I practice writing some lines of iambic pentameter in my notebook. As it turns out, it's not complicated. A person just has to figure out how to write a sentence in the rhythm of ba-*dum* ba-*dum* ba-*dum* ba-*dum* ba-*dum*). After a bit of trial and error between yawns, I finally come up with I *sim*ply *do* not *give* a *rat's* pa*too*tie.

At the start of the next lecture, Professor Kensington tells us Professor Xenakis isn't coming back until the following semester, if then.

A communal groan rises up from the 500 seats, but the professor doesn't seem to notice. Halfway through his lecture, people all around me are fidgeting, zoning out, and falling asleep. It's as if all of us are trying to cross a field of poppies on our way to Oz. I would have dropped the course like a hot potato if this windbag had taught the first lecture, but now the add/drop period has passed. As he drones on, I grow more and more cranky. But then he turns off the lights to show us a slideshow of classical art, and it seems like things might be looking up.

Unfortunately, he seems impatient as he clicks through the images. At one point, he pauses at a slide of Bernini's Apollo and Daphne sculpture. "This is an example of what *not* to do when sculpting a god," he informs us. "Don't make him look like a commoner."

But I can't figure out what he's talking about. It's one of the most gorgeous sculptures I've ever seen; Apollo looks utterly divine, and there's an insane level of detail in the bark and leaves wrapping themselves around Daphne's body. The agony written across her face as she's transformed into a tree makes it hard to look away.

Next, the professor clicks quickly through a series of ancient Greek mosaics, and my heart twinges in my chest. I want to call out for him to slow down. I want to study the technique and ask about the materials they used back then. Where did the smalti originally come from? What was the grout made of to make it last for thousands of years? I almost raise my hand, but then Professor Kensington says, "Of course, you've all seen these kinds of things many times before. My point here is to put the theories you'll be studying into a mythical context. If you want to know more, take an art history course, am I right?"

A few students around me laugh. Others shake their heads and roll their eyes. It occurs to me that the professor seems to take a perverse pleasure in presenting myth as something that's only for the special, ultra-smart and analytical/left-brained people. Maybe his graduate students eat this stuff up. Who knows?

That night, back in the dorm room, I look up the legend of Apollo and Daphne in the textbook as Natalie sits on the edge of her mattress waiting for her toenail polish to dry. She takes Intro to Myth, too, but her TA makes their entire section sit together, which means I never see her during class. "Man," I say when I'm done reading the legend. "Can you imagine being so gorgeous that the only way you can get a guy to stop chasing you is to beg your dad to turn you into a tree?"

"Duh," Natalie says, sticking out her chest and shaking her boobs from side to side. "Of *course* I can imagine that. I mean, *look* at me."

I consider throwing a pillow at her, but I don't want to mess up those toes. Instead, I just smirk. There's a small image of the Bernini sculpture next to their story in the textbook. "What the hell was Kensington talking about, calling this a subpar work of art?"

"He's got a pretty major ego," Natalie says. "But, man, is he hot for an older guy, or what?"

"You think so?" I ask her.

"Totally." She flings herself dramatically backward onto her bed. "I mean, he's not that handsome or anything. But there's something about his whole *I know everything* shtick. Or maybe I just have daddy issues. Who knows?"

At the beginning of the following class, the professor unfurls a large screen hanging on the front wall and motions for a nearby TA to turn off the lights. "We're going to watch a documentary," he announces. An audible sigh of relief can be heard all around.

The documentary is really well done. For the next hour, I learn about the doomed ancient city of Pompeii—how Mount Vesuvius was home to Zeus's son, Heracles, and how it erupted in 79 A.D. I marvel at the recreated images of the fiery cloud of volcanic debris barreling down the mountain faster than a jet plane, incinerating everything in its path. I cringe at the description of the two-thousand men, women, and children who tried to flee the pyroclastic flow of molten lava and deadly gasses in those moments but couldn't. Instead, they were cooked to ash in mid-gesture, carbonized while trying to escape. It wasn't until 1748 that explorers would finally unearth the remains of those ash people, many of whom were missing the tops of their skulls due to their brains exploding from the 750-degree heat.

The documentary is one of the most gruesome things I've ever watched, but that doesn't stop me from leaning forward in my seat. I'm completely captivated as things I haven't allowed myself to feel lately are unearthed—terror, for example, at how life can shift under a person's feet, causing the world to come crashing down in an instant. Also, gratitude that all the crap I've been through in the past few months hasn't charred me to a statue of human ash. Not yet anyway. I feel a bizarre sort of kinship with those citizens of Pompeii, relate to what they must have thought and felt in the final, brutal moments of their lives as they watched that death flow fast approaching. I'd never say this out loud, of course. The comparison between my problems and theirs would sound ridiculous. Still, watching that documentary makes me feel understood somehow. It makes me feel seen.

When the documentary ends and the lights come back on, I just sit there, slightly disoriented, trying to digest it all as Professor Kensington excuses the class. Eventually, still in a daze, I gather my things and head down the carpeted stairs toward the exit doors at the front of the hall.

Professor Kensington is standing at a table by the lectern, packing up his briefcase.

"That was…incredible," I tell him once I'm close enough for my voice to be heard above the din of exiting students. I don't realize how intensely I'm staring into his eyes until a wry smile forms on his lips, forcing me to look away.

"I'm glad you think so," he responds. "What did you say your name was?"

"I didn't," I say, glancing at his face again (Natalie's right: He is pretty cute). "It's Jill. Jill Jacobs."

A bottleneck of students has built up behind me, but I'm not aware of it until one of them says, "Sometime this *millennium* would be nice." Turning my head to look, I'm met with dozens of pairs of eyes, all of them staring at me.

"Sorry," I say, blushing as I snap out of whatever spell I'm under. Hurrying out the door, I glance back once, quickly. Sure enough, Professor Kensington is still watching me with the same amused expression on his face.

For the next class, I grab a seat as close to the front of the lecture hall as possible. I've been sitting way up in the back until now so the professor wouldn't see me stifling yawns. It isn't difficult to find a good seat in front; a ton of students have stopped showing up since he took over. Professor Kensington nods at me as I sit down just a few yards from the lectern.

The lecture is all about Hades and Persephone and how Hades has gotten an undeservedly bad rap due to the fact that so many modern scholars have refused to put the myth into its appropriate cultural and historical context. "This has occurred," Professor Kensington informs us, "due to the fact that it's long been assumed that Hades is the equivalent of Satan. It's interesting to note, though, that Persephone eventually came to love her abductor down there in the underworld...but that's a story for another day." He grins, and a few people around the hall chuckle. When class is over, one of the TAs approaches me in a rush and hands me an envelope as I'm heading out the door.

"What's this?" I ask him.

"Invitation to Prof Kensington's Poseidon party this Friday."

I glance at the front of the hall, but the professor is nowhere to be seen. "Poseidon party?" I look down at the envelope and then back up at the TA, perplexed.

"He holds one every year. It's this whole post-holiday, ancient Greek solstice shindig called a Haloea—one of those everyone-who's-anyone things."

"Why would he invite me?"

"I don't know," he says, looking mildly annoyed by my questions now. "Apparently, you've found favor."

"It's on my birthday."

The TA slings the strap of his messenger bag over his shoulder. "Well, isn't that neat-o," he says, not bothering to hide the sarcasm.

The thought of taking a bus all the way to Scottsdale on a Friday night and then trying to figure out how to get from the bus stop to Professor Kensington's house in high heels gives me a headache, so I splurge on a taxi. Taking a cab feels more adult anyway, and I've decided that doing more and more adult stuff is the best way to put everything that's happened in the past couple of months behind me.

It's a ten-minute ride to the part of the suburb noted on the invitation. From the back of the cab, I take it all in—the neighborhood watch signs and streets of immaculately maintained houses, most with at least one European car parked in the driveway. Professor Kensington's house is a stately Scottsdale adobe with expensive-looking xeriscaping complete with a couple of Saguaro cacti out front. Seeing it, I almost tell the driver to turn around and take me back to campus. I don't though. Instead, I summon courage from somewhere deep down, hand the driver a couple of bills, and head toward the front door.

When nobody answers my knock, I let myself in. The entry hall is empty, but I follow the sound of voices into what seems to be the main room of the house. It's full of people talking, laughing, and snacking from little paper plates full of crackers, cheese, and fruit. I don't recognize many of them, but I do recognize the group of TAs, mainly because they're always passing stuff out during class. The one who gave me the invitation is hanging out with a bunch of the others, all of them surrounding Professor Kensington.

It takes me about half a second to realize I don't belong anywhere near this place and that I never should have gotten out of the cab. *What an idiot,* I mutter under my breath. Slipping back into the entry hall, I think about what I should do. Calling another taxi will require asking to use the phone, thus drawing unwanted attention to myself. Then again, I could simply leave and just start walking. Even though it's dark outside, neighborhoods clearly don't get much safer than this one. As I ponder my options, a glint above my head and to the left catches my attention. When I turn and look up, my eyes widen. The bronze eagle statue seems bigger than it actually is, due to the way it appears to be exploding in mid-flight from the wall behind it. The eagle's sharp talons are outstretched, as if it's about to grab its next meal—a rabbit, or maybe a pony. At the base of the statue, a plaque is inscribed with the words AETOS DIOS.

"It means Eagle of Zeus," a voice from behind me says. I jump at the sound and at the feeling of hot breath on the back of my neck. When I turn around, Professor Kensington is standing there. Until now, I've only seen him at a distance (though less of one since I've started sitting closer to the front of the lecture hall).

"It's beautiful," I tell him.

"It was his messenger and companion. Some say the golden eagle was created by Gaia, but…I don't think so." He holds my gaze with his own, a flirtatious smirk on his lips now. "To some, it represents not just strength and beauty, but total loyalty and obedience."

"It almost looks like it's giving a warning or something," I respond, trying to make it seem like I actually know what I'm talking about. I don't tell him that the statue kind of freaks me out.

He curls a thoughtful hand around his mouth as he gazes up at the bird's expression. "I've never looked at it that way. But perhaps it is giving a warning. You definitely wouldn't have wanted to piss off Zeus. Just ask Prometheus."

"I'm sorry," I say, feeling myself blush now. "I'm really not familiar with myths other than the ones we've covered in class." What an idiot I am. He probably thought I was some up-and-coming classics scholar. That's probably why he invited me here tonight in the first place.

"Prometheus," the professor says, not seeming to notice my discomfort, "was chained to a rock on Zeus's order and had his liver eaten by an eagle every single day for eternity. His crime? Giving humans the gift of fire." He grins. "I guess Zeus wanted to be the one to provide it."

"That's…horrible," I say, strangely enthralled.

The professor lets out a laugh and then changes the subject. "So," he says. "Jill Jacobs. Hmm." He looks up at the ceiling, deep in thought. "Jill, short for Jillian, which is derived from Julian, Child of Jove. That makes you a daughter of Jupiter. But I won't hold it against you. I will, however, be calling you Jillian from now on, just so you know. And you should call me Lawrence."

Before I can respond, one of the female TAs appears from the living room. She gives him a long, questioning look before glancing at me and then back at him. "I'm leaving," she announces.

"Oh, must you?" His tone isn't overly concerned.

"I was actually just leaving, too," I say, sensing an opportunity to make a graceful exit.

"You should stay," Lawrence tells me.

The TA bestows an indulgent smile upon me. "Oh, I get it," she says, her eyes not leaving my face.

"Don't make a scene, Simone."

The TA laughs, but it's bitter. Some kind of icy sword passes between them like a baton. "Good luck to you," she says to me. "You're going to need it." Then her eyes shift to Lawrence, and her smile dissolves. "You can go straight to hell," she tells him.

When she's gone, I stand there, frozen in place, not knowing what to say or do.

Grinning, Lawrence makes the crazy sign with one finger near the side of his head. "She does know her ancient history though. So, tell me again why you were planning to leave?"

Three hours later, he pulls his car into a space behind my dorm and puts it in park. He'd convinced me to stay at the Haloea party, to partake of the mulled wine and the cheese board offerings, to mingle. He was by my side the entire time. When TAs approached to bend his ear or tell him a joke, I was right there, center stage. A few of them might have given me nasty looks, wondering why an undergraduate was even invited, but nobody said anything outright. After the party ended and there were only a few people left gathering their things, Lawrence offered me a ride home. I tried to decline, telling him that a taxi was perfectly convenient. But he insisted.

"Can I see you again?" he asks as we sit there, the BMW's heater warming my feet.

Normally, I'd be alarmed at this question from someone in his position, but between the mulled wine, the warm fire, and the general strangeness of the evening, I'm surprisingly relaxed. Flirty, even. "Isn't that forbidden?" I ask him.

"Possibly frowned upon," he says, his voice sly now. "But no. Not forbidden."

"And do you make a habit of doing that which is frowned upon?" The words meld together as they leave my mouth. I can't believe how brazen I'm being, teasing this man who's not only my professor but who's also significantly older than I am. Ten or fifteen years, I'm guessing—at least.

This time, he laughs out loud. "Hardly," he says. "Which is why I'm asking."

He takes me to a bar downtown the next night.

"I don't have a fake ID," I tell him as we approach the entrance.

"They won't check." He hooks an arm around my shoulders, tucking me securely against his torso. "You're with me."

Sure enough, the bouncer lifts his chin at Lawrence, says, "'Sup, Prof" as we saunter in.

We sip martinis in a dark corner booth, talking in low voices about things of little consequence—the warmth of the bar, the waitress's easy smile, the pianist playing smooth jazz. After a long while, we get up to slow dance with a few other couples on the grimy dance floor, under a disco ball.

"How old are you, anyway?" I ask, emboldened by the alcohol.

Lawrence is a good dancer. He smiles at the question. "You really want to know?"

I hesitate at first, but then I nod.

"I'm thirty-six. Is that a problem?"

Thirty-six, I think, glancing past his shoulder. Seventeen years older than me. It should creep me out more than it does. Why doesn't it? I've never been into older men. Looking into his eyes again, I shake my head.

A short while later, when we're outside the bar and he's about to drive me back to the dorm, we kiss. It's a little more restrained than I expected, not that I really knew what to expect or anything. "Come to my place," Lawrence insists.

In less than an hour, we're in his bed. Lawrence takes off my clothes and then just sort of…beholds me like I'm some precious artifact, a work of art. He tells me I'm beautiful, and I blush. "True, you have a little more meat on your bones than

I usually like in a girl," he continues, and my heart momentarily stops. "But that's okay. I could get used to it."

I don't know what to say to that, so I say nothing. Instead, as he positions himself above me, I focus on getting to know his body. It's different than Bodhi's (not that I'm going to think about Bodhi right now). For one thing, Lawrence isn't as tall as Bodhi (*who I'm not going to think about,* I remind myself). He's smaller in stature overall. Also, he has much more chest hair, some of which is already starting to turn gray. When it comes to the sex, he's masterful and fully in-command. I gaze up at him, wanting to know what he's feeling. He's looking off to the side, though, and I wonder if I'm disappointing him. Then it ends with little fanfare, and he drifts off without a word. I watch him sleep, studying the lines on his face, his salt-and-pepper five o'clock shadow. It's clear to me in that moment that Lawrence Kensington is a man who knows exactly what he's doing and what he wants—a man who is sure of both himself and of his place in the world.

In short, he's everything I'm not.

The next day in my dorm room, while Natalie's at class, I sit in front of the mirror on the back of the door and sketch myself nude. Then I walk to the Classics building with the sketch in my backpack along with a pomegranate I picked up at a local market this morning. Timing it so I'll show up at the end of his office hours, I'm relieved when there are no students waiting outside his office. I knock on the door, and he opens it; nobody's in there, either. At first, he greets me professionally. Then, glancing quickly up and down the empty hallway, he pulls me into the office, and closes the door behind us.

"How am I supposed to stay away from you?" he murmurs into my neck, sending a shiver down my spine as he kisses the spot just below my earlobe. "It's been only a little over twenty-four hours, and I've been going crazy."

It's indescribably good, being wanted in this way by a man like Lawrence—a man people look up to. Out of all the women he could choose from, he wants *me*.

"So, that thing I said about dating students being frowned upon rather than forbidden," he says, his voice slightly muffled against my neck as I unbutton his shirt.

"What about it?"

"As it turns out, that's not exactly true."

"Oh?" When his shirt is completely unbuttoned, I reach for the zipper of his pants.

"It's actually..." he says as I take hold of him, feeling, for the first time the power I have in the situation. "Forbidden."

I smile as our mouths close in on each other. "You don't say."

Afterward, when we're buttoning ourselves up, I hand him the pomegranate.

"What exactly is it you're trying to say with this?" he asks me, a wicked smile playing across his lips. "Am I Hades? Are you Persephone?"

I hand him the sketch, which he studies for several moments. "So, you're an artist." He breaks the pomegranate open and feeds me the seeds: One, two, three, four, five...I suck the tips of his fingers deeper into my mouth with each one.

Book 11: 2009

Sing, Goddess, Achilles' rage,
Black and murderous, that cost the Greeks
Incalculable pain, pitched countless souls
Of heroes into Hades' dark,
And left their bodies to rot as feasts
For dogs and birds, as Zeus' will was done.
~Homer

Hadley pops a Dar Williams cassette into the truck's old tape player as they drive down to Scottsdale. "So, I know you're, like, determined to figure stuff out on your own," she says, "but it would be awesome if you would just consider your stay at my place an indefinite one."

Jillian, who can think only of the knot of dread settling behind her ribs, nods, but she doesn't say anything. Right now, she has to focus on the task at hand—getting her things from the Scottsdale house. She'd wanted to make this trip alone, but Hadley insisted on driving them down.

"I'll take the day off. Need to use my vacation time anyway," she'd said. "Besides, you're going to need help packing stuff up. Also, this way, you can drive your own car back up the mountain."

All of it overwhelmed Jillian. The fact that Lawrence had asked her to agree to a set amount of time she would be in the house only added to the pressure. They'd finally settled on two hours, which Jillian initially argued wouldn't be enough time to pack up nearly two decades' worth of stuff.

"Don't worry," Lawrence had assured her over the phone. "Just gather your essentials. Nothing will be thrown away."

She called Evan this morning, before leaving Hadley's, to let him know what was going on.

"You shouldn't let him kick you out like this, Mom," he said. "It's your house, too."

"Not for much longer," Jillian told him.

"Then at least let me come help you move your stuff." Evan's voice was measured, careful. Since being down in Tucson, he seemed to have matured by about ten years.

"Don't be silly." Jillian kept her own voice as breezy as possible. "I have Hadley. And as much as we'd both love to see you, we'll do that at Thanksgiving, under happier circumstances."

Now, two and a half hours after they merged from I-40 in Flagstaff onto the I-17 off-ramp toward Phoenix, Hadley parks the truck next to the big saguaro by the driveway of the Scottsdale house. And then, with the simple turn of a key, they're inside. It's been almost a month since Jillian's been here, and the house smells unfamiliar, *other*, like a foreign perfume. She falters near the door of Evan's room but forces herself to open it anyway. Should she take his things for safekeeping? Righteous rage wells up at the thought, but then it dies back down. The truth is, Evan is going to be fine. He's probably fine already, even if he's upset with his father. He's a man now, after all, off and running with his own life.

The new couple's things are scattered throughout the house—from a portrait of Penelope and Lawrence on the mantle to a bright red G-string hanging from the shower curtain rod in the guest bathroom.

"Subtle," Hadley observes as she and Jillian stand in the hallway staring at it. "I wonder if she peed on all the furniture, too."

While Hadley goes back outside to grab some boxes and rearrange things in the truck to make space, Jillian heads toward the master bedroom. Everything looks basically the same as it did the last time she was here except for the fact that the room's been cleaned. Also, there are a bunch of unfamiliar toiletries in the bathroom. Not knowing where to even start separating the essentials from the nons, she looks in the closet, where her things have been shoved to one side to make room for Penelope's things: Silk blouses, strapless cocktail dresses, five-inch patent leather heels.

Good luck wearing those in a couple of months, Jillian thinks peevishly. Working quickly, she pulls a few of her own outfits from their hangers, tossing each item onto the bed. She gets down on her hands and knees to survey the messy pile of her shoe collection—the once-neatly arranged pairs of pumps, ballet flats, and espadrilles that were staples in her old life. The Sorel snow boots she's had (and barely worn) since high school are tucked in the back corner of the closet;

she grabs those along with the tennis shoes she bought for the gym and hardly ever used.

Next, she clears off the small wooden bench under the bedroom window that has always held various knick-knacks. She carries it over to the closet and stands on it so she can retrieve the boxes residing on the high shelf, the remaining evidence of her life before Lawrence. One old cardboard box is filled with photos, old sketches, and notes passed back and forth in middle school. Another's filled with her yearbooks, prom memorabilia, and diploma from high school. Jillian sweeps her hands as far back on the shelf as she can to make sure she got everything. When she does, her fingers connect with a third box. It's a small one, only about four-by-six inches, and she pulls it toward herself, frowning. She gives it a little shake, but still can't figure out what's rattling around in there. It's only when she opens it up and looks inside that she sees the broken pieces of her mother's dropped coffee mug from when Jillian was in eighth grade and things really started going south between her parents.

She starts to wonder what kind of misplaced sentimentality could have possessed her to keep the mug fragments all these years, but then a thought flashes across her mind: Broken things—herself included—have become her biggest fear. She's spent most of her life trying to hold things together, to keep them from breaking. Not just her parent's marriage, but her own. And what good has it done her? What has all her worry and effort ever kept from shattering? The question hits her like a bolt of lightning, leaving her in a sort of daze as she piles the boxes on the bed next to her clothes and then heads back out into the hallway.

Passing the window by the front door, she catches a glimpse of Hadley out near the big saguaro opening up the flattened cardboard boxes she brought from work and securing the bottom seams with packing tape. Continuing on through the kitchen toward the garage, she sees the china platter from the night of the faculty banquet last month. She'd arranged those Greek desserts so carefully, so lovingly, in her pathetic attempt to show her husband with this small, domestic gesture, how *there* for him she was, how undying her love and support had always been, would always be. A small but sharp surge of bile rises to the back of her throat. As she forces it back down, something else rises in its place. It's a vocabulary word she learned from the Pompeii documentary Lawrence showed her Intro to Myth class all those years ago: *Fumarole*—a crack in the earth's crust through which gasses and steam escape, indicating an active volcano beneath the surface. She whispers the word out loud.

In the garage, finding the boxes marked JILLIAN is easy; Lawrence has always kept their stored belongings separate. The first box she finds is filled with her old art clothes—denim overalls and various smocks. Others are filled with books and old framed photos, sketchpads, and small canvases she'd used in Madame Imre's class.

The last box, which Jillian hoists from the shelf and sets on the floor next to the others, contains the rest of the wedding gift china, the set with the entwined olive branch-pattern to which the platter in the kitchen belongs. Table setting for six, if Jillian recalls, reaching a hand into the open box. It was a hand-me-down set from Martha Bunston, who'd gotten it from another, older faculty wife when Martha and her husband Bill were first married. Jillian was the third recipient (at least) of the china, which had been re-gifted from one faculty wife to another—*A welcome, and a warning,* she thinks now. Lawrence had lugged the wrapped box home—this very same box, actually, since the platter was the only piece they'd ever used—and Jillian had unwrapped it, blushing at Martha Bunston's kindness. Back then, every belated wedding gift had reminded her afresh that she was no longer Jill Jacobs; that sad, lost girl who couldn't find her way had been replaced by Mrs. Jillian Kensington. It was a realization that alternately thrilled and terrified her.

Now, standing on the concrete floor of the garage, Jillian feels the sickness that comes from playing by the rules for decades and getting screwed anyway. She thinks about all the little ways she let Lawrence ride roughshod over her through the years, all the ways she let herself be trampled upon while feeling beholden to his moody "genius." She let herself be whittled away, grew accustomed to a thousand pinpricks. But the fatal stab wound came anyway. Hadn't she done her best? Hadn't she kept herself pretty, lost most of the baby weight, done everything required of her as a faculty wife and more?

She tries to cry, but it seems there are no more tears. Instead, it's the opening of *The Iliad* that comes to her, the rhythm of those old, familiar lines (Lawrence made the entire class memorize them) coursing through her bloodstream—lines about rotting bodies and the rage of a vengeful god. Morphing into a feral creature she doesn't recognize, Jillian shouts Homer's words as she holds a dessert plate aloft, draws back her arm, and lets the plate fly.

It shatters against the inside of the garage door a split second before all the shards rain down onto the concrete below. *I believed I was perishing with the world,* a traumatized Pliny the Younger wrote after watching the exploding guts of Mount Vesuvius destroy everything around him. *And the world with me.* Jillian might not have been the strongest student—especially after she and Lawrence started dating and she was constantly distracted by watching him at his lectern, memorizing his body, his movements, his voice—but she does remember Pliny the Younger's words. And she relates to the murderous volcano, to its boiling blood flowing toward Pompeii at top speed. She is heat. She is ash. She is a pyroclastic death cloud of rage and debris.

Revelations rise up within her one after another, flaming bursts of emotional magma. And with each one, she reaches for another plate, bowl, cup, saucer. All this time, she's been living a lie. It's not her happy marriage she's been pining for during the almost-month she's been on the mountain; it's the *illusion* of a happy marriage. *I've been missing a life that wasn't really there,* Jillian thinks, pausing with a saucer in her cocked hand. *I've been missing a ghost life.* The saucer explodes against the garage door. She's certain she has never felt more alive than she does at this moment, steeped in wrath. She is a warrior goddess, invincible, the fury somehow making her feel less replaceable. She reaches into the box of china for more ammo, but her hand encounters only cardboard.

Hadley finds her there several minutes later, squatting on the concrete floor, sweeping up shards with a whisk broom.

"Jill?" Her voice is hushed yet insistent, the kind of voice she'd use to coax an injured, feral animal into an enclosure. "What happened?"

Jillian looks up in a daze. "I just...got in touch with my anger a little, I guess," she says, sweeping a pile of shards into a dustpan and dumping them into the cardboard box.

Hadley comes toward her slowly. "Let me get this, okay?" She takes the dustpan and whisk broom from Jillian's hands.

"She's pregnant," Jillian says, utterly drained, her voice and eyes hollow now. "She's carrying Evan's baby brother or sister. I couldn't live with myself if she got injured on one of these pieces."

And then, without warning, a third person is there in the garage with them. "What. The. Actual. Fuck."

Jillian looks up to see Penelope standing in the doorway with a hand on one hip and her jaw hanging open in disbelief. The sight of her replacement is like a knife to the gut, but Jillian has no problem whatsoever seeing why Lawrence is smitten; Penelope is glowing, resplendent, radiant in her indignant shock at the scene before her. She's the picture of perfection from head to toe (except for being a bit fuller in the face since the last time Jillian saw her, and except, maybe, for her eyebrows, which are over-plucked to the point of looking penciled-in).

"Speak of the devil," Hadley mutters. Handing the dustpan and broom back to Jillian, she heads toward the door, where she gives the other woman as wide a berth as possible. "I'm going to load up those boxes from the bedroom."

Jillian can see the already-taut roundness of Penelope's stomach. She looks to be about four months along, and with that realization comes yet one more flash of understanding: This Other Woman, standing there with her elegant disdain while carrying Evan's half-sister or brother within her body, is not the enemy. How could Jillian have failed to see it before this moment? It was Lawrence, after all, who took their years as husband and wife, crumpled them up, and merrily lobbed them into the nearest trash can. For weeks now, ever since Jillian saw the two of them in Lawrence's office, she's been filled with something like hatred toward Penelope. So, why does she feel something different all of a sudden? Not pity, exactly, but...well, yes. It's pity. Penelope has no idea what she's in for. And she is so young. So very young. Twenty-five, tops. Though maybe Lawrence will be a different man with her. Maybe she'll bring out the best in him in ways Jillian wasn't able to do. There's just no telling. "I'm sorry for the mess," she says.

Penelope shifts her gaze to the floor and then back to Jillian. "Well, finish cleaning it up, and take it with you." Her voice is clipped and precise as she turns to go back inside the house. "We don't need it clogging up our trash bin."

We.

Our.

Jillian nods. She sweeps up the remaining shards in silence and dumps all the broken pieces into the cardboard box. Then, closing the box and lifting it up to hold it tightly against herself, she fully accepts defeat. All she wants to do now is sleep for a very long time.

Lawrence told her over the phone that he changed the lock combination of the side gate, but he didn't tell her what it was. So, she has to go through the house to get back out to the truck, which means she has to pass right by Penelope, who's standing in the kitchen with one arm crossed in front of her as she stares down at her phone, no doubt ready to call the police at a moment's notice. "I was careful to clean up as best I could," Jillian says, her voice weary as she readjusts the box in her arms. "But Lawrence will probably want to check it again."

Her words are met with a rolling of the eyes, a checking of the manicure.

Jillian feels another sudden, unexpected surge of protectiveness for this woman—who is only a handful of years older than Evan and not much older than Jillian herself was when she met Lawrence—that she almost wishes she could reach out physically. She remembers what happened when she'd tried to touch Penelope's scarf in admiration at the faculty banquet, though, and also, there's the box she's holding. "Please," she says instead. "Just...be careful." She almost adds, *...and I'm talking about so much more than broken china.*

"Whatever," the younger woman snaps. "Can you just leave now?"

Out front near the big saguaro, Hadley's loading the last box into the truck bed. Jillian's Toyota sedan has been parked in the driveway, waiting for her.

"Meet you at Cordes Junction," Hadley calls out before getting into the truck. "I'll need to stop there for gas."

Nodding, Jillian gets into her car. Before backing out of the driveway, she lets it warm up. Sitting there with the nose of the Toyota pointed at the house she's lived in for nearly half her life, she does her best to say a silent goodbye.

Just over an hour later, they're standing at adjoining gas pumps at the Cordes Junction truck stop by the side of the interstate. "I don't know what came over me," Jillian says, inserting her card into the reader.

Hadley, leaning against the truck as fuel gurgles into the tank, doesn't respond right away.

"I mean, you've basically known me my whole life," Jillian continues. "What do you think is wrong with me?"

"I think you're finally just waking up," Hadley says. "You've been asleep for a long time, and maybe you don't know quite where you are yet. It's…disorienting."

Jillian runs a hand through her hair. "I have to get my head back in the game. I need to get a job. I probably need to call a lawyer. How do people even do this?"

"They just figure it out, I guess," Hadley says, returning the nozzle to its slot. "And you will, too. I know you will. It's going to be okay."

Jillian laughs. "That's what you used to say whenever I'd start to worry about my parents splitting up."

"Well, I was right, wasn't I? You just need to get some rest. This day has been crazy, and you're exhausted. We both are."

Back at the A-frame after another hour and a half on the road, they unload the truck first thing. "Let's just leave all these on the floor," Jillian says as they stand in the barn, bleary-eyed. "I'll deal with putting them up in the loft tomorrow while you're at work."

Later that night, asleep in the Ovum, Jillian dreams she's back in high school biology. Except, instead of being a student, she's an insect. She's in a dish on one of the group lab tables, and all her old classmates are crowded around. One of them picks at her exoskeleton with a pair of tweezers as the teacher, Mr. Heinberger, tells everyone that Jillian's a cicada and that she's molting, transforming from an underground nymph into a fully-winged adult. "Until her new skin hardens," he says, "She'll be especially vulnerable to predators."

Jillian's awakened the next morning by the sound of Hadley's truck leaving the driveway. She allows herself a full five minutes to relive the awfulness of the previous day before hoisting herself out of bed, throwing a coat on over her pajamas, and stepping out of the Ovum to start organizing the boxes they unloaded last night.

It's hard to see inside the barn. As Jillian walks toward the light switch on one wall, Finster the pygmy goat approaches her silently, his tail twitching back and forth. "What are you doing here?" she asks him. He must have gotten in through a broken slat at some point after Hadley fed him this morning. He's being unusually quiet. Normally, he likes to greet her with a first-thing-in-the-morning bleat. Squinting at him in the dim half-light, Jillian realizes he's not making any noise because he's too busy chewing; she can just barely make out something papery hanging from his mouth. "What in the—" she starts to say, reaching down to pull on whatever it is. She succeeds only in tearing it in half. Looking down at the papery fragment in her hand, she gasps. It's a corner of the nude self-portrait she gave to Lawrence, the one she sketched in her dorm room when she was nineteen.

"Oh, no!" she cries, reaching for the goat, who stops chewing long enough to cock his head and behold her calmly through horizontal pupils. "No, no, Finster! Drop it!"

Startled, chewing frantically now, the creature gambols sideways toward a dark corner of the barn, leaving Jillian to stand there in shock. For the next several minutes, as rays of sunlight slant through the roof slats overhead, she waits for the tears. They don't come, though, not even when she tries to force them a little.

"Well's dry," she announces to the air in front of her.

As if in response, Finster reappears in her peripheral vision, cloven hooves thudding softly as he emerges from the shadows and draws cautiously near. *Beh,* he says when it's clear she's not going to yell at him again. Then he butts his head, ever so gently, against her leg.

Book 12: 1989

The pregnancy test comes back positive one day in late May, at the end of my freshman year.

For the past week, I've felt like I was fighting off a strange stomach flu. At first, I suspected food poisoning since I didn't have a fever. But then the nausea kept coming, and going, and then coming back again for days, hitting me at random moments. I made Lawrence keep his distance so he wouldn't catch whatever I had. It wasn't until I counted the days since my last period that I headed straight for the family planning aisle at the nearest drugstore.

As I walk toward the Classics department building less than an hour after seeing the little blue plus sign on that stick, everything around me seems unreal, like I've been roofied by a potent concoction of uncertainty, excitement, and terror: Can this really be happening?

I arrive right as Lawrence's office hours are ending and knock softly on his door. When there's no answer, I try the handle. It's unlocked, so I push the door open. At the sight of Lawrence sitting behind his desk, I almost break down. *This is the father of my child,* I think, feeling my eyes well up. *All of this is fate.*

He looks surprised to see me. A student is there, sitting in a chair across the desk from Lawrence. She looks like she's been crying, probably over a grade. I feel her pain; our professor can be strict that way. He did, after all, give me a C on the last test, even though I added up the wrong answers afterward and was pretty sure it should have been a B ("I don't want anyone thinking I'm doing you special favors," Lawrence said when I asked him about it). The girl's lips are puffy, and her makeup is smeared. She glances at me as I enter the office and swipes halfheartedly at her eyes with the back of her wrist.

"I'm sorry to interrupt," I tell them. "I should have knocked louder. I'll wait out in the hall."

"Don't bother," the girl says, standing up from the chair. "I was just leaving."

Once she's gone, I look at Lawrence. "She didn't seem very happy."

"Oh," he says, moving a hand quickly through the air like he's swatting away a bug. "It's nothing. She was just pissed off about an exam grade."

"That's what I thought." I glance at the door, which is opened just a little, and then I close it. I want to be sure we're completely alone. "Speaking of tests...there's something I need to tell you."

Lawrence tilts his head and frowns.

"I'm," I say. "We're...I'm pregnant."

At first, there's no reaction from him at all. Everything stops: Time, gravity, the rotation of the earth. Then, after an endless stretch of silence, he says, "I thought you were on the pill."

"I am," I tell him, my heart pounding. "I just think maybe, I don't know." I'm stammering now. I force myself to breathe. "Maybe I wasn't on it long enough or something when I…when we…conceived. Or maybe I took it later than usual once or twice." I'm not at all sure this is true. I can't remember taking a single pill even an hour late. Surely, I'd remember such a thing, right? Then again, I've had a lot going on for the past few months. I can feel my eyes tearing up. "I didn't mean to take it late, if that's what happened," I tell him.

Lawrence tents his fingers together and lays the tips of the first two across his lips. Squints at the wall behind me. After another long stretch of silence, he finally says, "It's going to be fine." His voice is cool, decided, as if there is nothing more to discuss and no reason whatsoever to be concerned.

A flood of relief washes over me. "I'm so glad to hear you say that," I tell him. "I thought maybe you'd—"

"I'll pay for the procedure."

His words knock the air from my lungs, leaving me speechless.

Seeing this, he frowns again, first in obvious confusion and then, finally, in understanding. "You can't actually be thinking of keeping it"

My brain takes several seconds to process his words. Until this moment, I haven't thought of anything other than getting to Lawrence as fast as I could. At nineteen, having a baby isn't something I've even remotely started to consider. I guess I thought that he, a full-fledged adult, would know exactly what to say to reassure me. But I was wrong. So clearly wrong. And with those two simple words—*the procedure*—something completely unexpected (and a little scary, to be honest) has awakened. Already, I realize, I am fiercely protective of the tiny life housed within me. It's an instinct that comes out of nowhere.

"Actually," I fire back, "that's exactly what I'm thinking." I move toward the door, my legs suddenly rubbery beneath me. How could I have been such an idiot? I'm not the love of this man's life. I'm just some coed he banged—one in a stream of many (I'm certain of it now). How typical of me to think it meant more than it did. With that thought, my hand is on the doorknob. And then I am walking, running, flying, down the main hallway of the Classics building, and then out into the sunshine, with nobody in pursuit.

He shows up at the dorm a week later, standing in the doorway of my room at dawn, hair disheveled, face hangdog.

"What are you doing here?" I hiss, looking around to make sure nobody else is nearby. Thank goodness Natalie slept in her new boyfriend's room last night.

"I can't sleep," he says, his voice a despondent croak. "I haven't been eating. I'm a mess."

"Somebody's going to see you here, and then what?"

"I don't care."

At that moment, a door opens and then closes around the far corner of the hall, and I pull Lawrence into the room. "You could lose your job!"

"Let them take it from me."

"You don't mean that," I tell him, placing a hand on his arm.

Lawrence clutches the hand with one of his own and looks into my eyes. "Jillian…I *need* you."

I open my mouth to respond, but he cuts me off.

"I was a fool. I...I think..." He's starting to stammer now, just like I did in his office. "I think I might be in love with you."

My mouth remains open for the longest time. "I love you, too," I tell him finally. And that's when the tears come. This is all such a relief. For the past week, I've been on autopilot, not going to his class and not allowing myself to even think about what I'm going to do, how terrified I am. I fall into his arms, weepy with gratitude as he rubs my back and squeezes me tight.

"There's something else, too," Lawrence says. "But I don't even want to tell you. You don't need the stress, and you'll probably just send me away, and—"

"My God," I say with a soggy little laugh. "I've never seen you in such a state." True, we've only known each other for about five months, but still.

"The girl," he continues. "The one who was in my office yesterday..."

"What about her?" A cold chill descends down my spine.

"Let's just say we used to be somewhat...involved. And when it came time to cut things off, she was...difficult. She wanted more than I was able to give. And now she's threatening to go to the administration and tell them about...well there was nothing serious between us, but..."

"Oh."

"She's delusional, Jillian." His voice is pleading now. "She's had a crush on me since she took the Intro course last year. But there's a chance they might believe her." He looks up at the ceiling, his eyes watery now. "It could mean the end of my career," he says, swallowing hard. "And what if they ask about my relationship with *you*?"

Something shifts inside me. I know I have to ask him when he and this other girl stopped seeing each other (was he seeing both of us at the same *time*?). But I also have to be careful not to get too crazy about this, not to get too paranoid. I've heard pregnancy hormones can do that. The last thing I want to do is drive away the father of my child. Our child. We need each other, no matter what obstacles the rest of the world tries to put in our path. "Well, I'll just deny everything," I tell him.

Lawrence seems overcome. He turns his face toward the floor, looking up at me with only his eyes after a few moments. "You'd do that?"

"Of course I would," I tell him, certainty surging within my chest now. "Like I said, I love you."

The OB-GYN doesn't want me driving up to high altitude too late in my pregnancy, so in July, when I'm about three months along, I take the bus up the mountain to visit Dad. He and Mom have both known about the pregnancy since last week. They're the only two people I've told, other than Lawrence. He wants us to wait a while to tell his parents. It's a beautiful day—about twenty degrees cooler than it was in Tempe—so I decide to walk home from the bus station rather than calling him from the pay phone to come pick me up.

I'm not used to the altitude anymore; I'm a little out of breath by the time I reach the house. The walk did me good though. It also made me hungry, which I realize only after stepping through the front door and smelling whatever it is he's cooking. Right away, standing just inside the family room, I notice that he's bought some new furniture and rearranged the house. It looks good. There's a new bookshelf in the living room full of books by Robert Bly and Sam Keen. *Zen and the Art of Motorcycle Maintenance* is wedged between *Call of the Wild* and *On the Road.*

Moments after I hear him rustling around in the kitchen, Dad appears.

"I thought I heard the front door open," he says, coming toward me with open arms.

For some reason, I feel like I'm about to cry as he hugs me. His reaction to the pregnancy is already so different from Mom's ("I have no idea what I'm supposed to even say to you right now," she said when I called her in California to share the news. "Other than you're throwing your life away.")

"I'm guessing it's not what you had planned," Dad says, glancing down at my just-emerging baby bump when he pulls away.

I shake my head. "Not exactly."

"Is he a good man at least?"

"Yeah," I say. "Yeah, he is." Then, to change the subject, "What smells so good?"

"Ah," Dad says. "I've made minestrone." He looks a little bashful all of a sudden.

"That's amazing," I tell him, happy for the change of subject.

"Well, you might want to hold off on the excitement. I'm pretty new to this whole cooking gig."

"Wow," Hadley says when I tell her the news about my pregnancy. "Bold move." She came over to the house after my dad left for work this morning, and we're hanging out on the living room couch.

"It's not like I'm trying to make a statement," I tell her.

Hadley smiles. "I should hope not. I mean, it's not like this was planned, right?"

Looking down at the floor, I shake my head. "But once I knew I was pregnant, it was like…I don't know." For some reason, I feel the need to explain. "It just seemed to make sense. And I couldn't ask for a more responsible, mature man than Lawrence."

"Well, hell," she says, smiling. "More power to you, then. Whatever floats your boat."

"What's that supposed to mean?"

Hadley shrugs. "It means I just can't necessarily relate to the life choices you've been making lately. But, you know, whatever. I'm sure Barb is thrilled."

I don't tell her how my mom actually reacted. I'm still stinging from her rebuke. And the last thing I need is for the two of them to form some kind of alliance against me. Instead, I say, "As if I relate to *your* life choices." I don't know why I even say it when I could have just said nothing. Maybe it's second trimester hormones. Who knows?

Hadley isn't smiling anymore. "Excuse me?"

Against my better judgement (which seems to be conspicuously absent more and more of the time lately), I keep talking. "Sleeping with women, Hadley? Seriously? And not bothering to tell me about it?" I wasn't going to bring up the subject of the girl in her bed again, was just going to let it slide, but here it is, bursting out of me.

Hadley stares. "Well, excuse me for not being the perfect hetero sidekick you've apparently always dreamed about. And are you suggesting I *chose* to be this way?"

"Oh, please," I fire back.

"Did it ever occur to you that you're not the only person on the planet who has problems? That maybe I've been trying to figure this stuff out about myself for my whole life, and the last thing I wanted to do was lose my best friend in the process? Based on what you just said, I'm glad I didn't open up to you earlier. I'm guessing it wouldn't have gone too well."

"That's not fair," I tell her. "I just...I'm concerned about you."

"Clearly," Hadley says, rolling her eyes.

A memory from when we were younger pops into my head. We were in seventh grade, and I'd been upset about how distant my mother had been acting lately, hurt that she never seemed to want to be around me and Dad anymore. Hadley had tucked me in and spooned me with the covers between us, stroking my hair. Later, she'd brought me tea. But it hadn't been a sexual thing. Had it? It suddenly feels extremely important to know the answer. "Just tell me this. Did you feel this way...I mean, did you know you were gay...when I came to your house that one time all upset, and you tucked me in, and then you...you know. spooned me?"

"Huh? What does that even..." Hadley looks confused, and then the light seems to click on. When she responds, it comes out in a rush, the words all jumbled together. "If you're talking about the time you showed up at my door when we were in junior high, convinced that your mother didn't love you, and that nobody else ever would, and if you're asking if I, like, took that opportunity to come on to you or something, then I'm pretty sure we seriously do not need to keep having this conversation."

"That's not what I'm saying."

"Not overtly anyway." Tears are welling up in Hadley's eyes now. "You were a complete mess, you know that? You were a wreck, and all I was trying to do was be your friend. I knew your mom loved you, and I also knew you'd never have a problem finding as many people as you needed to love you. But *you* clearly didn't know that, and so all I could do was try to comfort you. And now you're calling all of that into question, thinking I was being...I don't know. Some kind of sexual opportunist? God, Jill. I seriously can't believe you sometimes."

I feel sick to my stomach. Something big is happening between us right now, something not good. I'm not sure how much of what I'm feeling is morning sickness and how much is *mourning* sickness caused by shame and by what feels like the sudden end of a friendship that's been a huge part of my life for as long as I can remember.

"I'm outta here," Hadley tells me, getting up from the couch. And then she's gone.

Bodhi calls the next day. Bodhi, who I haven't spoken to for almost seven months.

"Just come over," he says. "Please? I know things have been weird, but I just...I just want to see you."

We meet at a park near his mother's house. I'm wearing a sundress, holding my purse in front of my belly; I didn't think first pregnancies were supposed to start showing this early.

His hopeful smile is the first thing I see when he gets out of his car and walks toward me. He raises a hand in greeting, a little shyly, like he did the first time I met him. I raise a hand in response, and my purse shifts. Bodhi glances down at my abdomen. When he looks back into my eyes, his face has changed. I can tell he doesn't want to say anything, though, in case the freshman fifteen I've gained has shifted from my butt to my gut. We're standing just a few feet away from each other now.

"I'm pregnant," I say, saving him from further guesswork.

"Are you serious?"

Looking away from him, I bite my lower lip. "Three-plus months," I tell him.

For the longest time, Bodhi just stands there, looking at the ground and shaking his head. He sniffs once, quietly, then swipes at his eyes with the sleeve of his hoodie. At long last, he looks up. "So, who is he?"

"You don't know him." Then, after a moment, because I might as well just get it all out in the open: "I'm engaged."

Bodhi staggers backward. "What? My God, Jill. How did this happen so fast? How could you not tell me about this?"

"You sound like Hadley." My voice is almost breezy, but the truth is, I feel like shit. I won't let myself cry though. And I won't let myself dwell on how it's possible to feel like such a horrible person when I'm carrying the very essence of love and life—an actual miracle—in the center of my body. The truth is, I've made my choice. Hadley and Bodhi have their lives, and I have mine. And one thing has become abundantly clear after seeing both of them in the past twenty-four hours:

It's time for all three of us to move on. It's time for me to burn those old bridges once and for all.

Book 13: 2009

No man or woman born, coward or brave,
can shun his destiny.
~Homer

"Hey, cool," Bodhi says, appearing through the back door of the studio. "You guys made it."

Standing once again just inside the entrance, Jillian and Hadley watch as he carries a curved piece of sheet metal over to the back of the space. Waiting there is the welding biker dude they saw the first time they showed up here. He takes the metal from Bodhi and sets it down on the workbench.

"Come on back," Bodhi says, motioning for Jillian and Hadley to join them. When they do, he introduces them to the biker. "Hadley and Jillian, this is Gunnar. Gunnar, these are civilized womenfolk."

Gunnar grunts in response, then turns back to the sheet of metal.

"He's a great welder," Bodhi tells them. "But we're still working on manners."

Gunnar shoots a glare at him, and Hadley smirks.

Jillian looks around the space. An easel is set up in a spot just beyond the square of natural light spilling in through big, west-facing windows. Next to it is a drafting table covered with sketch pads, graphite pencils, and a box of conté crayons. The wall closest to the easel is covered with sketches, most of them drawn from life—women and men (both nude and clothed), cows in a pasture, a couple of napping dogs curled up beneath an oak tree. There are industrial-type drawings, too: Machinery, vehicles, architectural renderings. Jillian stares at all of them in amazement. Bodhi was talented when they were in high school, but it's clear his skills have grown exponentially in the years since.

"I'm headed out to the shed," Bodhi says. "What can I grab?"

Gunnar taps the sheet without looking up. "Three more of these. Same size."

Bodhi looks at the women and raises his chin. "You two should come check this out." They're following him toward the back door when Jillian stops short. At the other end of the studio, hanging on a wall not far from where a futon and coffee table have been set up near a woodstove, she sees it—the self-portrait she painted in Madame Imre's class, the one she gave Bodhi for Christmas all those years ago. Not knowing quite what to do with the miniature tornado of emotions suddenly swirling around inside of her, Jillian looks away.

"It's still my favorite painting of all time," Bodhi says.

Once they're outside, he leads them down a wide, pebble-covered path to another structure about fifty yards away. This one's smaller than the studio, and it takes Jillian a couple of seconds to realize what she's looking at.

"It's the old cabin!" she cries. "The sheepherder cabin!" A senior prom memory arises—Bodhi's beautiful eyes fixed on hers from above as they lay together on those quilt-covered straw bales. "I…I thought the road out here seemed familiar," she adds lamely, trying to hide the furious blush rising into her cheeks.

Bodhi is watching her carefully. "Yeah, the main building hides it. Like I said, I wanted to give you guys the full tour when you came by on Labor Day, but…"

"But we were outta here," Hadley says with a laugh, glancing at Jillian and pointing a thumb behind her with a grand flourish.

Jillian looks down at the ground, completely mortified. It's been two weeks since she and Hadley drove down to the Scottsdale house to get her things. Two weeks since she made a complete scene by smashing all that wedding china in the garage. That's how long it's taken for her to feel balanced enough to start doing normal-person things, things like visiting an old friend's art studio. Apparently, it hasn't been long enough. She shouldn't have come back here. She's not ready to face the lifetime of memories and feelings that seem hell-bent on jumping her at every turn.

Hadley and Bo are both looking at her now. "We're just rattling your chain, Jacobs," Hadley says, giving her a little punch on the arm. "Builds character, right?"

Jillian smiles weakly as she raises her head and looks around some more. The dirt floor she remembers has been replaced with a cement pad. In fact, it looks like the entire structure has been redone on the inside—retrofitted and buffered against the elements. Where weather-beaten logs with gaps between them used to be the only thing separating the cabin's interior and exterior, there are now textured and painted walls. Heavy-duty storage units are lined up, side by side, around the perimeter, the shelves filled with scraps of metal in various shapes and sizes.

Bodhi clears his throat, his eyes following Jillian's around the space. "I didn't buy it to turn it into some sort of shrine," he says, grinning self-consciously as he walks over to one of the storage shelves and grabs three pieces of sheet metal. "In case that's what you're thinking."

Back in the studio, Gunnar's removing beads of slag from the long edge of a piece that looks almost finished. "So, what's this going to be anyway?" Hadley asks him, yelling over the noise of the grinder as Bodhi sets the metal sheets down on the workbench.

Gunnar turns off the grinder and lifts his goggles. "He's got a Utah thing," he mutters, jerking his head toward Bodhi.

"Huh," Hadley says. "Alrighty then."

"I've been hired to create a sculpture for one of the businesses near Zion National Park," Bodhi explains. "We're just working on a smaller scale mock-up right now. And this is just the base. We go into actual production in a couple of weeks, after I visit in person to get some pictures and sketches. They want something inspired by the park."

"That sounds so cool," Hadley says. "I love southern Utah."

"Wait a minute." Bodhi holds his hands up as if struck by sudden inspiration. "You guys should totally come with us."

"I'm in," Hadley says without a moment's hesitation.

Jillian looks at her, startled. "Just like that?"

Hadley shrugs. "Sure. Why not?"

"Uh…" Gunnar says. Straightening up, he shakes his head and makes a sawing gesture at his neck with one hand.

"I'll stay at your place and take care of things," Jillian adds.

"Oh, hell no," Hadley tells her. "I have a neighbor who can hold down the fort. You're coming with. Right Bodhi?"

Bodhi, who is clearly trying to look noncommittal, barely keeps his smile in check. "It's up to her."

"Not going to happen," Jillian says, avoiding eye contact with all of them.

"Agreed," Gunner chimes in.

Hadley's hands are on her hips now. "Why not?"

"Because it's ridiculous. And staying here will give me time to figure some stuff out, like where I'm going to live, for starters." Jillian closes her eyes. She so doesn't want to get into these humiliating details in front of the men.

"You're living here on the mountain for now," Hadley tells her. "Just deal with it."

It's Gunnar who finally tries to put a stop to the negotiation. "If she doesn't want to go, she doesn't want to go," he says to nobody in particular. Jillian's surprised by the little spark of gratitude she feels toward him as he turns his attention back to the piece he's been working on.

"It's a quick turnaround," Bodhi says, ignoring him. "Just two nights at a campground not too far from the park."

Jillian looks at him. "I can't just…leave."

"Clearly," Hadley says. "I mean, you have a schedule to keep, right? You social whore, you." When Jillian doesn't respond, she continues. "Look, I'm not trying to railroad you into going. Or maybe I am, a little. I just think it's not healthy for you to sit around ruminating."

Jillian shakes her head. "I don't have any camping stuff."

"I have an extra sleeping bag and tent," Bodhi says.

"But I'd need—"

"And I have hiking boots, socks…everything," Hadley adds.

Jillian releases a long sigh. "I'll think about it," she says finally.

Three days later, she stares out the window of Gunnar's van as the four of them cross the Painted Desert and the Navajo reservation. A crude, hand-painted sign zips past on the side of the highway: HAVE SOME REZPECT! DON'T LITTER!

Nobody has said much during the drive so far. Mostly, they've just ridden along in silence, Bodhi sitting up front in the passenger seat while Hadley and Jillian ride in the back. He'd asked if either of them wanted the front seat when they first set out, but both had declined. And so they'd driven out of Flagstaff, ponderosa forest dwindling until only pinyon-junipers dotted the landscape. Now, there's mainly just scrub brush and miles of bleached earth stretching out beneath a searing sun as far as the eye can see.

"Home Intruder," Bodhi says out of the blue.

"Axe murderer," Gunnar responds.

"Cannibal."

Hadley sits up. "What the hell are you two talking about?"

"Travel trailer that just passed us," Bodhi says, turning around to explain. He motions at the road ahead. "Logo on the back said *Invader*. Gunnar and I have a theory that the companies making those things use the most aggressive names possible as a marketing ploy."

They drive past the Vermillion Cliffs, which rise like a limestone army on the side of the road, and then into Colorado City right on the Utah border.

"Look at that," Hadley says, pointing to the roof of a huge cinder block house as they pause at a two-way stop sign. Two young girls in old-fashioned, full-length dresses with puffy sleeves and extra-high necklines are sitting on the roof waving at each vehicle that passes. The girls' hair is done up in looped braids with big, bouffant-type poufs on top. "What the hell century are we in?" Hadley wonders aloud as the girls seem to giggle to each other behind their hands. "Poor inmates," she mutters, waving back to them as Gunnar steps on the gas. "This must be their only fun."

But Jillian feels a strange flash of envy at the sight of those girls. They have a home, after all. They have their tradition, and they probably have big, supportive families and can look forward to having babies of their own someday. They know their place. As soon as the thought passes through her brain, she's horrified at herself. Horrified and exhausted.

"What's wrong?" Hadley asks her.

Jillian sighs. "I just miss my home. It's making me a little nutty, to tell you the truth."

"Yeah," Hadley says. "I get that." She watches Jillian for a long, careful minute before clearing her throat. "But I'm pretty sure you don't actually have a home anymore—at least not down in the Valley."

Jillian closes her eyes. "I know. But I can't help missing it anyway." She falls asleep without saying anything more, and when she wakes up, they're at the campground. The sun's already down, so they have to set up the tents in the dark.

It's not until the next morning, when she unzips her tent, that Jillian sees what the new landscape looks like for the first time. Their spot is right next to an enormous reservoir; a fall mist covers the water like smoke. Jillian can see Hadley's and the men's breath as they talk over cups of coffee, the three of them standing next to a small campfire, bundled up in flannel and denim.

"Morning, sleepy head," Hadley calls out.

"Morning." Jillian feels a little sheepish at what the others must be thinking: What kind of a lightweight diva sleeps in well past dawn on a camping trip?

A few minutes later, Hadley and Gunnar go off to explore the hiking trail that runs along the bank of the reservoir. "How does breakfast sound?" Bodhi asks when Jillian emerges from the tent.

"Sounds pretty good," she says, even though that's not completely true. Since the nightmare that was her recent trip down to Scottsdale, she's back to having hardly any appetite at all. "Have you eaten yet?"

Bodhi shakes his head. "I fed those two, but I thought I'd wait until you got up." He loads two tin pie pans with pancakes, sausage, and scrambled eggs, all of which have been kept warm in a Dutch oven perched high over the flames of the little campfire.

Jillian almost protests at the amount of food when he hands her one of the plates, but she doesn't want to be rude. Settling onto a couple of big rocks next to the fire, they set the plates on their knees. Bodhi pours some tar-black coffee into a mug before passing it to Jillian. "That'll put some hair on your chest," he says before producing a flask from his pocket and twisting off the top.

"Early start?" she teases him. She's a little surprised, actually; she doesn't recall Bodhi being much of a drinker.

He smiles. "It's maple syrup. Perfect for both flapjacks *and* coffee."

"If you say so." Taking the flask, she drizzles the syrup as directed before picking up her fork and taking a bite of pancake. The next thing she knows, she's closing her eyes to hide the fact that they're rolling back in her head as she chews. After swallowing, she lets out a small, inadvertent moan. "Holy moly," she says, looking at Bodhi. "I can actually *taste* this."

"That's good, right?"

Jillian nods as she digs enthusiastically into the eggs this time. "I know it sounds weird, but it's been weeks since I actually tasted food. I've been eating enough to get me through the day, but it's like I've been a robot or something. And once whatever I've eaten is gone, I barely remember what it was."

"I get it," he says. "Believe me."

"But you've never been married though." Her voice sounds more indignant than she means for it to. "Sorry," she says, covering her mouth with the tips of her fingers and looking down. "That was rude of me." Apparently, she doesn't even know how to make basic conversation anymore.

"It's okay," Bodhi says. "You're right. I haven't been married. I've had a couple of serious relationships end for various reasons though. I also broke off an engagement."

Jillian's head jerks up. "You did?" She doesn't like the chill that grips her chest at the thought of Bodhi being engaged. "I mean, not that it's any of my business."

"Hadley's definitely had her heart broken, too. And Gunnar—"

"Yeah, what's with that guy, anyway?" She's grateful for the chance to change the subject. "I mean, I know he's your friend and all, but..."

"He's a grouch," Bodhi says. "A big one. But try not to take it personally. Back in our early twenties, while the rest of us were figuring out what we wanted to be when we grew up, Gunnar was holed up in the Saudi Arabian desert not knowing how long his deployment was going to last or how many of his friends were going to die."

Jillian grips the edge of her plate. "Oh."

"Yeah," Bodhi says. "It wasn't easy for him over there, but things turned out pretty okay. Then, a few years later, he was deployed to Bosnia where he saw the kinds of things most people wouldn't be able to get over. He was married at the time. Came home from his deployment just in time for the birth of his daughter."

"He has a daughter?"

Bodhi's face is grim. "One night when she was almost a year old, Gunnar's wife broke down and told him the baby wasn't his."

"Oh, no." Jillian's hand goes to her chest as Bodhi nods.

"Honestly, I think that screwed him up more than the wars did."

Neither of them says anything for a while.

"And that," Bodhi finally announces, breaking the silence, "is how you ruin a perfectly good breakfast with stellar company."

Jillian smiles. "You didn't ruin it. But anyway…So, you were engaged?" (*Smooth transition,* she thinks to herself).

"I was," Bodhi says. "It was a long engagement, long enough for both of us to finally realize how totally incompatible we were. Look, you're just new to this kind of heartbreak. And I'm not going to judge your marriage. I don't know anything about it. But what I do know is that if you've been married for as long as you have, that means you've been sheltered from a lot of other stuff. The dating scene, for instance. Ugh, don't even get me started."

"I guess." She's looking off toward the horizon now. "So, you've dated a bunch?"

Bodhi picks a blade of grass growing at the base of the rock he's sitting on and holds it near his face for closer inspection. "Look who's up in my business all of a sudden."

Jillian reddens. "I'm sorry. I just…yeah, you're right. I'm being way too nosy."

"I'm messing with you, goofball," he says, tossing the grass away. "What about you? Think you'll date at some point?"

Jillian releases a long breath. "I don't know. Right now, I can't even imagine it. I'm pretty sure I'll want another relationship someday. But I have to find it with myself first, you know? It sounds totally *woo woo,* but I have this weird feeling that before I connect with another person, I need to find that thing that connects me...with me."

"It's your art," Bodhi says without hesitation.

Jillian looks at him. "Maybe."

"You know what I thought when I saw you at Hadley's place that day I came over to look at the water pump?"

"'Boy, that's one crazy loon?'"

Bodhi laughs. "I know this has been a terrible time for you, and I don't mean to romanticize it, or minimize it, in any way. But I thought *Jill's still got it. She still has the fire.*"

Jillian doesn't say anything.

"Most artists I've known let their creative passion die at the first sign of an engagement ring, or a mortgage, or a job with benefits. Do you know how rare it is for artists in their thirties to still have that spark?"

"I'm almost in my forties," Jillian reminds him.

"Even rarer!"

"...and I'm not exactly sure what spark you're talking about. I haven't made anything creative for almost twenty years. Unless you count desserts and centerpiece arrangements."

"Ah, but you're going to make something," Bodhi says. "I can feel it. I just hope I get to witness your big comeback whenever it happens."

As soon as Hadley and Gunnar return from exploring, the four of them load up into the van and head to Zion. Jillian's transfixed the moment they drive through the entrance of the national park and see the towering, rose-colored cliffs rising up before them. It's cold out and not as crowded with tourists as she expected, which is good; right away, she knows she wants to see as much of this wonderland as possible in the limited amount of time she has.

Bodhi brought his camera and a couple of sketch pads. The three of them follow him around until lunchtime, mostly on a bunch of the shorter trails where he'll have a good chance of capturing as many different views as possible. As they stand on a bridge, gazing in awe at the Virgin River flowing past a towering peak called The Watchman, Bodhi hands Jillian a sketch pad and a pencil. "In case you feel like drawing what you see," he says.

She tries, but not for long. It's too hard to get into any kind of artistic zone with the three of them standing there. Even though everyone's too busy marveling at the view to pay her any attention, Jillian senses a certain expectation. The weight of it feels crushing.

"I kind of want to hike alone for a bit," she says after they've eaten a late lunch. "Is that okay with everyone?"

Bodhi nods, Gunnar shrugs, and Hadley looks concerned. "You don't want any company at all?"

When Jillian shakes her head, Hadley checks her watch. "How about we meet back here at six then?"

"Okay, Mom," Jillian says with a smile. It won't be getting dark until well after that; three hours should give her plenty of time to clear her head.

She starts out on a trail leading to the Emerald Pools, marveling at the red earth beneath her feet and the lush vegetation all around. By the time she reaches the highest pool of the three and finds herself walking behind the curtain of a waterfall streaming from an overhead cliff, Jillian feels like she has stepped into another world entirely—some sort of Shangri La in the middle of the desert. Afterward, she heads back toward Zion Lodge, where she catches a shuttle that drops her at the head of the trail leading to Weeping Rock. She doesn't know what she'll find when she gets there, but the name alone is enough to make her want to see it. It's past five o'clock when she starts out. Looking at the map posted at the trailhead, Jillian calculates how much time it should take for her to do the loop. It's only a quarter mile or so. She should be fine.

Maple leaves adorning trailside trees have started to change color for the season. The lowering light makes them seem to morph further. Horsetails and maidenhair fern brush her ankles whenever she moves out of the way to allow descending hikers to pass by on their way down. The last part of the hike is a steep climb. Red-faced and breathing hard, she reaches the end of the trail, a spacious rock alcove where she finds herself alone. Jillian turns around to see a view straight out of a Bierstadt painting: Zion's famous Great White Throne rises mightily in the distance, the striated hues of the Navajo sandstone cliffs all around it an even deeper red now. Looking up, she beholds millions of water droplets falling from an enormous lip of rock jutting out high above her head. Acting as a sort of sieve for the setting sun's glow, the veil of rain casts persimmon flashes of light onto the curved wall behind her.

As she stands there, something shifts. Something inside her clicks into place without warning, as if the tectonic plates in her psyche are finally readjusting themselves after a major quake. Reaching both hands to the nape of her neck, she unclasps the delicate gold chain she's worn for years. Then she takes off her wedding ring, threads the chain through it, and refastens the necklace. Lawrence hasn't worn his ring for ages. Said it bothered the tender skin of his finger. "And like the patsy I was," Jillian informs the canyon stretching out before her, "I believed him."

Beginning to cry a little now, she wonders what it would be like to fly away through that canyon, to simply lift off from where she stands. She imagines great wings unfurling from her shoulder blades—wings made of fire and tears, breath and...acceptance. Wings that would carry her up and away, through the cascading mist and high over the valley beyond.

Five minutes into her descent back down the trail, she realizes how quickly it's getting dark. She'd foolishly neglected to ask Hadley or Bodhi for a flashlight when setting out earlier this afternoon; now, in the dusky dimness, she squints at the single-track trail to keep it in focus. She hasn't seen another hiker since a young European guy passed her on his way down, over forty minutes ago. Every once in a while, Jillian trips on a partially exposed tree stump or a rock in the trail. She tries not to panic. Walking faster will just increase her chances of falling down the steep drop-off to her right, so she forces herself to breathe deeply and to focus on each footstep. Then, without warning, she's brought up short by an ancient-looking doe that steps onto the trail as Jillian rounds a bend. Judging by the creature's stiff, careful steps, it's suffering from arthritis and maybe other things, too. Jillian can't imagine it will survive the rapidly approaching winter. She's filled with sadness, not wanting to startle the doe as it picks its way over the rocks.

Rounding another corner farther down the trail, she almost runs right into a tall, imposing man who's walking toward her with purpose. A surge of adrenaline shoots down her spine before she realizes it's Bodhi.

"We were getting worried," he says. "I couldn't reach you on your cell phone. Something told me you'd be here."

"I'm doing just fine." Her tone is more abrupt than it probably should be, considering how careless she was to stay out so late.

"I don't doubt that for a second," Bodhi says, holding a headlamp out toward her. "I just thought maybe I could bring you some light to see by."

They hike the short distance back to the bottom of the trail with ease, only occasionally stumbling on obstacles hidden in shadows cast by the artificial light.

As soon as the van comes into view, Bodhi stops walking.

Jillian stops, too. She turns to look at him with a questioning expression on her face. "What's wrong?"

"I just want you to know that there's plenty of space in the studio for another artist. We could set you up with whatever you need. Metalworking stuff, an easel, a work bench for mosaicking, whatever."

Jillian shakes her head. "Thanks, but that dog won't sail."

"Pardon?"

"It's just something my son used to say. Kind of a combination of 'That dog won't hunt' and 'That ship has sailed.'" Her heart clenches a little at the thought of Evan and how much she misses him. Thanksgiving break can't come fast enough.

"Ah," Bodhi says. "I see. But think about the offer anyway, okay?"

Once they're inside the van, Hadley turns around in the front passenger seat to reach back and grip Jillian's knee. "You scared the shit out of me," she says.

"I'm sorry."

Gunnar, narrowing his eyes at Jillian in the rearview mirror, doesn't even try to hide his annoyance. But there's something else in his expression, too, something she can't quite put her finger on. Could it be...yes, Jillian's pretty sure it is: It's relief.

The four of them are quiet as they sit around the campfire that night. After leaving Zion, they'd stopped at the first pizza joint they could find and gorged themselves on two extra-large supremes; now they have full bellies to go with their tired legs. Having already showered and brushed her teeth in the campground bathroom, Jillian watches the flames illuminating Bodhi's face as he sits across from her, staring into the fire. Without a doubt, she's coming back to Zion someday. There's so much still left to discover. "I could konk out right here," she says when overwhelming sleepiness descends without warning.

Next to her, Hadley slings an arm around Jillian's shoulders and gives her a hug. "I love you," she says.

Jillian rests her head on Hadley's shoulder. "I love you, too, Hads." Excusing herself, she returns to her tent where she unhooks the blackout panels at the top, leaving only a layer of mesh through which she'll be able to see the stars before falling asleep.

Soon, she hears Bodhi saying goodnight to Hadley and Gunnar, too. And not long after that, as her eyelids are fluttering closed, Jillian senses something to her left, where the walls of her tent and Bodhi's tent almost touch. Turning her head, she sees the outline of his open hand pressed lightly but clearly against the nylon. She presses her hand against his and holds it there until her arm grows heavy.

"Night, Jacobs," Bodhi finally says as shadows outside flicker and sway in the glow of the dying campfire.

Instinctively, Jillian's mouth opens to say, "Kensington," but she doesn't say it. Instead, she just says, "Night, Bodhi."

The next morning, after breakfast and before packing up the van, Bodhi challenges Gunnar to an arm-wrestling match. In a sudden outburst of macho competitiveness, the men remove their shirts and crouch on either side of one of the big campfire boulders.

"Can't argue with that," Hadley says, watching from where she and Jillian are stuffing their tents and stakes into tubular nylon bags.

Jillian looks at her, surprised.

"What? I'm gay, not dead."

A few minutes later, when the van is all packed up, Jillian sees Bodhi standing alone at the edge of the reservoir, looking out over the water. "I wanted to thank you for yesterday," she says, walking up behind him. "For this whole trip, really. It's been…inspiring."

Bodhi shifts his gaze to her face. "I'm really glad to hear that."

"In fact," Jillian continues, taking a deep breath. "I feel like I might even want to dip my toes back into the whole art thing, after all."

"Tell me what you need."

"Space."

Bodhi looks momentarily crestfallen, but he covers it up quickly and looks back out at the water. "I can give you that," he says. "No problem. I won't call or try to touch base. I mean, I haven't really been doing a ton of that anyway, but—"

"No," Jillian says with a laugh. "I mean studio space. I want to take you up on your offer."

Back in the van, forty-five minutes into the drive home, she falls asleep to the drone of wheels on pavement. She's woken up sometime later by Gunnar's voice: "Hell," he says with a sigh, "having a chick in the place'll harsh the whole vibe. C'mon, dude."

Jillian blinks hard to clear her head of restless dream fog.

They stop somewhere between Marble Canyon and Gray Mountain for gas. There's a little repair shop with an attached retail space a short distance from the pump—The Epic Motorcycle, it's called. Gunnar heads toward it. "Gonna poke around a bit," he says. "See if I can find anything interesting for my Hog."

Hearing Tracy Chapman's "Give Me One Reason" playing loudly somewhere nearby, Hadley and Jillian peel themselves instinctually from the back seat to investigate. It turns out the music is coming from another small building attached to the gas station, a bar this time. Without a word, the two women wander inside the dimly lit, untended space, find an open spot on the floor, and start dancing to the music pouring out of the jukebox. They dance close, like lovers—under the spell of road weariness and without a care. Done with pumping gas and whatever the hell else men do, Bodhi and Gunnar eventually come looking for them. For the remainder of the song, the two of them stand in the doorway, slack-jawed, watching.

By the time they get back to Hadley's and haul their stuff out of the van a little over an hour later, Jillian's exhausted to her very bones. Stumbling out to the Ovum, she collapses into dreamless sleep without bothering to take off her clothes or even the hiking boots Hadley loaned her.

Book 14: 1989

Young women spill out into the late October sunlight as if being birthed, fully formed, from the double-doored forehead of the Classics department. They're unfailingly sylph-like, these women, leaving the lecture hall at the end of Lawrence's class in their long flowing skirts and ballet flats, or mini-dresses and heels, or short-shorts and flip-flops. The prettiest ones are sullen, pouty, as if their beauty, their effortless way of moving through the world, are burdens nobody else could possibly understand.

And here I am—twenty-four weeks pregnant and waddling up the steps like a spawning salmon making its way upstream—a different species entirely, as I bring Lawrence the homemade lunch I packed for him on a whim. My body, encased in a yellow, form-fitting maternity dress, looks like one of those marshmallow Easter peeps that's been microwaved for about ten seconds. I remind myself that it's temporary, though, and that how I look doesn't really matter. What does matter is that the baby inside my womb is (according to the tests) perfectly healthy. And also, that I am engaged to Professor Lawrence Kensington. He asked me to marry him last week, which means soon I'll officially no longer be that lost, sad girl who has to do everything on her own. My heart swells thinking of my soon-to-be husband. He has basically made me who I am, and I owe him more than I could ever repay.

Lawrence isn't in the lecture hall, and he's not in his office yet, either. One of the Latin professors, who I met briefly at an awards luncheon last month, nods as he passes me in the hallway. Professor Kemp, I think his name is. After a while, I make my way back out into the sunshine and across the quad to the little coffee shop adjacent to Humanities. Lawrence isn't there, either, but a Sanka packet with my name on it is. All I need is a cup of hot water. I get in line behind an older woman whose back is turned toward me. I'm admiring her beautiful silver hair when she turns around as if to check for a lover's presence. It's Madame Imre.

"Jill!" she cries, opening her arms wide and wrapping me in a hug. "I was just thinking about you not so long ago."

"I'm pregnant," I blurt out in response. "In case, you know, you thought I just got fat." Could I *be* a bigger doofus?

Her eyes widen for a moment in confusion. It's clear she's putting some effort into arranging her expression. "Oh?"

"I took a break from school after freshman year was done," I say, the words gaining momentum as they leave my mouth. "It was exactly the right choice, mainly because it gives me the opportunity to fully support Lawrence before the baby comes. He's been working so hard on his new book."

"Lawrence?" Her face is a blank.

"Professor Kensington," I tell her. "He's the father. It's hella awkward, I know. But it's okay. Everything's fine. Everything's *great,* actually."

If she's shocked or disappointed in me, she doesn't let it show. Instead, she puts a hand on my arm, looks into my eyes, and smiles broadly. "Of course it is okay. This is the ultimate creation you're working on now, after all."

"Right," I say, forcing a smile. The line has moved, and Madame Imre turns to the guy behind the counter to place her order. Once I've placed mine, we stand off to the side to wait.

"Just remember," she says, giving my arm a squeeze. "You may leave your art for a time, but it will never leave you."

"Aliz," another guy behind the counter calls out.

"That's me," she says. "And now I must run. Class starts in five minutes. Congratulations on the baby! I am so happy for you!"

Once she's gone, I could kick myself for not telling her more about Lawrence and how wonderful he is: I've already begun to notice, for instance, how being with him stabilizes me. He's regimented and disciplined, and…let's face it…just plain experienced. He's taken control of my life—in a good way, of course. He has some great ideas, for instance, on how I might dress to better fit in with the other faculty wives. He even took me dress shopping when it was time to introduce me to his parents. And he's convinced me to put away all the ratty overalls I used to wear before I met him. "Who knows?" he said after I'd boxed them up with some of my other art stuff and stuck them on a shelf in the garage next to the wedding gift china set (minus the platter I pulled out at the last minute because it looks useful). "Maybe we'll use them for rags or something later."

Even when it comes to sex, Lawrence exhibits near-perfect control. He never looks at me during the act, for example, not even when he's tipsy (and definitely not now that I'm hugely pregnant). Instead, he closes his eyes or looks off to the side, past my head. My theory is that this new life we've created makes him feel more vulnerable than he's used to. Plus, I'm sure I'll eventually get used to how he is in bed. It's just…different than the wide-eyed adoration I became used to with Bodhi. Not that I let myself dwell on those memories anymore—it's been almost a year since Bodhi and I broke up, after all. Even if I did let myself dwell on them, it would be an unfair comparison. Next to Lawrence, Bodhi's an inexperienced youngster in just about every way.

"I stopped by the department today," I mention when he comes home that evening. "But I couldn't find you.

"I left right after class ended," he says. "Must have just missed you. I actually went to see my lawyer."

"Oh?" A slight quickening of the pulse. Because I'm silly.

"There is the issue of the prenuptial agreement for you to sign."

I pout. "That sounds so unromantic, and I don't even know what it is."

"It's basically a friendly document that protects both of us," he says. "A minor inconvenience at best. But since this house will likely become mine someday…"

"What? It isn't yours already?"

Lawrence shrugs an apology. "It belongs to my parents. I'm sorry to tell you that I am not, in fact, a millionaire."

I almost tease him that I might just have to find another guy who *is* a millionaire, as any gold digger worth her salt would do. I don't want him to misunderstand though. Drawing close to his side, I nudge him playfully with my hip. "You do remember that part about me loving you, right?"

"Rest assured the house will be ours in spirit," he says, "thanks to my parents' generosity. But it's still theirs on paper." He sighs again. "These things can be so complex and unpleasant. And you're such a good person. I know you'd never want to jeopardize their home."

"Oh my gosh, of course not! I just assumed you'd trust me to not do something like that."

Lawrence kisses the top of my head and sighs. "I would. It's just..."

"What?"

"Well, don't take this the wrong way, but they're a bit concerned. You've already broken my heart once, you know."

I think about that day in his office when I'd fled after he'd not-so-subtly suggested I get an abortion. I'm not totally sure that the shame I feel now at what I've put him through is warranted or not, but I feel it anyway.

"I know they're going to love you completely," he continues, "as soon as they get to know you the way *I* know you. But until then..."

"Say no more," I tell him. I can't blame my future in-laws for being protective of their only son, considering how protective I already feel about a baby I haven't even met yet. Besides, Lawrence is right: I'll definitely be able to win his parents over. I'm giving birth to their grandchild, for crying out loud! How could they not end up loving us both?

It will probably take a little time though. The first and only time I met them was a few weeks after Lawrence begged me to come back to him. Mr. and Mrs. Kensington came through the door of the house not knowing I was standing near the entry hall, waiting in the wings. Lawrence had thought it would be best to surprise them.

"The house looks lovely, dear," Lawrence's mother said, pausing to kiss him on the cheek.

"Hopefully, we won't have to sell it," his father added. "It would be a shame if our almost middle-aged child had to finance his own life for a change."

They still hadn't spotted me. I would pretend I'd heard nothing.

"Oh, we won't have to sell it," his mother said (a bit nervously, it seemed to me, but what did I know?).

Lawrence still hadn't said anything. His back was toward me, so I wasn't able to get a look at his face.

"Times are tough," his father continued, shutting the front door. "They can get tougher at the drop of a hat. Especially when a kid decides to go into classics rather than finance."

I couldn't stand it anymore. "Lawrence is very responsible," I piped up, stepping out from the shadows. Something in me wanted it known that I was ready to leap to his defense. And also, that while I intended to respect my soon-to-be in-laws, I was strong enough to stand up to them, if need be.

Silence stretched for a good five seconds before both men turned to singe me with simultaneous, withering glares. Lawrence's mother opened her handbag and looked down as she fussed around inside of it.

"Who the hell is this?" Lawrence Senior demanded.

Things never defrosted during that visit, and I haven't seen them since. Lawrence wants to wait until after we're married to tell them about the pregnancy.

"Of course I'll sign the prenup," I tell him now.

Lawrence wraps me in a brief hug and kisses the top of my head. "I'm going to pay off your student loans," he says. "I know it's not much of a consolation prize, but—"

"You'd do that for me?"

"Oh, don't worry." He reaches down with both hands to draw me closer to him and to stroke my hips. "I'll get my pound of flesh."

It's an overcast day in the Phoenix Metropolitan Area when we head to the county courthouse. I'm a little disappointed at not having a fancy wedding with the vows, and the cake, and the bridesmaids, but this is fine. One of Lawrence's male TAs, the one who gave me the invitation to the Poseidon party back in January, is our witness.

"This'll be you someday," Lawrence tells him. "Just don't do what I did and get yourself into a shotgun situation." He laughs, indicating that it's a joke, but I'm still a little embarrassed by it.

"Thank you for coming," I tell him.

"I'm honored to help," he says, smiling at me for a quick moment before looking away.

The following Monday evening, Lawrence comes home from work bearing gifts that were waiting for him in the faculty lounge. One of the gifts is a box of china from Bill Bunston and his wife, Martha. She was the youngest of the Classics department faculty wives before I came along. *Welcome to the Club!* the gift tag reads.

And then, on Wednesday, we get the greatest wedding gift ever: An official letter stating that the university wants to publish the book Lawrence has been working on for years. It's a thin but no doubt very important treatise called *Castration of the Father: Zeus, Cronus, and the Dysfunctionalization of the Paternal Olympian Bond.*

I'm so excited for him that I can hardly stand it. "It's going to be a real book!"

Lawrence bestows one of his patient smiles upon me. "More or less," he agrees. "It's not like being published by one of the Big Six, but at least there's a chance for reviews—perhaps even for building a readership."

"New York will come knocking at your door someday," I assure him. "Just you wait." Honestly, the magnitude of our good fortune makes me a little dizzy. To steady myself, I make some celebratory cupcakes to bring to the Classics building for Lawrence and his colleagues to enjoy. Given the momentous occasion, I take considerable care in decorating them, even going so far as to create little laurel wreaths out of green fondant before arranging the finished cupcakes on the china platter.

We go back and forth about names for the last few weeks of the pregnancy: "Zeus!" Lawrence suggests on my twentieth birthday. "Heracles!"

At first, I assume he's kidding.

"Homer?"

That's when I put my foot down. "How many times would he have to hear people exclaim 'Doh!' in his lifetime? And what if it's a girl?"

Lawrence thinks about this. "Aphrodite, then. On second thought, strike that. It would mean I'd have to have my genitals cut off and tossed into the sea."

When I finally go into hard labor one late January evening a few hours after being induced, Lawrence quotes Homer: "And even as when the sharp dart striketh a woman in travail, the piercing dart that the Eilithyiae, the goddesses of childbirth, send—even the daughters of Hera that have in their keeping bitter pangs; even so sharp pains came upon the mighty son of Atreus."

I stare at him, wild-eyed. Even though I agreed to the induction due to being a full forty weeks along, I wasn't prepared for the out-of-the-blue agony: A contraction comes, and then another. They keep coming, closer and closer together, until I am pushed out of my old life, out of my old skin—nearly out of my mind from the pain. And then—finally, finally—they lay that baby against my sweaty chest, and there's my new life's entire purpose.

The moment I lay eyes on him, everything that came before is over and done with. Anything that I thought actually mattered is instantly vaporized by this tiny creature. There's little choice involved. It's as if my ancient, oceanic, fish-with-feet ancestors are calling out to me across the millennia: *This is your spawn. He shall be your life now*. The fact that he is still slick with the substance of another world makes the moment feel especially fleeting—evanescent, even.

"Evan," I say, looking up from the baby and into Lawrence's eyes.

"Pardon?"

"I think that's his name."

Pursing his lips and looking up toward the ceiling, Lawrence considers my words. "I like it," he says finally. "Evander of Pallene, the wise hero who founded pre-Rome Rome. He was featured in Virgil's *Aeneid*, you know."

But I'm not paying attention. I can't stop staring at our new son, already the most important thing I've ever accomplished—and likely ever will.

Afterward, once everyone has gone home, the baby and I are alone. Evan's tiny head is burrowed against the side of my neck, the rhythm of my femoral artery perhaps like a lullaby at his ear, beckoning him toward sleep. Right then and there I make a promise that I'll never try to fly away like my own mother was always trying to do when I was a kid. I promise him that, no matter what happens, I'll stay.

Mom comes into town when Evan is just a few days old. Waiting for her arrival, I can't settle down. "Do I look okay?"

"You look fine," Lawrence assures me.

"Does the baby look okay?"

"Jillian."

I don't know why I'm such a wreck. Maybe it has to do with the post-partum hormone crash I've read about. It doesn't help that she and I had a tense exchange over the phone a few days before Evan was born. She asked me if I'd be interested in having her splurge on a housecleaner. "Even

I had one after you were born," she said. "Once a week, no big deal, but it was such a help."

"Taking care of my family and my home is my job," I told her.

"I'm just saying it would free up your time."

"To do what?"

Mom laughed. "I don't know," she said. "You tell me. To study, maybe? To go to class? Maybe you'll be ready to start up again when summer session rolls around and Evan's a little older."

I didn't have the heart to tell her that there will be no more starting up, not where college is concerned, anyway. I officially withdrew from the university in early December. Because what's the point of continuing, really, when it comes right down to it? No degree can possibly compare in importance to my new job of being Evan's mommy. Besides, Lawrence is the scholar, not me. Not that I'm a horrible student or anything, but I've come to realize that I'm just not cut out for school. There's too much stress, too much striving, and for what, exactly? Lawrence's Intro to Myth course was a perfect example. The gods and goddesses, the battles and victories, who spawned whom, who dragged whom down to hell, and who rescued whom, got all bungled up in my brain, mismatched pieces I could never quite make heads nor tails of.

"What about your art?" Mom pressed.

"When have you ever been concerned about my art?"

There was a long silence at the other end of the line. "I'm going to chalk that comment up to post-pregnancy hormones."

The moment she walks through the front door and sees her new grandson, it becomes abundantly clear that I needn't have worried about her visit; the instant she sees the baby, my mother falls instantly, transparently in love. Lawrence, who comes in after her, carrying her suitcase, doesn't stay long. In fact, he tells us, he's going to have to work extra hours pretty much during her entire visit. I'm disappointed; I was hoping he and my mother could spend some time bonding while she's here.

For the three days she's in town, Mom cooks, cleans, and stays at Evan's beck and call while I try to catch up on sleep. When I'm awake and the baby's asleep, we talk about the things she experienced after I was born, like how hard it was for her to figure out how to pin a diaper, and how painful it was when her uterus started contracting back to its normal size.

I sit at the kitchen table, listening in wonder. How has she never told me about these things before? How have I never realized how much she actually knows? I'm shocked at how starved I am for this kind of information. My memories of my mother from when I was a little girl are of a woman running, always running—usually in the opposite direction from me and Dad. Now I understand, fully and for the first time, that she once went through almost exactly what I'm going through right this second, this shift from being a person in one's own right to being completely responsible for the life of another.

Mom even watches the baby so I can make a solo trip to the grocery store. Unfortunately, as I'm standing in the check-out line, I have a mini panic attack about leaving him. It's no small miracle that I'm able to hang in there long enough to actually pay for the groceries before practically running back to the car, loading everything up, and driving home.

Evan's asleep when I get there. "He's been asleep since you left," Mom tells me. My shoulders, which have been hiked up near my ears for the past half hour, drop down to their normal position. And then, as I stand there feeling relief washing over me, my milk lets down. In an instant, my breasts transform into udders.

"How do I get a handle on this situation?" I ask Mom, showing her the front of my drenched shirt.

"You were a bottle baby," she says with a shrug.

When it's time for Lawrence to drive her to the airport so she can go back home to California, we make the goodbye short and sweet. Mom lowers her face to Evan's and whispers something, her hair forming a protective curtain around the two of them. When she looks back up, tears are shining in her eyes. Minutes later, as the car backs out of the driveway, I stand at the window by the front door, holding the baby and waving goodbye, even though she can't see me. Reaching into the blanket for Evan's tiny wrist, I carefully help him wave, too.

And that's when the tears start to fill my eyes. "Don't go," I whisper to the window glass. "Please don't go." I have never felt more alone in my entire life.

When Lawrence returns from the airport, he finds me on the couch, pumping milk while the baby naps in his bassinet nearby.

"We have the house to ourselves again," I tell him, looking up from the plastic cone encasing my boob.

Lawrence arranges his coat over the back of a chair. "Yes, indeed," he says, rubbing his hands together and turning to head into his office. "And now, if you'll excuse me, I need to get back to work."

I'm not expected to perform faculty wife duties for those first few months, which means I'm able to stay home with Evan, the two of us in a cocoon of domesticity, as I dive into motherhood, housekeeping, cooking, and baking. It doesn't take me long to realize that I wouldn't ever leave the house if I didn't have to. I also realize that I have to stop snacking on the things I bake: Not long after establishing the new routine, Lawrence places his open hands on my stomach and wiggles the newly loose flesh there. "Where's my hot young wife?" he asks with a pout.

I'm speechless as my brain scrambles for a response.

"When we met," he continues, "your body reminded me of Aphrodite from the Hellenistic *Aphrodite with Pan and Eros* sculpture." He gives a little laugh. "Now it looks more like those paintings of Venus by Rubens. Still classic, but you know..."

No, I don't know, I think as he kisses the tip of my nose before disappearing into his office to work for the rest of the evening.

A few days later, I stand next to my car under a shade tree at a local park, getting ready to transfer Evan from his car seat into the front pack. Just yesterday, I saw a flyer on the community bulletin board at the grocery store. It was for a new mom exercise group that meets here weekly. *Work off your post-natal flab & blues in a FUN, supportive & DISCIPLINED atmosphere!* the flyer read. I've just finished strapping Evan into his front pack when I hear a single voice yelling out: "I said a boom chicka boom!"

Other voices repeat the phrase. If I didn't know better, I'd think it was some local high school cheerleaders practicing.

"I said a BOOM CHICKA BOOM," the solo voice shouts, louder this time.

Again, the other voices respond.

"I said a BOOM CHICKA ROCKA CHICKA ROCKA CHICKA BOOM! Let's go, ladies. Work it!"

I wander halfway across the parking area to get a better view. What I see is a small army of young mothers in spandex and tennis shoes lined up near a stone wall at the entrance to the park. A bunch of strollers are parked parallel to them, one for each mom, and the women are doing squats. The yeller, an ultra-fit woman with a high, blonde ponytail and a salon tan, marches up and down the line like a drill sergeant, the response to her call clearly too anemic for her liking. Several of the mothers look unsure about how to respond. *What am I doing here?* their faces seem to say. *Someone please remind me who I used to be.*

That's when I realize I can't go through with it. Instead of joining the other mothers at that wall, I return to my car, strap

Evan back into his seat, get behind the wheel (baby flab and all), and drive away.

At the end of May, when Evan is almost six months old, I'm recruited to work my first big university event. The post-graduation ceremony buffet for classics majors is one of the key celebrations we faculty wives are expected to help with, and I'm actually excited. It's going to be nice to spend a little time among adults again.

One of the first people I see on that glorious spring day is Natalie Edelmann, my old roommate, who's just finished her sophomore year. Natalie's there with her family to celebrate her older brother's graduation. She gives me a big hug before turning to her parents, who I met once or twice. "You guys remember Jill, right? My roommate from last year?"

"Of course!" her mother says. "So nice to see you, Jill." Her cheerful voice can't hide the fact that she's looking at me with obvious pity. Natalie's father, meanwhile, looks off toward the horizon, avoiding the awkwardness completely.

Just then, one of the other faculty wives calls my name from over by the hors d'oeuvres table. "I could use a little help," she says.

"I have to go," I tell Natalie. "Congratulations to your brother." I flash a big smile, but it's forced. I'm going to ask the wife in charge of these things to assign me to a more behind-the-scenes role for this event in the future; I'm not sure I'll be able to handle watching Natalie and my other former classmates walk across the graduation stage when the time comes.

After helping with the hors d'oeuvres, I'm asked to man the nametag table at the entrance of the hall. Each attendee is supposed to fill out a large rectangular sticker with the words *HELLO, I'M* ______ printed on it. A young woman comes up, grabs a marker from the table, and writes *Bridget* on the blank line in curlicue script before unpeeling the sticker from its backing and pressing it against her left breast. She holds her hand out to me. "What's your major?"

"Motherhood," I reply. I crumple the waxy square of backing into a ball and toss it into a nearby cardboard box full of trash as Bridget looks at me, clearly confused. She probably thinks I'm helping out as part of my sorority's community service requirement or something.

"Oh, like early childhood development?" she presses, tilting her head.

My first instinct is to sigh at this new, impassable chasm between me and every other twenty-year-old female on campus, but I force another smile instead. "You could say that." At that moment, my milk lets down, as it tends to do when I haven't fed Evan or used the breast pump in the past hour or so. "Excuse me," I tell Bridget. Clamping a forearm across my breasts and grabbing my tote bag from under the table, I make a dash for the nearest bathroom. It's not such a big deal when this happens at home. Milk routinely drenches my shirts, drenches the sheets, shoots halfway across the room whenever I dare to remove my nursing bra, or even to change the pads in the nursing bra. And God forbid I hesitate to wake Evan from a nap to nurse him at the exact time rigidly predetermined by my mammary overlords. Even Lawrence—who was utterly fascinated at the end of the pregnancy, drawn like a moth to a flame to the rapidly growing bosom that seemed so clearly designed for his pleasure—is put off lately by how leaky and unpredictable the "fun bags" (as he used to jokingly call them) have become. Now, as I run, I realize that I (stupidly) haven't brought another shirt since I'm not yet used to leaving Evan at home with Lawrence. If I don't find a place to sit down and pump in the next minute, the blouse I'm wearing will be completely soaked through.

Five minutes later, I'm sitting on a toilet with a plastic cone affixed to a nipple, feeling like a postpartum Han Solo—encased in carbonite, frozen in time, while the world and all the people I once knew in it move on.

Book 15: 2009

There is nothing impossible to him who will try.
~Alexander the Great

"Care to share details, or are you afraid of jinxing your idea?"

"Both," Jillian says. She and Bodhi are standing in the doorway of the old, retrofitted sheepherder cabin, looking over the stuff he has stored out here. "Also, I don't completely know what the idea is yet. It's not fully formed."

Ever since the Zion trip, she hasn't been able to stop thinking about making something, even though it's probably ridiculous to even entertain the idea. Does she really think she's going to return to some bygone dream of becoming an artist? Hadley won't let her pay rent for the two months she's been squatting in the Ovum so far; the most she'll let Jillian do is buy food once in a while. At some point, sooner rather than later, Jillian knows she's going to have to return to reality. And reality is probably going to look a lot like a centrally located studio apartment somewhere down in Phoenix where she'll be close to as many substitute teacher's aide jobs as possible.

She also needs to deal with finances. For the past several weeks that she's been on the mountain, she's continued to use the joint checking account she and Lawrence have always shared. Soon, she'll no doubt have to get her own individual account set up. Then she'll need to approach Lawrence about funding it with the money she's made subbing over the years. The thought fills her with dread.

"Look," Bodhi says, still talking about art. "At some point, you're going to have to choose between self-doubt and just, you know, going for it. It's that whole one-foot-on-the-dock and one-foot-on-the-boat thing. You need to commit to one or the other if you don't want to end up in the drink."

Jillian's been pulling at the corner of a pinky nail with her teeth, but she stops now. He's right, of course. "The dock's just so familiar," she tells him, only half-joking.

"Sure it is," Bodhi says. "And you can totally stay there. I don't recommend it though. We have all sorts of cool stuff on the boat. Including cookies."

Smiling, Jillian turns from the doorway and points to one of his unfinished steel sculptures sitting outside in the shade of a pine tree. It reminds her of a grouping of stalagmites trying to come to life, rooted-looking but somehow in motion, too. "What if I want to do something like that?"

"Music to my ears," he says.

They walk over to the sculpture so Jillian can inspect it up close. "This is really cool," she says, running her finger along a welded seam. "What's it going to be?"

Bodhi shrugs. "Just something I've been messing with for a few months. It's not a commission or anything, so I get to just play around with it whenever I have some spare time. It started as one thing, and now it's turning into another. I'm not quite sure what yet."

"You don't want to overwork the metal though, right?"

"Right," he says. "Especially since Gunnar's already welded these spots. But I can still change it up a little here and there. And if it doesn't work..." He shrugs. "I scrap it. Turn it into something that does."

Jillian stares at the work-in-progress. "I think I want to start with a sheet of metal," she says. "Something I can work by hand as much as possible, so I don't have to rely on big power tools."

"Now you're talking."

"I don't want it to look manufactured, you know? I want to go for a more organic vibe."

"Far out, man."

Smirking, she ignores him. "Also, I need to be able to stick stuff onto it."

"Okay, ouch," he says, reaching up with both hands to rub his temples. "Slow down. You're getting too technical."

Jillian puts her hands on her hips, tries to look stern. "You know what I mean."

Bodhi laughs. "I do. I'm pretty sure you want to mosaic it."

"Maybe not the whole thing," Jillian answers. "But at least some of it, yes." She shakes her head. "The truth is, I didn't even *know* what I wanted until just now. But being out here, it just seems to be coming to me all at once."

"Yeah," he says. "I've always found this to be a pretty inspiring spot." He looks off at a line of trees in the distance before shifting his gaze back to her face. "For more reasons than one."

Jillian blushes and looks away. She waits a beat before asking the next thing. "So, do you think what I'm describing is doable?"

Bodhi looks thoughtful. "Sure," he says. "You definitely need something like sheet metal. I'm thinking light gauge, cold rolled steel, thin enough that you can bend and hammer it by hand but with enough integrity to keep its shape and not collapse when other materials are attached to it. I used to have some lying around here, but it got used a while back."

"That sounds about right."

"Of course, the more you hand work it, the more primitive it's going to look. I have machinery you can use, even for just some parts of the process, if you want an end result that's more polished."

Jillian shakes her head. "I don't mind primitive. Like I said, there's something about using my own two hands...it's hard to explain." She thinks of the stuff she used to make as a little kid. She'd find the most random materials—wooden planter bottoms and pinecones, old wrapping paper and beads from a broken plastic Mardi Gras necklace. There was always something magical about repurposing the finds into entirely new creations. And now, the same intense need to make something, an impulse Jillian felt at eight, twelve, nineteen years old—right up through her first semester at college—is driving her once again. It turns out she's missed it.

Bodhi scratches his chin. "I might have just the thing," he says finally. "It's out at Gunnar's place. Unfortunately, I need to leave this afternoon to meet a client down in Mesa. I'll be gone for a few days, but it'll be easy enough to load into the bed of Hadley's pickup if you want to get started sooner than that. She's going to be driving some scrap to Gunnar's for me anyway, in exchange for help winterizing her place."

"He makes me uncomfortable," Jillian says two days later as Gunnar walks toward them wearing desert camos. They're inside Hadley's truck, which sits idling in Gunnar's driveway.

"He's not going to hurt anyone," Hadley says.

"I didn't say he scares me. I said he makes me uncomfortable."

Gunnar, scowly as ever, directs them to a massive pile of old scrap metal, and Hadley backs the truck up to it. After they've unloaded some leftovers from one of Bodhi's big residential projects, Gunnar walks them over to a twisted hunk of raw sheet metal that's been pulled from the pile.

"What is it?" Hadley asks.

Gunnar shrugs. "Dunno. It came in a big shipment of reclaimed metal. I'm guessing it was originally some kind of decorative overhang for a store, or a theater, or something. Who knows?" He looks at Jillian. "Bodhi said you wanted it."

Jillian nods. She's mostly stayed quiet the whole time they've been here. Gunnar doesn't like her and doesn't want her in the studio; he's made that abundantly clear. And she's pretty sure he knows that she knows.

The hunk of metal is more awkward than heavy. After the three of them load it up and tie it down, Hadley navigates the truck out of Gunnar's driveway. Just before they get to the road, Jillian spies a hand-painted plywood sign that's facing inside the property like some kind of parting reminder. BE NICE, the sign reads in big block letters. Jillian turns to look back at Gunnar, but he's already walking toward his small house at the far end of the property.

Back at Hadley's after dropping the hunk of metal off at the studio, Jillian goes through a box of her Scottsdale clothes that's been stored on a high shelf in the barn. Taking off her shoes and standing barefoot on the dirt floor, she pulls a pair of her old overalls from the box. After shaking them out, she strips down to just her underwear and top and steps into them. The denim is softer than she remembers, but it still feels sturdy.

Before leaving for Mesa, Bodhi sent her home with supplies—steel scraps, an anvil and hammer—and gave her some pointers so she could start figuring out basic metalworking techniques while he was gone. After changing into the overalls, she sits on a stump out back in the fall light, figuring out how to twist and bend and crimp and fold the small scrap she's using for practice. She experiments with hammering it into various shapes, too, figuring out the effects of different types of strikes.

Hadley sits on the porch nearby in her faded Wranglers, a flannel shirt, and a fleece vest, watching Jillian work. After a while, she gets up, grabs her bulky old video camera from inside the A-frame, and starts taping. "Just like old times," she says with a wink when Jillian looks up from her hammering.

"You've been at it for hours," she says later, as the sun lowers in the sky.

"I guess I have," Jillian agrees, setting down the hammer and the metal sheet. "Still haven't beaten this thing into submission though." She looks at her palm where a few blisters have formed.

"Let's go for a walk," Hadley says, getting up from her stump. "Come on. Stretching our legs will do us some good."

They're about half a mile down Hadley's road when they see a white-tailed doe with her fawn starting to cross the pavement. "Oo, look," Jillian says, remembering the old doe she saw at Zion. "How cute."

Just then, a black Camaro comes roaring around the turn at the end of the road, straight toward the deer.

Jillian's hand goes to her heart. "Oh, no. He's going to hit them."

"Sun's in his eyes," Hadley says. "We better get further off to the side."

The car speeds up.

Jillian waves her arms to signal the driver, but there's no change in speed. "Hey!" she shouts at the top of her lungs. Both deer stop to gaze in her direction as the Camaro bears down.

"Don't look," Hadley says, grabbing Jillian's arm and dragging her onto the grassy shoulder.

Jillian clamps a hand over her eyes. When she doesn't hear the expected tire screech and thumps though, she peeks through her fingers just in time to see the pair bounding off the road and toward a cluster of nearby pine trees.

As the Camaro approaches where she and Hadley are standing, Jillian can see that the driver's side window is open. A man who looks to be not much older than they are is behind the wheel. "Slow down!" she warns as he passes.

The car screeches to a halt about thirty yards past them. Then it just sits there, engine rumbling ominously, as the women watch.

"Harpy ass *bitches*!" the driver finally yells, his voice dripping with something like hatred. He sounds like he'd happily murder both of them with his bare hands, right there on the spot.

Hadley snorts. "We must remind him of his ex-wives."

But Jillian, too utterly pissed off to laugh, marches toward the Camaro, which is peeling away now. The driver's arm is out the window, his middle finger thrust into the air.

"Jill, hey," Hadley calls after her. "Dude, it's not worth it."

Jillian is undeterred. "As if *you're* some kind of catch!" she yells. "You horrible...puckered...*butthole* of a man!" One of her fists is planted firmly on a hip; the other is held high in the air like his, the middle finger outstretched. Once again, the car screeches to a halt. This time, though, the driver revs the engine before starting to make a U-turn.

"Shit," Hadley mutters.

Lowering the hand, Jillian looks back at her, panicked. "He's turning around."

"Let him," Hadley responds, her voice deadly calm. She rests her fingers on a spot near her hip where the butt of a pearl-handled pistol just barely peeks out beneath her vest. After a few more seconds, the Camaro's tires squeal against asphalt as the driver reverses his turn, steps on the gas, and disappears down the road away from them.

"Puckered butthole," Hadley says thoughtfully as they walk back to the A-frame. "That's original."

Jillian lets out a nervous little laugh. "I guess I still have some rage."

Inside the Ovum that night, she stares at herself in the mirror above the tiny bathroom sink. *A harpy?* she thinks. *Is that what I am?* She remembers learning about harpies in Lawrence's class. They were described as beautiful, winged women soaring like elegant birds, or, alternately, as hideous, vengeful hags, swooping down to snatch their unsuspecting victims from the earth at Zeus's request.

There's an old phonebook in the cupboard Hadley stocked with gossip magazines. Retrieving it, Jillian turns to the Beauty section of the yellow pages. With her finger marking one of the listings, she sits on the bed, staring straight ahead for a minute before punching the number into her phone with her thumb. She leaves a message for them to call her back tomorrow to make an appointment.

"Gussying up for anyone special?" the stylist asks as Jillian reclines in the shampoo chair two days later. Roz is her name.

"Not really." Jillian's eyes are closed in bliss as Roz massages her scalp. She's worn her hair pulled back into a hasty ponytail for so long that she's almost forgotten what it's like to have an actual style.

"Well, every woman wants to feel at least somewhat human for the holidays, right?" Roz drenches Jillian's hair with hot water, works a heavenly smelling shampoo deep into the roots, rinses, and then massages conditioner in.

"Well, maybe there's someone I'm gussying up for," Jillian admits, her tongue loosened by the pampering. "Kind of. Not really though."

"Dish it," Roz commands, wrapping Jillian's head in a fluffy white towel and helping her sit up before leading her to a chair.

And so Jillian does, starting with high school and working her way through her marriage and the betrayal to what's happening now that she and Bodhi have reconnected. Which, truth be told, isn't much. "It's mainly just a bizarre feeling being back up here," she says, finishing the story.

Roz separates a section of Jillian's hair and clips it into a loop. "Sounds like he's your placeholder guy."

"My what?"

"You know," Roz says. "That guy who knew you back when." She holds the sides of Jillian's head with her fingertips to keep it from swiveling around. "That one guy who's held onto a piece of your old self and kept it safe all these years while so many other parts of you were being blown to pieces. Placeholder Guy."

An odd little shiver works its way down Jillian's spine. She's quiet for the next few minutes as Roz brushes on the color, wraps each section of hair in foil, and leads her over to the drying hood. Sitting there under what always feels like a sensory deprivation dome, she tries not to overthink what the stylist said. Still, she can't help but wonder: *Is* Bodhi her placeholder guy?

"Roll tape," Hadley jokes the next morning. They're outside the studio, and she has the video camera again. She brought it here knowing this would be a sight—Jillian draping the reclaimed sheet of metal they got from Gunnar's place over a fallen tree before climbing up onto the trunk and strategically stomping on the metal until it folded more or less in half. Jillian grunts as she hops down, pulls the metal from the tree, and turns it over. With one half propped against the trunk, she beats at it with a rubber mallet until it more or less assumes a convex bowl shape.

"Want some help yet?" Hadley asks from behind the camera.

Shaking her head, Jillian turns the metal over once more. After putting the other half through the same propping and pounding routine, she drops the mallet and stands up. Arching her back, she grimaces. "I'm beat," she says, wiping sweat from her brow with the back of her hand.

Together, she and Hadley carry the piece (which now looks pretty much like a fat, misshapen clamshell) inside the studio to the space Bodhi designated for her. It's at the opposite end of the room from Gunnar's workbench.

They're standing there staring down at it, when they hear a car pull up outside: Bodhi, back from Mesa.

"Wow," he says, coming through the door and walking toward them. "Look what you've done!" He's dressed semiformally, in an Oxford shirt and slacks. He's also freshly shaved, and his hair is moussed into a more urban style than usual. Jillian tries not to stare. "I knew this piece of scrap would work for you."

Feeling self-conscious all of a sudden with her friends looking at the start of her new creation, Jillian blushes. "We'll see if I can actually turn it into something halfway decent."

"It's already on its way there," Bodhi says. Then he claps his hands together. "Oh! I brought you something." Walking quickly back toward the door of the studio, he disappears outside only to reappear a minute later. This time, he's holding a pink cardboard pastry box tied with gold twine. He sets it on a table near Jillian's work area. "I had a feeling there would be something to celebrate when I got back here."

Jillian looks mildly concerned. "What are we celebrating, exactly?"

"Your return to art," Hadley says. "Right, Bo?"

Bodhi nods as Jillian goes over to the box. Untying the twine and lifting the lid, she gasps at the half-dozen extravagantly designed cupcakes inside. When she looks more carefully, she can see that each one represents a different art movement. There's the Impressionist cupcake, with its frosting done in a riot of pastels. And the Cubist one, covered in geometrical, multi-colored chocolate shapes. There's even a Frida Kahlo-inspired cake, upon which a portrait of the artist has been painstakingly airbrushed. Whoever decorated it got Frida's eyebrow just right. "Oh," Jillian says, gazing lovingly into the box. "They're so beautiful. Too beautiful to eat."

"We should definitely eat them though," Bodhi says, smiling at her. "They're probably pretty perishable. Best bakery in the southwest. Or so I was told by the guy who owns it."

Halfway through the Dadaist cupcake with its airbrushed x-ray of a mechanical human head, Jillian licks her fingers and groans. "This is the most amazing thing I've ever tasted," she says.

"And the frosting is the lightest thing ever," Bodhi adds. "Like clouds, see?" He smears some on her forearm.

Jillian looks down at the arm and then back at him. "Really?"

"What? I was just demonstrating the fluffiness."

"It is fluffy," Jillian says, licking the frosting from her arm. "Now demonstrate this." Using her finger to scoop a dollop of frosting from her own cupcake, she reaches up and dabs it onto his nose.

"Oh, okay," Bodhi says, standing his ground as a diabolical grin spreads across his face. "If that's how we're playing it." He reaches his frosting-covered fingers toward the top of her head, but she holds his wrist with her free hand.

"*Not* the hair!" she cries. "I just had it done."

They remain in a deadlock, both of them grinning like maniacs as Hadley calmly uses her teeth to scrape the last crumbs from her Pop art cupcake's liner, which is printed with a portrait of Marilyn Monroe in DayGlo colors.

"Don't give me that look," Jillian says after she and Bodhi have called a truce and he's out in the storage cabin grabbing some paper towels.

"I'm just saying," Hadley responds, working the muscles of her forehead up and down. "Or, rather, my *eyebrows* are just saying…"

"There's nothing going on," Jillian insists, trying to keep her smile in check.

"Whatever you say, punkin."

"Seriously. There is no way I'm ready for something like that."

Hadley laughs. "Something like *what* exactly? Having fun for a change, rather than feeling like death on a cracker?"

"You have a point."

"Yeah, well, don't I know this."

"All kidding aside," Bodhi starts to announce as he reappears through the back door of the studio with a roll of paper towels in his hand. He looks from Jillian to Hadley, both of whom have fallen suddenly silent and are staring at him. "What?"

"Nothing," Hadley says. "We totally weren't talking about you."

Bodhi shakes his head and smiles. "I gotta tell you, Jillian," he says after a while, good-naturedly changing the subject. "I really do think you're onto something with that hunk of steel."

She's about to say thank you. She's about to tell him how much she owes him for everything—the studio space, the metalworking tips, the cupcakes with their fluffy masterpiece frosting. "You know what?" she says instead, wiping a final crumb from the corner of her mouth. "Call me Jill."

Book 16: 1990

It happens in early December. Having already checked everywhere else, I'm rooting around in the back seat of Lawrence's car for Evan's favorite plush toy, the floppy little manatee my mother bought for him when she visited Marine Land in California. He can't sleep without it, which is why I've been shining a flashlight across every inch of the car's interior. I'm running my hands inside the spaces around the seats when my fingers finally brush against something soft. *At last,* I think, pulling the item free and holding it in the beam of the flashlight. When I do, my blood runs cold.

It's Saturday, and Lawrence is sleeping in. Evan's not sleeping in though. Evan was up at five a.m. realizing that the manatee was missing. Now, as I come back into the house from the garage, he's waiting expectantly. He's hoisted himself up by grabbing the top edge of his playpen, something he just learned to do this week. "Sorry, buddy," I say, forcing a cheerful smile and showing him my empty hands before lifting him out of the pen. "I'll keep looking."

Evan whimpers for a moment in response, but then I pause by the Christmas tree, jouncing him on my hip to distract him. I can't let him sense how I'm trembling. My beautiful boy beams as he reaches toward a shiny red ornament and then reaches up to pat my face. When he rubs his eyes and yawns, I carry him to his room to try, once again, to put him down for his late morning nap. We were planning to go to the park later, the three of us, assuming it didn't rain. First, though, I was going to make a small brunch. I have ingredients for waffles and fruit salad already set out on the counter. Evan doesn't fuss as I lay him in his crib.

Heading toward the master bedroom, I think of the recent get-together Lawrence and I hosted here at the house for his new batch of grad students—beautiful young people, most of them just about my age, some slightly older. One TA was quiet the entire evening. She had a really cute 1940s-type outfit on, complete with seamed stockings and a veiled pillbox hat, but she hardly said a word. Instead, she just stared at me, as if I was intruding on their gathering. Stared at me and then at Evan. Upstairs in the nursery toward the end of the evening, trying to nurse Evan to sleep while the scholars talked and laughed downstairs, I couldn't help but feel like an outcast in my own home.

"That one girl creeped me out a little," I told Lawrence as we got ready for bed an hour later. "What was her name? Angelica?"

"Who?" He was lying on his side with his back toward me. "Oh. Yeah, I think that's right."

And I knew. Without him saying another word, I knew.

Now, standing in the doorway of the master bedroom, I watch Lawrence sleep for a minute as I think about what I'm going to say. He must sense me standing there, because he wakes up and says, "What is it?"

I pull the seamed stocking from the front pocket of my pajamas.

Lawrence stares at it. Swallows. Glances at my face. Flings an arm across his eyes.

"Why?" I ask him, my voice already faltering, already betraying me, with that one tiny word.

Lawrence sighs heavily. It sounds like a cross between annoyance and resignation.

"It's Angelica's, isn't it?"

"Let's just have a calm discussion about this, okay?" He's sitting up in the bed now.

"Isn't it?"

When he doesn't answer, I turn and walk back down the hallway.

"Jillian," he halfheartedly calls after me.

In the guest bedroom, I sit on the edge of the queen-sized mattress and place a hand on my heart. It's not thumping as madly as it should be, all things considered. In fact, I feel suffused by an almost eerie calm. All I know is that I have to get away. I have to go someplace where I can actively not think about any of this, where I can put all of it out of my mind. Not knowing how long the calm I'm feeling might last, I take the opportunity to return to the master bedroom. Lawrence is still sitting in bed, looking up at the ceiling.

"I'm going back home for a while," I tell him.

"All right," he says.

"I'm taking the baby." My heart does start pounding a little harder at those words. "Don't call us."

"All right," he says again, looking at me now.

If my father is surprised to see me and Evan show up on his doorstep out of the blue, he doesn't let on. I called before leaving Scottsdale, but it went straight to voicemail. "See you in a few hours" was pretty much the message I left.

Dad's been living alone in my childhood home since he and Mom split. This past spring, though, all his personal ads and blind dates finally paid off: He found the love of his life in Helen Winchell, a widow who never had kids. They came down to Scottsdale for a visit when Evan was about three months old, and right away I could tell Helen was one of those people who was in Heaven when she had someone to spoil and nurture (which meant Dad was in Heaven, too). I was almost embarrassed at how goofily in love they so obviously were with each other—embarrassed and a little jealous, to be honest.

Just a few weeks ago, Dad called to announce that he was planning to move into Helen's place in Prescott, halfway between Flagstaff and Phoenix.

"That's great," I told him. "You'll be closer."

I felt a pang when he told me the Flagstaff house would have to be put on the market, and that if I wanted any of my remaining stuff, I should come get it ASAP. But at least I have a plausible excuse for showing up with his grandson without warning.

"I ran into your old friend Hadley Wallace at the supermarket after I got your message earlier today," Dad tells me that evening as we're sorting through the guest room closet.

I only hum, "Mm hm."

He has to know something's up based on how quiet I've been since Evan and I arrived, but he doesn't pry for details. "Told her you're in town. She's going to come by and say hi."

"Oh." My stomach does a weird little flip. I almost start to protest, but then I clamp my mouth shut. I don't want to make a bigger deal out of this than it is. So what if the last time Hadley and I saw each other she thought I was accusing her of being a pervert, and I thought she was accusing me of being an idiot for getting pregnant? She's probably forgotten all about it, as I mostly have until this moment.

When we're done in the guest room, I head down the hall to clear out the last few things remaining in my own closet. Fortunately, it doesn't take long; over the years I've either thrown stuff out or brought it with me to Scottsdale. One of the last things I find is a small box that rattles when I shake it. Peeking inside, I discover the shards from Mom's old broken coffee mug. For just a split-second, my pulse skips a beat. A quick memory of that morning in the kitchen when I was in eighth grade flashes through my brain, and then it's gone. That's just as well; I'd rather not deal with any drama—past or present—while I'm here on the mountain. I've already designated three piles on my bed for the stuff in my old bedroom: Keep, Donate, and Dump. Without a second thought, I put the box of shards in the Dump pile.

"Damn, Jill," Hadley says when I open the front door the next morning. "You're so thin." She doesn't even try to hide her shock.

"Benefit of new motherhood, I guess," I tell her with a shrug. "I barely have time to eat. Also, I go by Jillian now."

"Oo," Hadley raises one eyebrow and gives me a *How shi-shi* look until she realizes I'm not joking and resumes her neutral expression.

"It was Lawrence's idea. He says it sounds more like a name befitting a professor's wife." As soon as the words leave my mouth, I hear how snobby they sound. I also realize I'm talking too much. "I can't argue with that, I guess. I mean, I could argue, but what would be the point?" The laughter leaving my mouth sounds a touch manic; I make a mental note to take a deep breath and tone it down. I chalk up my behavior to how strange it is seeing Hadley in this context of my childhood being emptied out, turned upside down, and shaken to see if anything of value still remains.

"Ah," she says with a nod.

Just when I think things can't possibly get more awkward, I'm saved by the baby: Evan lurch-crawls into the room, softly chanting *muh muh muh* as if driving invisible troops into battle. When he sees Hadley, he lifts one of his arms, points a chubby finger at her, and sets his smile phasers to stun.

"He's so big!" she cries, visibly melting as she reaches her arms out toward him. In response, Evan *vrooms* toward her on all fours, instantly smitten.

As soon as she got here and realized what Dad and I were doing, Hadley offered to help haul stuff away. I show her the piles on my bed, and together we bag up the Donate pile. The Dump pile is next. Hadley holds a trash bag open while I throw things into it. At the last possible second, just before we close up the bag and carry it out to her Pinto, I pluck the little cardboard box with Mom's mug fragments out of the Dump bag and set it back on my bed, on the Keep pile.

Around noon, after our run to the landfill and to Goodwill, Hadley suggests we grab some food at her favorite burger joint. She orders a double cheeseburger, fries, and a large coke. I order a salad with dressing on the side. I've started eating salads almost exclusively lately, for lunch and dinner. It was Lawrence's idea. I don't tell Hadley this though. No doubt she'd think I was married to some kind of monster.

"This feels so grown up, going out to lunch," Hadley says, digging into her fries. "I hardly ever go out to eat."

"I have to do it pretty often," I tell her.

"Have to?"

I allow myself a bit of a dramatic pause before explaining. "You might say it's part of my job description." What I don't tell her is how hard I've been struggling to learn the code of the faculty wife (dress in a more mature fashion, avoid hair and makeup that looks too young, and don't dare to even give the impression that you might be competing with the older, more experienced wives).

"Ah," Hadley says again. For the next minute or so, we focus on Evan, who's sitting in a highchair, playing with his fries. "So, I ran into Bodhi the other day."

It takes a little effort to control the look of surprise that jumps across my face. "Oh?"

"Yeah, he was in town visiting his mom. It sounds like he's doing really well. He got a grant to study sculpture with some bigwig or other in New York, apparently."

I put down my fork and look at Hadley. "Is there a reason you're telling me all this?"

"Sorry?"

"I just don't know why you think I'd be interested. Bodhi was my high school *boy*friend. I'm married now. I'm a mother."

Hadley puts down her burger and wipes her mouth with her napkin. "I know that," she says quietly.

I pay the lunch tab, even though Hadley tries to protest. "Feel like going for a little walk?" she asks me once we're back in the car.

"Sure," I respond, even though I don't feel like it, not really. The truth is, it's taken everything I have to not check my watch for the past half hour. Hanging out with Hadley has been good for nostalgia's sake, and I'm grateful for her help getting my piles of stuff moved out of the house. But the main reason I came up here was to clear my head. The complications of hanging out with my old best friend aren't helping. Still, I really do appreciate her help. I can indulge her in this one thing.

Fifteen minutes later, we're standing on a single-track forest trail. It's a popular hiking spot in the warmer months, about halfway up to the local ski resort where Bodhi tried to teach me to snowboard (another memory I'd rather not think about). I was carrying Evan until about a minute ago, but then he started squirming so hard in my arms that I had to put him down. All around us, the earth is strewn with fading gold aspen leaves that no doubt fell a month or so ago. As Evan sits on the trail, captivated by them, I imagine how the leaves must have looked at the peak of their golden color in early-

October, raining down by the thousands whenever a fall breeze picked up.

"So, tell me the truth," Hadley says as we stand there.

Uh oh, I think.

"You're not just up here to get your stuff out of the house, are you?"

"I'm not sure what you're—"

"Jill," she says, holding up a hand. "Please. Can we just be honest for a second here? You've been going on like a Stepford wife since the moment I first saw you."

I act like I didn't hear her correctly. "What did you say?"

"You know what I said," she answers,

My hands get fidgety, and tension starts to work its way up the back of my neck. This is where I'm supposed to open up to the only best friend I've ever had about what's really been going on in my marriage. It's where I'm supposed to tell her the story of the stocking I found in Lawrence's car, and how I came up here to the mountain to reevaluate the situation.

Just as I'm about to open my mouth and spill everything, Hadley looks past my shoulder, toward where Evan's playing in the leaves. Her eyes grow wide. "Oh!" she cries. "Look!"

I've had my back turned to Evan for the past minute or so; I didn't see him crawl about ten feet away from the spot where I first set him down. Now, when I turn around and look to where Hadley's pointing, he's on his feet solo for the first time ever, lumbering toward us like a drunken sailor.

It's one of those extreme slow-motion moments that I immediately know will be etched in my memory for the rest of my life. Heart leaping, I start toward him.

Evan falls on his butt and then looks up at us, startled. At first, I think he's going to cry, but then he plants his hands among the aspen leaves, raises his butt high into the air, and hoists himself back to standing. He lurches toward me and Hadley like Frankenstein this time, arms akimbo and with a manic smile on his face. And something unravels in my heart. This is the beginning of his moving away from me. I know it on an instinctual level. When I squat down, he launches himself into my arms with a squeal, and I breathe in the scent of his hair. When I'm done planting kisses on him, I look up to see Hadley standing there with her arms held out in front of her.

"May I?" she asks.

Nodding, I scoot out of the way so she can squat down and wrap Evan in a bear hug, too. Delighted toddler squeals ensue.

"*You,*" Hadley says, holding him at arm's length and pretend-glaring into his eyes like she's about to read him the riot act. "If you don't give your mother adequate hell from this point forward, Aunt Hadley is going to be sorely disappointed. Got it?"

In response, Evan throws his head back and cackles.

"You and Evan could stay with me," Hadley says twenty minutes later, as she parks the Pinto in front of my dad's house. Her voice is verging on desperate.

"What are you talking about?"

Hadley sits there in the driver's seat with tears in her eyes. "I'm sorry about what I said earlier with my whole Stepford wife comment. I really am. It's just…I'm worried about you, Jill. I feel like something's not right with this whole situation. There's just something…off about it."

Evan starts to fuss in the back seat. "I'm fine," I tell her. "Really. It's been a long day. For all of us."

Hadley takes a deep breath as I reach for the passenger side door handle. "I would just ask you one question," she says. "What exactly is it that you're trying to teach your son?"

My hand falls to my lap. She's being melodramatic, but I think about what she's said for a minute anyway. "I guess," I say finally, "I'm teaching him that when two people love each other, they find a way to work it out."

"And you're sure there are two people loving each other here?"

I don't even try to hide my disbelief this time. "What the hell is that supposed to mean?"

Hadley just shakes her head. "It means I agree that there are two people loving. Unfortunately, both of them love Lawrence. From the little you've told me, he sounds like a complete narcissist. He's manipulating you, Jill."

"It's Jillian," I tell her. "And I didn't know you had a degree in psychology."

"I don't need a degree to know a toxic relationship when I see one."

"Wow," I say, my voice flat now, chin thrust forward. "Don't hold back. Seriously, tell me how you really feel."

"This stuff isn't exactly hard to figure out."

"Well, I don't care if my marriage is *toxic*, as you call it," I fire back. "Lawrence is my *husband*." With that, I open the passenger side door, get out of the car, and walk around to Evan's side. I unbuckle him from the car seat, taking deep, calming breaths as I lift him out and start working on the seat-belt attachment holding the car seat in place. "Thanks for helping out today," I tell Hadley before settling Evan on my hip, yanking the car seat from the Pinto, and slamming the door.

That night, Evan sits up in the portable playpen I've converted into a makeshift bed for him, resisting sleep as hard as he can. To help him settle in, I sing to him in a soft voice from under the covers of my old bed while fighting back tears. It's the only thing I can think to do that might both lull my child to sleep and help me say goodbye to my childhood home—my entire childhood, really—once and for all.

Book 17: 2009

Gratitude is the sign of noble souls.
~Aesop

Jill waits inside the old downtown bus station the day before Thanksgiving, just like she waited here during her freshman year of college. Only this time, she's waiting for Evan's bus from Tucson to arrive. She paces back and forth across the grimy floor until a bus pulls up outside the windows with a dramatic sigh. Passengers disembark, and Evan is there among them, everyone crowding around the driver as he heaves open the luggage doors on the side of the bus. Jill has to keep herself from running toward him. He looks tired from the six-and-a-half-hour ride, but when he glances up and smiles at her, all is immediately right with the world.

"Hi, Mom," he says, giving her a hug.

Half an hour later, they're at the Flagstaff Municipal Airport to pick up Barb. Jill remembers when it was little more than a glorified shack in the middle of nowhere, with Formica flooring and elk heads mounted on one wall above an old woodstove. Now it's a modern airport with a real terminal and multiple daily flights between Flagstaff and Phoenix. The moment Barb comes through security and spots Evan and Jill standing there, she makes a beeline for her grandson. "I haven't seen you since graduation!" she cries, wrapping him in a grandmotherly hug. Then she hugs Jill. Holding her at arm's length, Barb studies her daughter's face.

"Hi, Mom," Jill says.

Barb winks. "Hi, yourself." As usual, she looks like a million bucks—hair and nails done, flawless makeup, tailored outfit, the works. She even smells good.

Before long, the three of them are standing in the kitchen of the A-frame. "Just as I thought," Hadley said when Evan first walked through the door. "Way too handsome for his own good." Now she grills him about college life as Jill prepares a snack tray.

Glancing at the two of them as she arranges a row of crackers next to some cheese slices, Jill can't help but remember the day Evan learned to walk on that leaf-covered trail not too far from here. It seems impossible that eighteen years have passed since then.

Hadley asks Evan about his girlfriend Tabitha, the one who went to school back east. "How long did you guys last after college started?"

"A month," Evan says, his voice glum.

Jill winces. She only recently learned about Evan and Tabitha's split. She's reminded again that she should have been there for him more these past couple of months. She should have known what was going on immediately instead of being so wrapped up in herself and her unraveling life.

"It's okay, Mom," Evan says, looking at Jill as if reading her mind. "I really haven't even wanted to talk about it until…well, until Aunt Hadley here basically forced me to."

Hadley grins. "What can I say? I have a gift."

The next day is Thanksgiving. After heading into the A-frame for coffee and a light breakfast with Hadley and Evan, Jill returns to the Ovum for a nap while Evan takes the Toyota to go see some of his high school friends for a few hours before picking Barb up at her hotel. She wakes up around midday to put the finishing touches on her makeup and hair. Hearing a vehicle pull up out front, she peers out one of the Ovum's tiny windows to see Bodhi helping his mother from the passenger side of his car.

When she emerges a few minutes later, she feels like a new woman. Her hair is styled, her makeup is done, and she's wearing high heels. It's the first time in almost three months that she's put more than a passing thought into what she's wearing. Gingerly, she navigates the cinder path leading to the kitchen door of the A-frame, trying not to break a heel—or her neck. When she finally reaches the door and steps inside, all conversation ceases. Jill stands there in the doorway, looking from Bodhi to his mother to Hadley, feeling the heat of sudden self-consciousness rising into her face.

Bodhi's the first one to break the silence. "Wow," he says.

"Damn," Hadley adds. "Hot mama."

Not only does the blushing not abate, it grows into a brief flush of guilt as Bodhi's mother approaches; since arriving here on the mountain, Jill hasn't made time to see Evelyn yet. But the older woman is as gracious as she always was. "You came back," she says, holding both of Jill's hands in her own. She has deep lines worn into her face now, and long, gray hair streaked with white.

"I did," Jill responds, smiling at her. "It's been so long since I've seen you."

"Since the summer after you three graduated high school," Evelyn says, beaming at Bodhi and Hadley. "I understand Barbara will be joining us today as well?"

Jill nods.

"Your wonderful mother. Such a strong, vital woman. A warrior. You got a lot of that from her."

Jill is more than a little taken aback. She never thinks of her mother this way. Quite the opposite, in fact.

"Sorry about that," Bodhi says a few minutes later when they're briefly alone together in the living room. "My mom gets a little…intense about things sometimes."

"No, it's okay," Jill tells him. "She's wonderful." She changes the subject by asking if Gunnar will be joining them.

Bodhi shakes his head. "He's volunteering at the community food center today," he says. "Cooking meals, hanging with people he knows, that kind of thing. It's sort of a tradition for him. A bunch of the regulars there are vets."

Just then, Evan and Barb walk through the door. "You look nice," Barb says, giving Jill a peck on the cheek.

Jill's surprised by the little wave of nervousness that overcomes her as she introduces Evan to Bodhi, but the men greet each other warmly, not seeming to think anything about it. Before long, Barb and Evelyn are settled on the couch together, getting reacquainted.

After setting the table, Jill wanders into the kitchen where the older women are now helping with last-minute preparations. Over by the stove, Barb's trying to teach Evan how to make cranberry sauce.

"This is kind of lame, Grandma," he says good-naturedly, trying to push her buttons.

"Lame?" Barb retorts in mock horror. "You know what's lame? A young man going out into the world helpless as a baby, not able to even feed himself because his mother has always waited on him hand and foot."

"Thanks, Mom," Jill says as Barb aims a pointed look in her direction.

"Spare the cooking lessons, spoil the grandson," Barb continues. "That's all I'm saying."

Jill snorts. "This coming from the least domestic woman I've ever known." Everyone in the kitchen stops and stares at her. Wincing at the unintended bitterness in her voice, she forces herself to take a slow, deep breath. "Sorry," she says, looking at the floor.

Soon, the table is laden with more food than the six of them could ever hope to finish. There's a massive turkey, a vat of cranberries, mashed potatoes, green beans, hot rolls, and a sweet potato casserole topped with a layer of browned marshmallows.

"I'm about to bust a button," Bodhi says when everyone's done eating.

"Not so fast," Hadley tells him. "We still have dessert to get through: Pumpkin pie, apple pie, berry cheesecake…"

Everyone groans.

That night, after Bodhi and his mom have left and the kitchen's clean, Jill and Evan drive Barb back to her hotel.

"I'll walk you up to your room," Jill tells her mom as Evan maneuvers the Toyota into the hotel parking lot.

There's something sad about Barb's hotel. Not that her room is dirty or outdated or anything. It's just the single suitcase sitting on the luggage stand, the upside-down glasses next to the ice bucket, the double bed, still made up and with a mint on the pillow—they give Jill the impression of a transient, uprooted life.

"Do you want to maybe visit for a bit?" Barb asks her.

"I shouldn't keep Evan waiting too long down there."

Her mother nods. "Well, it was a lovely night."

"That it was," Jill agrees. They stand just inside the room, neither of them saying anything further for several seconds. Then, finally: "Mom?"

Barb raises her eyebrows. "Hmm?"

"Why did you leave?"

More silence.

For a moment, Jill thinks her mother's going to play dumb: *Leave where? Leave when? What are you talking about?*

But instead, Barb just sighs. "I married too young," she says, looking straight ahead, at nothing in particular. "Before I knew who I was, when I was still *afraid* to know who I was." Now she looks directly at Jill. "I never wanted that for you."

"Who said I was afraid?"

Barb raises only one eyebrow this time.

"You weren't there for me," Jill says. She knows she sounds more than a little whiney. She also knows it's not the most skilled way to shift the focus back to Barb, but it works.

"You're right," Barb says. "I wasn't. I could have stayed home, been a housewife. I could have modeled exactly what society was still telling women they were supposed to model for their daughters. Instead, I realized I could model for you what a woman *could* be, that she didn't just have to cook and clean. Not that I should have *had* to model it. You were born during the sexual *revolution*, for heaven's sake. But I could see you falling into that trap when you met Lawrence. Maybe it's just in your nature, I don't know. Maybe I should have honored that more."

"Some women think taking care of a house and raising a child is pretty damn noble," Jill fires back, indignant. "I happen to be one of them. Maybe I learned it by taking care of Dad when I was a kid." (*Shots fired,* Evan would say if he was here listening to her.)

Barb's expression is unreadable. "It wasn't your job to take care of your father."

"Well, nobody ever told me that. I was a *kid,* Mom. What did you think I was going to do? Sit in my room and refuse to clean? Refuse to cook? Refuse to listen to him tell me how his day went? You were the wife, but you were nowhere to be found. Dad still needed someone to keep the house clean and cook the meals."

"I think that's overstating things a bit. He was a grown man."

"That's beside the point!" Jill's gesticulating now, her voice louder than it needs to be. "You weren't *there*. How would you know if I was overstating things? You were too busy with your job. And then you divorced a good man who worshipped you."

"Is it making you feel better?" Barb asks, her voice surprisingly calm.

Jill envisions herself coiled up like a snake, but not a snake ready to strike. A sick, tired snake that just wants to take a nap. "Is *what* making me feel better?"

"Enumerating all the ways I failed as a mother," Barb says. "All the ways your dad was martyred. Is it helping you? Because if it is, I think that's a good thing. You need whatever help you can get at this point."

That's it, Jillian thinks. "You know what, Mom? Screw you."

Barb sighs as if she's been expecting this response for a long, long time. "Well, my darling daughter," she says, leaning forward to kiss Jill's cheek before the latter can pull back. "With all due respect, screw you, too. Also," she adds, guiding Jill to the door and gently ushering her out of the room, "I love you. Do try to get some sleep."

"Everything okay?" Evan asks when she gets back to the car.

"Could be better," Jill tells him, still in a daze. "But it could be worse too."

"Well, that's good," he says cautiously. "Right? So, where to?"

Jill sighs. "Tell you what. How about using those muscles of yours to help your mom out with a project?"

"This place is awesome," Evan says as they walk into the studio about twenty minutes later. He's carrying the box of broken china that's been riding around in the Toyota's trunk for the past few days. Jill shows him where to set it down, and then she shows him the metal sculpture she's been working on.

"Whoa," Evan says as they stand there looking down at it. "Cool."

"I don't know," she says. "It needs…something. It needs to be a little more open, or aired out, or…hell, I don't know. Honestly, I feel like kind of a dunderhead for even starting this thing."

"I think it's pretty badass of you to try something new," Evan says. "Promise me you won't give up on it unless you seriously have to, for whatever reason."

Jill smiles. "Okay," she says. "I promise. Help me pry this monster open a little, will you?" She hands him a pair of leather work gloves before pulling on her own.

Evan works his hands between the two edges of the metal, and Jill does the same. Pulling upward and outward like her life depends on it, she feels the muscles in her back stretched taut. It took her full weight to fold this thing, she reminds herself; it's going to take at least that much effort to open it back up. When the two of them finally pry the metal open a few inches, she gets the toe of her work boot wedged in there and holds down the bottom edge of metal while grabbing the top edge with her gloved hands and pulling upward as hard as she can. Finally, the metal groans and releases a bit further, until there's roughly a twelve-inch space between the two edges. It looks more like her intuition tells her it should, even if it's still not quite right. "It'll have to do for now," she says, covering the piece with a big drop cloth before she and Evan head for the door and turn out the lights.

In the car, on the way back to Hadley's, she says, "We should probably talk about, you know, the situation with your dad."

"Oh, yeah," Evan says, his hands tightening on the steering wheel. "That. He called me about it last week."

Jill's breathing becomes very slow. "Oh? How did it go?"

"Great. I told him he was an asshole."

"I can't imagine he reacted well to that."

"He told me," Evan says, "to keep my attitude in check."

"What did you say?"

"I told him I'll start keeping my attitude in check when he starts keeping his dick in his pants."

Jill can't help but crack a smile. She also can't help being a little concerned. "That doesn't sound like you."

Evan shakes his head as the dirt road transitions to pavement. "How can you do it, Mom?" he asks, his voice quieter now. "How can you be on his side? It's like you've just...forgiven him or something."

At this, she lets out a long breath. "I don't think I have, to tell you the truth. That said, I'm pretty sure staying mad at your father is just going to keep me stuck in a really bad, unhealthy place. And that's the last thing I need. Also, he loves you, and I can't fault him for that." She's surprised to hear herself, yet again, defending Lawrence. But it's the truth, and she knows it.

"Yeah, yeah," Evan fires back. "I get it. He just doesn't know how to express that love in a 'selfless, healthy way,' right?"

Jill is silent.

"Sorry, Mom. It's just that you've always made so many excuses for him."

"You're right," she says, thinking of the conversation she and Barb just had in the hotel room. "I have. I did model a certain kind of woman for you—a woman who gives up everything, gives up herself. There's such a thing as too much sacrifice, and I didn't do you any favors by sacrificing the things I loved to raise you. But here's the thing: All of this stuff with your dad and his particular way of being in the world. It's just...who he is. It's a fact of life, kid." She pauses. "Kind of like Penelope's pregnancy."

Evan lets his head fall back against the seat as he navigates the car onto the main road leading to Hadley's place. "Ugh. Don't even go there."

"Hey," Jill says, putting a hand on his shoulder. "Like it or not, that baby is going to be your little brother or sister."

"I still don't know how you can be so okay with it."

"Did I say I was okay with it?"

He shakes his head again.

"That said, acceptance of reality can be a really useful skill."

Evan nods as they pull into Hadley's driveway, but he doesn't say anything further.

He gets a ride back down to Tucson with a friend who also spent the holiday up in Flagstaff. Before he leaves, Hadley cooks him a massive breakfast. "What kind of auntie would I be if I didn't make a fuss over you?" she asks him.

Grinning, Evan shrugs.

Jill drops him off at the friend's house. "Bye, sweetie," she says, getting out of the car to give him a proper hug. "I love you." One of these days, she'll get used to how tall he's gotten in the past couple of years.

"Bye, Mom," he says as he heads toward the friend's front door. "I love you, too. I'll see you soon. And hey," he calls out as she's getting back into the car. "I'll think about what you said, okay?"

Next, Jill heads to Barb's hotel to pick her up and take her back to the airport. They arrive there early; Barb's flight back to the Bay Area isn't for another hour.

"Want to get some coffee?" her mother asks.

Jill nods, and they head toward the little airport café where they settle in at one of the tiny tables after placing their order.

Barb looks nervous. "Look," she says, drumming her fancy fingernails on the laminate tabletop. "I was probably too flippant last night at the hotel. Too breezy. I have something important to say to you."

"Okay," Jill says cautiously, drawing out the word as a waitress brings their coffee.

"Here's the thing," Barb says. "I knew my marriage wasn't going to work out pretty early on. Then I got pregnant, and it seemed important for me to stay. And that's not your fault, okay? That decision is on me, not you. But as it turned out, you were perfect. You were just what I needed."

"I don't even know what you're telling me right now."

"Jill." Barb's voice is firm as she looks into her daughter's eyes, reaches across the table, and covers Jill's hands with her own. "You grounded me. And I was a young woman who needed grounding. At a certain point, though, I also felt like I needed to be free. I needed to explore what else was out there for me. Unfortunately, that meant I was not always the mother you needed. And I definitely wasn't the wife your father needed. You've always been a good daughter. When you were growing up, I suspected I didn't deserve you. To tell the truth, I still suspect that sometimes. I don't take any credit at all for the woman you've become."

"Oh, I've become some kind of woman, all right," Jill interjects, her voice heavy with sarcasm.

"That's correct," Barb says sternly. "You have. You were able to temper your own needs for nearly twenty years to focus on your child and your marriage. I wasn't able to come close to doing that."

Again, Jill scoffs. "My *failed* marriage, you mean? Yeah, there's a great success."

"It doesn't matter. And I don't say that to minimize your pain. But look at what does matter. Look at what you've done, what you continue to do." Barb is gesturing with her hands now. "Look at the spectacular young man you've raised. Look at your talent, your art. Look at these gifts you've given to the world!"

Boy is she stubborn, Jill thinks. At this point, she knows she can either keep fighting what her mother's saying, or she can just surrender. "Thank you," she says simply as pre-boarding for Barb's flight is announced over the loudspeaker.

Barb smiles at her as they gather up their things and toss their empty cups into the recycling bin. A floor-to-ceiling mirror separates the café from the rest of the terminal. Jill touches her mother's shoulder, motioning for her to stop. "Stand here with me for a second," she says as she puts an arm around Barb's shoulders and gives her a squeeze. The two of them behold their reflection in the glass, Jill dressed down in her working overalls and Barb in a crisp, professional pantsuit.

"Maybe not so different underneath it all," Barb says.

They head for the gate, where other passengers are already lined up, waiting to board.

"You have everything?" Jill asks, giving her mom a hug.

Barb nods. Tears are shining in her eyes, and she blinks them away. "See ya around, kid."

It's only after she's crossed over the security checkpoint tape on the carpet and is shoelessly waiting her turn to pass through the x-ray machine, that Jill thinks of something else she wants to say. "Hey, Mom?"

Barb turns around.

"Lighten up on yourself a little, okay? You did the best you could."

Barb gives a thumbs-up as she slips her feet back into her heels. Smiling at the TSA agent, she collects her things and joins the other passengers. Jill watches, blinking back her own tears now, as all the passengers file through double glass doors to the outside and head across the tarmac toward the waiting plane.

After seeing Barb off at the airport, Jill thinks about the sculpture. She thinks about what Madame Imre told her in college, how the great surrealist, André Breton, said Frida Kahlo's work was "a ribbon around a bomb." Turning onto the dirt road that leads to the studio, Jill shakes her head. If she put a ribbon around the hunk of scrap metal she's been trying to beat into submission, she knows for a fact there would be no explosion. The piece is missing something vital, and she has no idea what it is. If she hadn't made that promise to Evan about not quitting, she'd seriously consider ditching the entire project.

An artist's model is sitting for Bodhi when she opens the studio door. It's an old man wearing a T-shirt and jeans. He's posed on the stool in the center of the space in a forward-leaning position with his elbows on his thighs and his hands clasped together. "I'm so sorry to interrupt," Jill says. "I'll come back later."

"No," Bodhi tells her, setting down his sketching crayon and standing up from his easel. "We're almost done. It's fine with me if you're here." He turns to the model, who cups a hand by his ear. "Is it okay with you Jack?" Bodhi yells.

"Fine and dandy," the old man hollers back, beaming at them.

Jill walks over to her work-in-progress, pulls the drop cloth off of it, and then just ponders for the next few minutes while Bodhi finishes up his sketches. When he's done, Jack stands up and stretches slowly before wandering over to where Jill is now sitting on the floor in front of her project, lost in thought.

"I like what you're doing here," the old man yells. "Something about it reminds me of being a little kid, the way I'd come across interesting things when I was playing outside.

Birds' nests, snake skins. You name it. Do kids still discover those things?"

Jill grins up at him. "I don't know," she says with a shrug. "I hope so."

After Jack leaves, Jill goes over to Bodhi's easel to check out the sketches. "These are incredible," she tells him. "I'm impressed by how you see the beauty in people."

"It always surprises me how much people need to be seen," he tells her. "Really seen. Not gawked at. Not judged. Just...acknowledged. Appreciated."

Jill knows exactly what he means. She has lived that need. She lived it all those years Lawrence insisted on looking off to the side when they made love. She lived it every time he told her to please not surprise him at his office for lunch and to not bother attending events with him.

Bodhi is looking at her strangely. "Are you okay?"

Jill snaps to attention. "Yes," she says. "Yeah, I'm fine."

He settles down on the wooden bench behind the easel and turns to a fresh page of his big sketch pad. "What are you doing right now? Working on the piece?"

Jill lets out a disgusted sigh and shakes her head. "I'm not doing anything."

"Good," he says, picking up a conté crayon and nodding toward the bench in the middle of the studio. "Because I'd really love to sketch you."

There's no way this mom bod can possibly live up to the one in his memory.

That's what Jill's thinking as she sits on the stool in the center of the studio with a fresh sheet draped strategically across certain parts of her body. Fortunately, Bodhi's just restocked the fire with a few aspen logs; otherwise, she'd be freezing her butt off. Sitting there, with the heat from the woodstove warming her bare skin, Jill can't help but momentarily regret all the catch-up eating she's done lately, thanks to Hadley's magnificent cooking. Since she's gradually learned to stop resisting and just give herself up to the pleasures of food in the past several weeks, there have been elk steaks and crab cakes, cookies and wild berry cobblers. Not to mention yesterday's over-the-top Thanksgiving feast. "Draw me like one of your—" she starts to say. It's an attempt to neutralize some of her tension, but Bodhi, grinning evilly, cuts her off.

"Don't you dare say it."

She'd started out wearing her overalls. Posing stiffly at first, shifting this way and that on the stool.

"It's probably too much for me to ask you to undo those top straps so you look like you're in a T-shirt and jeans," he said after she'd been unnaturally perched there for a few minutes.

"It's fine," Jill told him, reaching for the little brass buckles by her shoulders. Back in high school, she'd loved drawing the human form. Bulky clothes made it almost impossible though.

"One of these days," Bodhi said, "maybe I'll convince you to do an actual nude figure drawing session. You can have whoever you want here with us—Hadley, the National Guard..."

Jill smiled. "We can do it now, if you'd like." She didn't know where this boldness was coming from. No doubt, she'd live to regret it.

"I would like," Bodhi said.

Hence, the sheet currently covering her breasts and pelvis. She wishes she'd arranged it to cover more of her body—the pale stretch marks on the sides of her abdomen, for example, and the little dimples of cellulite on her upper thighs.

But Bodhi doesn't seem to notice her flaws. *Of course, it's possible he's just doing a really good job of hiding his revulsion,* Jill thinks. She doesn't actually believe it though. If anything, the intense yet removed expression on Bodhi's face tells her he's focused on the details of her unique human body, and on getting those details right as he commits them to paper.

"Now you," she says when he's finished the sketch. She pulls the sheet around her like a toga as she gets up from the stool.

Bodhi, who's using a shop rag to wipe sepia crayon marks from the heel of his palm, looks up at her, surprised. "Excuse me?"

"This is the part where we trade places," she tells him.

"Are you serious?"

"As a heart attack."

He sets the rag down. "Hoo boy. You're really going to make me do this, aren't you?"

"Well, I'm not going to *make* you do anything, but…"

"No, no," he says, holding up a hand. "I get it. Turnabout is fair play."

"It's probably too much for me to ask you to unbutton your shirt," she says five minutes later, mimicking him as he sits on the stool looking only slightly less awkward than Jill felt when he first started sketching her.

"Hell," he says. "I'll go full Monty, if you'd like."

Jill stares at him, momentarily at a loss for words. She's about to screw her courage to the sticking-place and say *I would like,* but he cuts her off.

"Strike that," he says. "I'll use the sheet."

"That works, too."

She focuses hard on arranging the miscellaneous drawing tools on the drafting table next to the easel as Bodhi pulls his Henley shirt over his head and then starts unbuttoning his jeans. Eventually (according to Jill's unintentional peripheral vision), he's wearing just boxer shorts as he grabs the sheet from a nearby wall hook and heads back to the stool in the center of the studio. Then the boxers come off, too. "It's chilly in here," he says, glancing down as he sits. "Just so you know."

Jill is blushing to beat the band. Truly, he has nothing to apologize for. For years, she's been married to a man of smaller physical stature; compared to Lawrence, Bodhi's built like a Viking. As she sketches, Jill notices the details. His shoulders are broader than she remembers from when they were eighteen. Also, his arm muscles have a different sort of definition than they used to, and his chest is thicker. Some of the dark hair there is salt-and-pepper gray now. Her eyes wander downward.

"You always had more natural talent than me, you know," he says, interrupting her observations.

Jill looks up at him, embarrassed. He's been watching her. "Not true," she says, shaking her head. "But even if it was, you're the one who kept going. You stayed with it."

After that, there's mostly silence, the only sound coming from Jill's pencil on the sketch pad. She'd forgotten what it was like to lose herself in the moment, forgetting everything but the project at hand. It's a specific kind of quiet euphoria. She doesn't know how long it is that she glances back and forth between the details of Bodhi's body and the sketch pad. At one point, laser focused on getting the definition of a specific abdominal muscle shaded in just right, she realizes that she's lost all sense of time. "I'm so sorry," she says, looking up at him. "You probably need a break."

"It's no problem. The blood supply to my lower extremities died off twenty minutes ago, but who needs legs anyway?"

Jill covers her face with her non-sketching hand.

"I'm *kidding,*" Bodhi says. "Keep going. I can tell you're in the zone."

"I'm almost done." She finishes shading the abs, fills in a few more areas of the drawing, and then sets down her pencil.

"You know," he says as she picks up the sketch pad to flip it around and show him. "There was never anything going on between me and that girl who kissed me during freshman year of college."

The sketch pad hovers in mid-air. "Theresa," Jill says, her smile hovering somewhere between surprised and bemused. "You're seriously going to bring that up now?"

Bodhi grins and readjusts the sheet. "Why not? I've only been wanting to tell you for…oh, about two decades."

An aspen log pops like a gunshot in the woodstove, making both of them jump. Not knowing what else to say, Jill glances over to where the fire Bodhi built has started to grow a bit in intensity. It's not blazing full force yet though; for the time being, it's more of a slow, steady burn.

Book 18: 1990

Hadley's been calling ever since Evan and I got back to Scottsdale from our visit to the mountain. When I finally respond, it's when I know she'll be at work. I leave a message on her answering machine. "Sorry I haven't gotten back to you," I say, keeping my voice as breezy as possible. "You must be out. I'll try again later."

But I won't try again later. I've already decided this. I've made a decision once and for all about who I am going to be, where my allegiance will lie. Hadley and I have been friends since before I can remember, but my husband and my child have to be top priorities now.

"That whole thing with whatshername," Lawrence says out of the blue, after Evan and I have been home for a few days. "It was nothing."

I just sit there on the edge of our king-sized bed, not saying anything. Until now, the *whatshername* in question—Angelica, owner of the seamed stocking I found in Lawrence's car—hasn't come up. I've assumed we were just going to let bygones be bygones.

"I was acting foolish," Lawrence continues. "I guess this whole new fatherhood business has made me a little nuts, that's all. Plus..." He stops talking for a minute, and just looks at me with imploring eyes. "...so much of your attention goes to the baby now."

I look down, chagrined. He's right, of course.

"And there's this," Lawrence says, switching gears as he picks up a copy of the student newspaper that's been sitting folded up on his nightstand.

"What is it?"

"A review of *Castration of the Father*." He grabs a pair of reading glasses and puts them on. "'It's almost as if Dr. Kensington is being intentionally obscure,'" he reads in a mimicking *I know you are, but what am I* kind of voice. "'...as if he's determined to make these already well-known Greek myths as inaccessible as possible.'"

"But that's the farthest thing from the truth!" I protest (even though I'm not actually sure about this; I've been too wrapped up in new motherhood to find time to read Lawrence's newly published book. Another wave of shame washes over me at the thought).

Lawrence tosses the review aside. "It's because I'm not willing to sell out and make myth sensationalistic," he says, removing the reading glasses and tossing them onto the bedside table. "Nobody really cares about analyzing the great ancient classics anymore. It's in the hands of academics such as myself to guard these texts—to guard the brutality, the reality, even though so many of them are based in myth." He's standing now, claiming the center of our bedroom the way I remember him claiming the front of the lecture hall when he took over the Intro to Mythology class from old Professor Xenakis. "To keep them safe from smaller minds who would soften them in the name of accessibility. Well, I'm not willing to modernize the classics like some of those other hacks." His shoulders slump a little. "My God, this whole nightmare has thrown me into an utter *anhedonia* of the soul."

I know better than to ask what that means.

"It means an utter absence of pleasure," he explains anyway.

"What about therapy?" I ask, sensing an opening to address our marriage head-on. "It might be helpful for you to talk to a professional about this. And I've heard it can also be a good thing for married couples to—"

"I hardly think that's necessary," he says, cutting me off.

"But if I decide to go, will you go with me?"

"Jillian," Lawrence says with a patient, almost fatherly smile (His eyes don't match the smile though; his eyes, in fact, are as flat as the eyes of the reptiles Evan and I saw when we visited a pet store recently). "Let's face it. I'm not the one with issues here."

When the first bump appears on the bridge of my nose nine days later, my first thought is that I've been bitten by a spider. I spend the day baking for a get-together for new classics majors at the provost's residence. By the time I arrive, another bump has appeared next to the first one, and my nose is somewhat swollen.

"Spider bite," I say with a little laugh to the first faculty wife who asks what happened.

I feel like I'm finally starting to be accepted by these women. Most of the other faculty wives are so much older; I swear they've looked at me like I'm a complete idiot since I joined their ranks. I'll be damned if I'm going to let an insect bite keep me from making a good impression today (*Spiders are arachnids, not insects,* Lawrence would no doubt correct me).

"You have shingles," Martha Bunston says after taking one look at my nose.

I'm still holding the platter she gave me and Lawrence as a wedding gift. "I'm fine," I tell her. It's just…" A wave of pain slices across the center of my head, and I scrunch my eyes closed. "I'm sorry. All of a sudden, I have a terrible headache."

"I've had chicken pox," Martha says, "so you're no threat to me. You should go back home, though, just in case. And definitely get some antivirals in your system, stat."

In the days that follow, I'm the sickest I've ever been. Lawrence's mother moves into the guest bedroom for a week to look after the baby. Evan's had his chickenpox vaccinations; his doctor assured me when I called that he's safe. Still, I don't want to expose him to anything unnecessarily. Plus, with my swollen, red-streaked face, I look terrifying. If I end up dying, which it feels like I might, I don't want his last memory of his mother to be an image of the monstrosity I've become.

"Would you mind sleeping on the couch?" Lawrence asks me in the middle of the worst night, four days in. "I really have to be rested for the conference tomorrow."

I've been moaning uncontrollably, practically hallucinating from the itching and pain emanating from the raised, red rash covering half my face. I nod in the half-dark, raise myself to sitting as a meat cleaver slices through my brain without warning. At this point, I don't know what's worse, the shingles or the antiviral medication I started (too late, it turns out, for them to do much good). I make my way toward the living room, one hand on the hallway wall to steady myself. And without warning, something happens. I don't know what it is, exactly. Maybe I'm hallucinating for real this time. Or maybe I'm having a stroke. Whatever the case, I suddenly feel like I'm not inhabiting my own body anymore. It's almost as if I'm quite literally beside myself—or maybe above myself—suspended from wires and in third person—not an "I" at all.

More like a *she*.

Book 19: 2010

A woman who does not blush is a champion in battle.
~Theano

A regional blizzard moves in without warning just after the new year, stranding Hadley in Durango on the last leg of her multi-day trucking run to and from Oklahoma City.

But it's okay. There's something therapeutic about being snowed in at the A-frame alone. With icy rain falling outside and a fire roaring in the wood stove, Jill runs a hot bath in Hadley's old-fashioned, clawfoot tub. She adds some organic lemongrass body oil she found under the sink; citrusy-smelling steam rises up as she lowers herself into the water. Lying there with her eyes closed, she thinks about the past month, the rush of the holidays. Getting to see Evan for Christmas so soon after she'd seen him at Thanksgiving was a treat, as was their visit to Prescott to see Jill's dad and his wife, Helen. A few days later, she got to visit with Hadley's parents, who live a few hours away in the White Mountains, and with Hadley's brother, Chuck, who's now married with two kids.

"How about a noogie for old times' sake?" he asked Jill with a playful grin, holding up the knuckle of his index finger as soon as he saw her.

As much as she loved seeing everyone, there had been little time for rest until the snow arrived this morning. Now, Jill soaks in the tub until the palms of her hands turn pruney and her eyelids grow heavy. It's not until every single one of her muscles has reached the limp noodle stage, though, that she finally allows herself to get out of the water. After wrapping her hair in a towel and her body in the plush robe Barb sent her for Christmas, she wanders into the kitchen to set out the French press, coffee beans, and grinder in preparation for her morning brew; she wants to be able to hit the ground running and caffeinated tomorrow. She's decided it's time to start getting serious about the metal sculpture, even though she's still not entirely sure of the direction she wants to take. A few ideas have been forming in her head lately, though, which is promising.

As she reaches up to pull the grinder down from its cupboard shelf, the back porch security light clicks on outside. Turning to look, Jill sees the silhouette of a man standing out there, snowflakes racing slantwise to the ground behind him as he peers in through the glass-paneled door. Jill gasps, the grinder nearly landing on her head before she rebalances it in her hands and hastily places it on the counter. Her brain scrambles to figure out her next move. Hadley keeps the little pearl-handled .45 derringer in the pantry, but there's no way Jill could get to it in time to defend herself should this man intend to do her harm.

The silhouette shifts so that the face becomes visible. Jillian blinks once and then blinks again, frowning. She knows that face. It's Lawrence, showing up on Hadley's back porch the way a hungry coyote will sometimes show up near the fence line at dusk—silently and without warning, rarely with good intentions. Then something else occurs to her: Evan. Rushing toward the door, she unlocks it with trembling hands and flings it open. "Is he okay?" she demands, her voice frantic.

Lawrence appears clueless. "Is who okay?"

"Evan," she shouts, completely beside herself now. "My God, who else would I be talking about?"

In response, Lawrence shakes his head and looks (Jill notes with mild fury) somewhat amused. "Of course Evan's okay. Why wouldn't he be? Aside from the fact that his entire personality has changed, and he barely speaks to me."

Jill breathes deeply, allowing herself a moment to regroup. "Your behavior might have something to do with that," she says finally.

Lawrence's shoulders drop. "May I come in?"

"Fine," she says, her voice intentionally acidic as she steps aside and pulls the robe closed more tightly. "But first tell me why you're here. What is it this time? Another pregnant TA?"

"Jillian," he says.

"I go by Jill now."

Lawrence smirks. "Ah. I see."

He looks older than he should, Jill thinks. Especially considering the obvious steps he's taken to look younger—new cologne, a more youthful haircut and dye job (which isn't quite working for him; his gray roots already need redoing).

"I suppose I should get right to it," he says. "May I sit?" He motions to the kitchen table.

Reluctantly, she nods.

"You look good," he says. "You look...luminous. Evanescent."

Jill narrows her eyes at him. He knows her weak spots. "What is it you need, Lawrence?"

"I've come to ask you to take me back."

Cocking her head in stupefaction, she stares at him. "Pardon?"

A wooden bowl filled with pomegranates and clementines sits in the center of Hadley's kitchen table. Lawrence removes one of the pomegranates and turns it over and over in his hand like some kind of Magic 8 Ball. "I've been doing a lot of thinking," he says. "And I want you back. I want *us* back. Maybe I needed to see that you'd let me go if you had to. That you'd retreat in order for me to advance toward you." His eyes meet Jill's. "Well, it worked, because here I am. I'm here for you, Jillian."

"Wow," she says with a little laugh, not bothering to correct the name this time. "Do you mean for that to sound as diabolical as it does?"

"You think I'm not serious?"

"Also," she says, ignoring his question. "Are you...*hitting* on me? Because, if you are, I can't tell you how long I've waited for this."

Lawrence sits up a little straighter, a look of satisfaction on his face now.

"I mean, you're my husband, after all, right?"

He nods, smiles encouragingly.

"The man who's always been there for me when the chips were down."

At this, his smile falters, but just barely.

"I'd be a fool to not at least consider it," she tells him.

"I'd never call you a fool, Jilly."

Jilly? She shivers at the sound of that nickname he'd so rarely called her over the years. Mostly, he'd used it during those first months after Evan was born: *How's my Jilly Jelly today?* he'd ask, placing a hand on her abdomen to agitate the postpartum flab there. So why choose that particular term of endearment again now?

As Jill ponders this question, Lawrence leans forward and takes one of her hands. Bringing it up to his face, he kisses her palm. She knows she'll probably hate herself later for the vague fascination she allows herself to feel regarding what he might do next. It keeps her from taking the hand back as quickly as she should.

"We can start over for the new year," he says, laying his cheek against her hand now (a tiny shudder of revulsion travels through her at the feel of his stubble). "What do you say?"

At that moment, the motion sensor porch light clicks on again outside, seemingly in tune with the lightbulb turning on inside her head. This time, when Jill glances toward the door, nobody's there. Probably the light was just triggered by the snow, which is falling more heavily now. If she doesn't get Lawrence out of here soon, they could be snowed-in together, like two characters from a Stanley Kubrick film; she's quite certain it wouldn't end well. The porch goes dark again, and she returns her attention to Lawrence. "You would seriously abandon a woman who's pregnant with your child?"

"Penelope's not you, Jilly," he protests. "She's not...selfless."

The laugh that comes out of Jill is more like a bark. "So, she's not making you the center of her universe. Is that what you're telling me?"

Lawrence returns the pomegranate to its bowl. "You make me sound like an unreasonable person."

"Goodness knows I wouldn't want to do that."

"Penelope will be fine, believe me. I'm sure she'll find someone else more suitable for her."

The silence that follows is broken only when Jill shakes her head and makes a small sound of disbelief. "It amazes me," she says, "how you can be even more of a complete bastard than I thought."

"So, who is he?" Lawrence demands.

"Pardon?"

"You heard me. I said 'Who is he?' Or perhaps it's a *she*, now that you've apparently moved to the isle of Lesbos."

"What are you even talking about?"

"I assume this new 'clarity,'" he says, making air quotes with his fingers, "or whatever you want to call it, is due to the fact that you've taken a lover."

Jill fights the impulse to rub her temples. "This isn't the Victorian Age, Lawrence."

"What's that supposed to mean?"

"It's just that you never hear anyone say that anymore. *Taken a lover*."

"Forgive me for using a classical manner of speech," Lawrence snaps, his voice and his face—his entire being, really—utterly devoid of humor. As usual.

Jill closes her eyes for several seconds. She can't help but continue to feel pity for Penelope. But more than that, she feels tired—just 100% stick-a-fork-in-her DONE—to the very center of her bones. "You know, Lawrence," she says, "All these years I've been desperate for your approval. Starved for it. But it turns out the only approval I need is my own. And make no mistake about it. I intend to do what it takes to earn back my own approval."

"Don't be so theatrical."

Jill stands up from her chair and motions for him to do the same. When he does, she walks to the kitchen door, not saying a word.

Lawrence's features rearrange themselves yet again, this time into the reptilian coldness she's grown so familiar with over the years. "You're going to regret this," he informs her.

Jill flings open the door with a ferocity that surprises even herself. Snow flurries rush in. "I already do," she says. "But not for the reasons you imagine. You've been wasting my time for two decades. It ends now."

"In that case," Lawrence says. He reaches into his coat as he walks toward her, and for a crazy split-second, Jill thinks he might have a gun. It's not a gun he pulls out though. It's a business card. He hands it to Jill, and she glances down at it. "That's the contact information for my divorce attorney. You'll be hearing from him shortly."

"Get the hell out," she hisses, feeling almost like a reptile herself now. She's still holding the door open, her gaze glued to his. The hand holding the business card is hidden behind her back so he won't see it shaking.

"There's something so distinctly unappealing about a middle-aged divorcée," Lawrence quips as he moves toward the door. He opens his mouth to spew further venom, but the second he's across the threshold, Jill shuts the door, hard, behind him and locks the deadbolt.

Twenty minutes later, she's still wound-up. Instead of going back out to the Ovum and trying to fall asleep (which she's pretty sure would be impossible anyway), she makes herself a cup of chamomile tea and turns on Hadley's TV. Apparently, a nature channel was the last thing anyone watched; images of morphing insects fill the screen as a male narrator drones on about the stages of larval development. "Oh good," Jill says out loud, settling onto the couch. "This'll put me to sleep." Then the narrator starts talking about butterflies, how they enter the chrysalis only to become a sort of "butterfly jambalaya," melting down so newer versions of themselves can take shape. *Gross,* she thinks, giving the tea a stir and then setting the spoon on the saucer next to the teabag.

"Continuously transforming," the narrator drones as she inhales the aroma of chamomile and honey before taking a sip, "the creature bides its time within the cocoon until, one day, it realizes it has wings. Finally ready to leave the chrysalis, it pumps fluid from its body into these new, graceful appendages."

The teacup stops halfway to Jill's mouth. For several seconds, she just sits there staring at the footage of a *Menelaus blue morpho* butterfly doing everything it can to leave the only home it's ever known.

"Thus enwinged," the narrator continues as Jill sets down her cup, "the newly reconfigured creature cannot help but fly."

She sits up, ramrod straight, on the couch. Then she stands, turns off the television, and walks quickly to the back door of the A-frame, where she pulls on her snow boots.

"Flight of Icarus" blasts from the massive old boom box when she lets herself into the studio forty minutes later, having just survived a harrowing drive in near-blizzard conditions. Immediately, Jill thinks of the group of metal heads in her eighth-grade class. She can see them now with their feathered hair and Iron Maiden T-shirts, singing about flying as high as the sun, fists held high as they'd banged their skulls against an invisible wall.

Gunnar's over at his workbench using the plasma cutter on a thick sheet of steel, oblivious to her presence.

She knows they're on a strict deadline for a piece commissioned by a small town in Wisconsin. Bodhi showed Jill the sketches for it a few weeks ago. She wouldn't be surprised if both men are stressed out trying to get it done on time. "I'll stay out of your way," she yells over the music, just to make sure Gunnar knows she's there.

When there's no response, she walks over to where her own piece hangs, suspended now, from a tow chain slung over a roof beam thanks to Hadley's help hoisting it the other day. It was getting too hard for Jill to work on the thing while it was lying on the ground; her back had started killing her.

Jill reaches her arm through the vertical opening between the two edges of metal. As she feels around, her fingers searching for a good contact spot where another piece of metal might be attached, the delicate gold chain she wears around her neck gets snagged on a rough patch of the outside steel. She doesn't realize it's caught; when she pulls her arm from the sculpture and steps back, the chain breaks. Her wedding ring goes flying.

"Damnit," Jill mutters, holding the broken necklace against her chest. She probably shouldn't even care about the ring, not after the stunt Lawrence pulled this evening. Still, it's gold. She might have to pawn it someday if she persists in her current life choice of being an unemployed wannabe artist squatting in a friend's travel trailer. She's pretty sure the ring rolled under the wood stove, not that she could hear it over the Judas Priest song that's now blasting from the boom box. Walking over there and getting down on her hands and knees, Jill scrambles around, feeling along the floor underneath the stove.

Before long, a bright beam shines behind her, illuminating the search. She squints upward to see Gunnar holding a high-powered flashlight. His welding mask is perched on top of his head, and he's clearly annoyed at the inconvenience.

"Thanks," she shouts over the music once she's found the ring, tucked it into a pocket of her overalls, and stood back up. "You didn't need to do that."

He grunts in response.

They're both heading back to their respective places in the studio when Jill stops. Changing direction, she walks to the boom box and hits the pause button. "Can I ask you something?"

Halfway back to his workbench, Gunnar stops walking, too. "Sure," he says without turning to face her in the new silence. "Why not?"

"What the hell is your problem with me?"

Now he does turn around, slowly. "You want to know what my problem with you is?"

Forcing herself to stand her ground, and keeping her eyes locked onto his, Jill nods.

"My problem," Gunnar says, his voice a low growl, "is that I don't like seeing my friends get screwed over."

"What are you even—"

"I'm guessing you're doing that thing women do."

Jill waits for him to elaborate, even though this is more than she's ever heard him say at one time. When he doesn't, she tries to prompt him. "And that would be..."

"Setting the stage to screw Bodhi over once again, just like you did when you guys were kids." Gunnar raises a hand in the air and then lowers it, wiggling his fingers to symbolize rain. "Lining up all the pieces just to get your rocks off watching them fall."

He's completely insane, Jill thinks. "My rocks?"

Gunnar rolls his eyes in disgust. "You know exactly what I'm talking about." His voice is dripping with sarcasm now. "How are things on the home front?"

Jill can't help but wonder if he's having some kind of flashback or breakdown. She decides the best course of action is probably to just answer him honestly. "Well, technically I'm homeless, so..."

"That's not what I heard."

She laughs. "What, did Hadley tell you she's going to add my name to her deed or something?"

Turning away from her, Gunnar shakes his head like she's a lost cause. "You may be good at art, but you suck at lying."

He thinks I'm good at art? Jill thinks. "Wait," she says, giving up on whatever game this is they're playing. "Gunnar, please. I really don't know what you're talking about right now. Is there any way you could give me a hint, or...you know, draw a picture?"

Gunnar releases a heavy sigh, like it's taking everything he has to engage in conversation with her. "I heard you were working things out with your old man," he says.

Jill freezes. "Well, one part of that is true. My soon-to-be ex-husband *is* an old man..." She stops, closes her eyes, and presses fingertips to her forehead as he walks the rest of the way to his workbench and picks up the plasma cutter. "Okay, that was uncharitable. But as far as working things out? God, no. That's not going to happen." Something inside her sort of ...lifts when she says it.

"Hmph," Gunnar says, bending back to the task at hand. "Interesting."

"Where did you even hear this?"

"A mutual friend."

"Gunnar! I'm serious. Who told you?"

For a long moment, he doesn't say anything. Then he looks up at the ceiling and shakes his head. "Bodhi told me. I was on the phone with him right before you got here. He was at Hadley's earlier tonight. He saw you sitting in the kitchen with your guy."

Jill's mind flashes back to the motion sensor porch light switching on out of the blue as Lawrence held her hand to his stubbly face. "First of all," she tells Gunnar, "he's *not* my guy."

Gunnar doesn't look convinced. "So, why—"

"Lawrence showed up at Hadley's in a last-ditch effort to try to 'win me back,'" she says, making air quotes. "Probably because his new gal got tired of his bullshit. When I shut him down, he had a little hissy fit and left."

Gunnar chuckles. "Well, you might want to tell Bodhi that. Not that it's any of my business. And hey. Sorry for being such an ass. I have a little trouble with filters. Which is to say I don't have one."

"You can make it up to me," Jill says without hesitation.

Gunnar squints at her, clearly suspicious. "How so?"

She motions for him to follow her out to the storage shed where she holds up a misshapen piece of sheet metal as he brushes snow from his shirt. It's one of the long, narrow pieces she practiced on at Hadley's after Bodhi sent her home with some metalworking tools. She started thinking about it again earlier tonight when that nature program came on. "Can you cut and weld this for me?"

"It's crumpled," Gunnar says.

"That's okay. It's perfect, actually. Crumpled is good."

Gunnar shrugs. "Sure."

After he goes back to the studio, Jill stands out there in the shed for a minute longer. She remembers being out here with Bodhi on prom night. She remembers the bright blue feather she spotted on the ground when he was about to turn off the lantern.

"Don't look at the flame," Gunnar commands half an hour later.

Jill nods and averts her eyes as he lowers the welding mask over his face, transforming himself into a sort of fire-handling warrior. "Think it'll hold?"

"Oh, it'll hold," he yells back, his voice muffled behind the mask.

After carrying the piece of practice sheet metal in from the storage cabin, she'd traced the shape of a crude-looking wing on it with a white conté crayon, and then Gunnar had cut the wing free. Now she forces herself to look away, focusing on the painting she gave Bodhi all those Christmases ago, as he welds one end of it inside the sculpture.

When he's finished, Gunnar turns off the welder and raises his mask. "You can look now," he says.

And so she does. Jill doesn't know what to say as she stands there looking at this new version of her creation—her and Gunnar's creation now, if she's going to give credit where it's due. Add Bodhi, for providing the metal and the workspace, plus Hadley and Evan for their help shaping and hanging the thing. The sculpture looks just the way she'd envisioned it on the snowy drive out here tonight—like a single wing has just emerged from a chrysalis, the first indication of an entirely new life about to take shape.

And that's when it hits her: For the better part of two decades, Jill's been pouring her creativity into home projects—baking cookies, redecorating the dinette, painting a mural on a wall in Evan's bedroom—a mural that consisted of various wild creatures in a jungle with the black night sky overhead, filled with stars. Those things were wonderful in their own way. They were meaningful. Now, though, there's this new thing. Jill never could have seen it coming, this return to a pursuit she loved so much as a younger person—the act of creating something just for the fun of it. Just because it quietly asks to be created. Until recently, she'd thought it was gone forever.

Gunnar grabs a couple of beers from the mini-fridge and twists the caps off. "Time to call it quits for the night, boss," he says, handing one of the bottles to Jill.

"I agree. But there's just one more thing I need to do." Reaching into the pocket of her overalls, she retrieves the wedding ring and sets it inside the sculpture, on a curve of the new wing that's visible from the outside. *Forget about pawning it,* she thinks. *This ring has an even greater purpose.*

Gunnar takes a swig of beer. "You gonna want that thing soldered in there, too, or what?"

"Eventually," she says, taking the bottle he's holding out to her. "When the time is right."

An hour later, the two of them are sitting on the unfolded futon with their backs against the studio wall.

"So," Gunnar says, "what is it you're trying to do with that sculpture of yours, anyway?"

"What do you mean?" A small headache has started working its way up the back of Jill's skull; she's never been much of a beer drinker.

Gunnar lets his head roll toward her. "You know what I mean. Are you trying to change the world, or maybe just change yourself?"

"Wow," Jill says. "Deep."

"It's just a question," he drawls. "You don't have to be such a smart ass."

"Whatever," Jill's voice is peevish, but then a memory of her old art professor, Madame Imre, rises up unexpectedly. "I'm going more for 'ribbon around a bomb,' actually."

Gunnar doesn't respond right away. "You know," he says after a while, readjusting the pillow behind his back. "I studied at a funky artist colony in New Mexico after I got back from Iraq."

Jill takes a swig of water from a plastic bottle next to the futon. "Oh, yeah?" Outside, snow is still coming down, but not as fiercely as it was earlier. It taps softly against the studio windows. A Navajo blanket is stretched across the foot of the futon; grabbing it, Jill tosses one half to Gunnar's side and covers her feet with the other.

Gunnar nods. "Yeah," he says. "It was part of my PTSD treatment—Art Recovery Therapy, they called it. Let's just say it was...somewhat involuntary. And by that, I mean I didn't want anything to do with it."

"How come?"

"Are you kidding me? Holed up on some commune with a bunch of artsy-fartsy hippie types? I'd rather remove my own appendix with a pair of ordinary chopsticks."

"So, why'd you go?"

Gunnar shrugs. "It was part of the deal. If I refused, there went my treatment funding. Anyway, long story short, we did all sorts of stuff: Painting, sculpture, mixed media, writing. Turned out it wasn't a hippie commune at all. It was more like I imagine those old salon gatherings in places like Paris used to be back in the day."

"Sounds cool."

"Yeah," he says. "It was. It actually turned my life completely around. And when I moved back here and saw an ad for some local artist looking for a part-time assistant, I applied. That's how I met Bodhi. But my whole point is that the Taos program made me step outside myself. Saved my life, actually."

Jill feels simultaneously cranky and woozy from the beer. *Croozy*. "I can't help wonder where you're going with all this."

"I'm just saying maybe you could find something like that for yourself," Gunnar fires back. "If you'd get off your pity pot for about half a second."

"The hell are you talking about?" The words are more than a little smooshed-sounding as they leave her mouth. Apparently, she did overdo it with the beer.

"You know what I'm talking about." Gunnar's voice is slurred, too. Whether from booze or tiredness, it's hard to tell. "You're just mourning the way you thought life was supposed to be."

"Oh, gee. Well, thanks for that, *Oprah*."

"You know I'm right." Gunnar closes his eyes and slides down the futon so he's reclining more than sitting. Jill does the same. For the next few minutes, the two of them lie there in silence as a Veruca Salt song plays out. It's followed by *Sweet Jane*, the Cowboy Junkies version. At some point, the boom box must have gotten unplugged; now its batteries are clearly running low, making the band sound even more like junkies than usual.

"Damn," Gunnar murmurs, his voice a slo-mo growl, interrupting her drowsy thoughts. "I forgot how depressing this song is." He finds Jill's hand with his own and gives it a squeeze. Then he rolls onto his side with his back toward her and almost immediately starts snoring.

"Hey, you're snor—" Jill starts to say, but before she can finish the sentence, sleep overtakes her, too. Instantly, she dreams about falling from some unidentified high place. Instead of hitting the ground in her dream, though, she looks down and sees her own self looking up at her, mouth open in surprise. *What the*—Dream Jill thinks a split second before crashing back into her own body. In an instant, it's like she's no longer beside herself—or above herself—suspended from wires and in third person the way she's been for the past couple of decades. It's like she's no longer a *she* at all.

More like an *I*.

I wake up a few hours later when Gunnar shifts on the futon, yanking the Navajo blanket off me.

"Damn," he groans, turning over so we're facing each other. "Please tell me we didn't have sex."

"Thanks a lot." Lifting the covers, I glance down at my jeans, which are fully zipped and buttoned.

Gunnar lifts the covers on his side. "Mine are still on, too," he says. "No way I would have gotten dressed afterward. Thank the good Lord. I'd have to put a bullet through my brain if I messed around with you."

I just stare at him, bleary-eyed. "Again, thanks so much for sharing." I don't even care that my stale beer morning breath is probably just about knocking him out.

"You don't frickin' understand," he says. "Typical woman."

"Piss off, asshole."

"No, you piss off."

"No, *you* piss off," I mutter, flinging a forearm across my eyes. "Infinity."

After a while, Gunnar clears his throat. "It's because of Bodhi," he explains. "The last thing he needs is for you and me to—"

A blast of cold air washes over us. Gunnar and I turn our heads in unison to see Bodhi standing in the open doorway of the studio like he's riding out an earthquake.

"Oh," he says, his voice both glum and resigned as he stares in disbelief at the two of us lying there on the futon together, clearly recovering from a wild night.

Book 20: 2005

"Jillian? Jillian Kensington?"

Car keys in hand, Jillian stops in the hallway of Desert Vale Elementary, one of the larger public schools in the district. When she turns around, Martha Bunston is walking toward her.

She hasn't seen Martha ever since her husband Bill left the Classics department a couple of years ago. Before that, Jillian and Martha worked on tons of faculty functions together. And, of course, the china platter the Bunstons gave Jill and Lawrence as a wedding gift was always a topic of conversation at those functions, laden as it usually was with various Mediterranean treats.

"How long have you been subbing?" Martha asks now, glancing at the laminated tag hanging from a lanyard around Jillian's neck.

"It's my first day, actually. And I'm just a substitute aide, not a full sub."

"Well, what are you doing for lunch?"

Jillian glances down at the keys in her hand. "I was going to eat in my car," she admits. "I don't really know anyone here."

"You do now," Martha says, placing a hand on Jillian's arm. "Follow me."

Minutes later, they're settled into the reading corner of Martha's flawlessly decorated third-grade classroom. Jillian sits in a rocking chair holding the turkey sandwich she brought from home while Martha lowers herself onto a nearby beanbag chair and pulls the lid from a Tupperware container. "How's Lawrence?" she asks.

Jillian shrugs. "He's good. Working hard, as always. How's Bill?"

Martha looks taken aback. "Didn't you know? I left him last spring. The divorce just became final a few weeks ago. I assumed everyone already heard about it through the university grapevine, even though I'm not part of the faculty wives club anymore."

"Oh, my goodness," Jillian says, shaking her head and placing a hand on her chest. "I'm so sorry."

"No need." Martha takes a bite of chicken salad and chews thoughtfully for several moments. "He was sleeping with students. Had been for our entire marriage."

"I don't..." Jillian's voice drops off. She feels suddenly queasy.

Grinning, Martha leans forward in the beanbag chair. She looks around and then cups a hand near her mouth, even though nobody else is in the room with them. "I've been *online dating,*" she whispers. "It's *fantastic.*"

Jillian swallows hard and tries to smile. Glancing down, she realizes that she's been gripping her sandwich so firmly with both hands that the tips of her index fingers and thumbs are touching through the bread and lunchmeat.

"Anyway," Martha continues, leaning back and taking another bite of chicken salad, "enough about me. What made you decide to start subbing?"

Jillian wipes her fingers on a napkin. She doesn't quite know how to answer this. It was when Evan started middle school that she first began to feel more and more adrift. Cut off. Parents weren't as welcome in the classroom as they'd been in previous years, for instance. And forget bringing cupcakes for the entire class on his birthday or contacting other parents to arrange sleepovers; Evan strictly forbade her from doing both. He still wanted to hang out with her occasionally, though, so there was that. Then he became a freshman, and Jillian realized she might as well kiss mom-kid time goodbye. In the months since starting high school, Evan's been so perpetually wrapped up in girls, and friends, and homework that Jillian hardly ever sees him.

"I'm thinking about getting a job," she told Lawrence one night in October. He'd just come in after another late evening at work, and they were sitting at the kitchen table.

"Is there anything you're qualified to do?"

Jillian didn't respond at first. When she did, her voice was quiet. "The school district has some substitute aide positions listed on their website. You don't need experience or a diploma for those."

"Well, it sounds easy and pleasant enough," Lawrence said, getting up from the table. "And it should be a good fit for your level of education."

Jillian pushes the memory of that conversation out of her mind and takes a bite of her sandwich as Martha looks at her expectantly. "I just thought it would be a good way to get out of the house and work with kids a bit," she says.

Martha nods. "Well, I think that's great. Hey! A bunch of teachers are going to one of those wine-and-painting things downtown tomorrow night. Do you want to come?"

Jillian's hand goes to her chest again, fingers fiddling with her gold necklace this time. It's been so long since she really did anything social without Lawrence. "I don't know if—"

"At least think about it," Martha says. "It'll be fun!"

The noise level in the wine bar the following night is such that the Pinot Noir in the fat, stemless glass next to Jillian's easel is actually trembling. Who knew elementary school teachers could be this boisterous? According to Mitch, the handsome young artist leading their group for the evening, they're supposed to be painting whatever it is they see when they look at the collection of fruit that's been set up in the center of the circle of easels and stools. As it turns out, several of the teachers have some interesting interpretations, particularly of the bananas and the peaches. Bawdy laughter erupts from time to time as Mitch tours the room, stopping to squint at each canvas.

"Fun, huh?" Martha yells across the circle.

Jillian nods and raises her glass, but she feels a bit like the nerd of the group; it's hard for her not to take the painting assignment seriously, even though the materials they've been given to work with are basically just dollar store acrylics and brushes with plastic bristles. Still, it's fun being out and about with a bunch of other women on a Friday night. When she'd run the idea by Lawrence yesterday, he'd told her she should go. "It's not like we have any other plans," he said. "And I'll be working late anyway."

When Mitch gets to Jillian's canvas, he stops and says, "Whoa." Crossing one arm over his chest and resting his other fist against his mouth, he just stands there in silence for what seems like an unusually long and awkward amount of time. "Where were you trained?" he finally asks her.

Jillian laughs nervously. A few of the other women have started to gather around.

"That's amazing," one of them says.

"Dang, girl," says another.

"Are you a working artist?" a third one asks her.

Jillian's face feels like it's about to burst into flame. "Just a mom," she manages to say as more women crowd in to see what all the fuss is about.

Seeming to notice her discomfort, Mitch moves on to the next easel. "More wine for those of you who are drinking, ladies?" he calls out.

Some members of the group respond with enthusiastic whoops and hollers, paint brushes held high. As the space around Jillian clears, a teacher she hasn't yet met approaches. "I'm Laila," she says, resting a hand on her enormous belly.

"How far along are you?" Jillian asks her.

"Seven and a half months," Laila says with a congenial roll of her eyes. "It feels like fifteen. Obviously, I'm one of the DDs tonight. Hey, Martha says you sub. And your painting is fantastic. Any chance you'd want to take over my classroom during the first part of my maternity leave? I teach at Desert Vale, too. I'm the art teacher."

Jillian sighs. "I'd love to, but I'm just an aide."

"That works for now," Laila says. "The school can find a long-term sub after the baby comes, but in the meantime, I need someone who can move a little faster than I can. There will also be some light lifting involved, cleanup, stuff like that."

"Wow," Jillian says. "It sounds amazing."

Laila laughs. "I don't know about that."

But Jillian can't believe her good fortune. She glances across the circle at Martha, who points at Laila and then at Jillian before making an "OK" sign with her thumb and forefinger.

Two weeks later, she finally feels like she's settling into the new position. Laila's a taskmaster with the kids, but she's easygoing with Jillian. "It's just so nice to have another adult down here," she said on the first day. The art room is housed in what was the school's original auditorium from the 1970s, and it's huge. It's also on a lower level than the rest of the school, at the opposite end of campus from the other classrooms. It feels like its own world.

The kids seem to sense this, too. All grades from kindergarten through sixth have art twice a week, which means the room is a revolving door of ages and energies. No matter how rowdy the kids are when Jillian sees them at lunch or recess, though, it's almost like a hush passes over them when they file into the art room. Laila, who always has soothing music playing during class, meets each group at the door with a stern expression until everyone is silent. Only then, does she allow them to file into the room and take their places at the communal tables.

"I'm basically the love child of Mary Poppins and Nurse Ratched," she tells Jillian one day as they clean up after a group of fourth graders. Well, Jillian cleans up. Laila sits in the plush office chair with her legs splayed out, cradling her belly with one hand and fanning herself with the other. The kids have been working on a Day of the Dead unit; Jillian is amazed (and exhausted) by their enthusiasm. One little girl, a second grader named Madison, reminds Jillian so much of herself at that age that it's almost...well, spooky. Without fail, Madison has a hard time containing herself as she picks out the colors she's going to use. She's a perfectionist when it comes to her designs, planning everything out beforehand. And when she's working, nothing distracts her—not the girl sitting on her right picking her nose, or the boy to her left who's having a hard day and starts to cry when his paper rips. Watching Madison makes Jillian remember that same spark she used to have all the way up through high school (until she met Lawrence, really).

Not that he was to blame for her stopping. Life just changed. That's all.

Book 21: 2010

...There is the heat of Love, the pulsing rush of Longing, the lover's whisper, irresistible—
magic to make the sanest man go mad.
~Homer

The Toyota skids on a patch of ice and slides toward a tree on the side of the road. I correct it, but I'm shaken. If I run off the road and get stuck, I'll be a popsicle by the time anyone finds me. *A chilly Jilly*, I think, cracking myself up for a fraction of a second before a massive creature steps out onto another patch of ice about fifty yards ahead. Gasping, I slam my foot down on the brake pedal. In response, the car once again slides crazily sideways for a couple of eternal seconds before correcting itself and then rolling to a stop. The enormous white-tailed buck stands there, calmly resplendent in the glow of the headlights, staring at me as if to say, *Dude, slow down.*

I'm not too surprised to find the studio completely dark when I pull up in front of it and shut off the car; Gunnar doesn't like driving all the way from his place on the wintery Interstate at night, and I haven't seen Bodhi since he walked in on me and Gunnar doing exactly nothing on the futon. I shake my head at the memory.

"I'm so sorry, man!" Gunnar had cried, leaping to his feet as his best friend stood in the doorway staring at the two of us. In the process, Gunnar ripped the blanket off of me completely, wrapping it around himself like some sort of Garment of Shame.

"You're not naked," I reminded him.

But Gunnar didn't seem to hear. "We slept together," he blurted at Bodhi, turning to point an accusing finger my way. "I mean, *next* to each other. But nothing happened, I swear!"

"No," Bodhi said, not looking at either of us by that point. "I mean, it's fine. I wish you guys lots of happiness. I guess." He rubbed both hands up his face and let out a long, whispered groan: "Damn."

And that was when I'd had enough. "For crying out loud," I muttered, getting up from the futon to clean up my workspace and then hit the road. Clearly, it was going to take a while for them to iron out the misunderstanding. Bodhi wouldn't look at me as I cleaned, and I haven't seen hide nor hair of him in the two days since. Neither of them said I'm no longer welcome here at the studio anymore, though, so I'm going to just assume the whole thing will eventually blow over. If that's cold-hearted of me, so be it. I've had enough of all the drama.

It's a little spooky being all alone way out in the middle of nowhere at night without Bodhi working on his sketches, or Gunnar sawing and hammering at his workbench, or Hadley getting in my face with a video camera. I'm intent on finishing this piece, though, so I tromp up the walkway in my snow boots, open the studio door, and step inside where my breath continues to plume in the frigid air. I've gotten pretty good at building a fire, thanks to Hadley's teaching; before long, a few logs are crackling inside the big woodstove as I unpack the provisions I brought with me—a hunk of goat cheese, some crackers, a bar of dark chocolate, and a gallon of ice-cold water. I'm anticipating a long night.

I head for the boom box first and pop open the lid of the CD changer. Marvin Gaye's in there, along with Roberta Flack and some others. If Gunnar had an Aaron Tippin or Bellamy Brothers CD lying around here somewhere, I'd pop that one in, too. I'd do it in memory of what happened yesterday. I was in the hardware store, picking up some extra-strength epoxy, when I spotted him: Herman, my almost-one-night stand from the Zoo. He was near the register, paying for his own stuff, and I froze, unsure of what to do next. I probably should have just spun around like one of those reining horses on the TV above the bar at the Zoo and walked fast in the other direction, but that felt too extreme. As Herman slid his wallet into the back pocket of his Wranglers, I did a quick calculation in my head: *It's been about four months since that ill-fated night,* I thought. *Maybe he won't recognize me.* As if in response, Herman turned from the counter, his eyes immediately locking onto mine. Smiling that meltingly slow drawl of a smile, he touched the brim of his cowboy hat and winked before making another quarter-turn toward the entrance and leaving the store.

Shaking my head and grinning a little now, I close the plastic hatch on top of the boom box and press play. Roberta Flack sings about being killed softly as I drag the cardboard box of ceramic fragments I've been storing in a corner of the studio over to where my work-in-progress hangs from its chain. Pieces of my broken wedding china are in that box along with pieces of my mother's broken coffee mug from more than a quarter century ago. My vision for the piece is finally crystal clear now: I want to see snow collecting on this sculpture when it's done. Rain dripping from it during a monsoon downpour. Hence, the epoxy from the hardware store, which is much more suitable for outdoor-type pieces than the non-toxic adhesive I'd otherwise prefer to use. With the temperature in the studio getting more comfortable, I open the big nearby window to get some fresh air circulating. Then I put on a ventilator mask and safety goggles and get to work.

I've decided to just do mosaic accents, rather than trying to mosaic the entire piece. For one thing, the metal isn't really a thick enough gauge to handle the weight of all that ceramic and grout. Also, I like the look of the reclaimed steel—world-weary and full of dents and dings, full of character. I work quickly at first, affixing fragments of various sizes and colors to the steel wherever I feel like they belong. After a while, though, as the pattern starts to solidify, I'm more careful about the pieces I choose, sometimes trimming them to precise shapes and sizes with my nippers before epoxying them into place. I need to be sure they're all firmly attached so they'll survive not just weather but also the grouting process, when I'll work that wet, gritty substance into all the crevices before sponging it off and clearing the haze.

It's so good to be immersed in a project like this, not running from anything, and not clinging too tightly to anything, either; not going anywhere and not in any kind of a hurry. At one point, I glance up at the wall clock and see that two hours have passed since I got started. I haven't so much as touched the food I brought yet. I am thirsty, though, so I gulp some water from the plastic jug, using the back of my wrist to wipe away the drips escaping down my chin. I'm standing thusly near the boom box table, eyes closed and head back, doing a little blissful sway as Bryan Ferry sings to me about the sea on the tide having no way of turning.

I don't hear the door open. I only know someone is there by the gust of air pushing into the studio and stroking a little icy tendril across the nape of my neck. Opening my eyes in surprise, I see Bodhi standing just inside the doorway.

"Gunnar told me about what happened—or rather, what didn't happen—between you and your husband," he says. His five o'clock shadow and windswept hair make him look a little wilder than usual, a little more raw.

"My ex," I correct him, setting the water jug on the table and walking over to the boom box to turn down the music.

"Yeah. Apparently, I...misinterpreted something I saw."

"You thought Lawrence and I were back together."

"I did," Bodhi says, his eyes meeting mine.

A trickle of sweat travels down between my breasts, raising goosebumps on the exposed skin north of the tank top's neckline. It occurs to me that I never put on a bra before leaving Hadley's; I cross my arms over my chest as I walk to where he's standing. "And then you thought Gunnar and I were actually...I mean, *really*?"

Bodhi runs his fingers through his hair and winces. "Yeah. I'm pretty embarrassed about that, too."

"Well, just so you know," I tell him, the words tumbling unexpectedly from my mouth. "I don't consider you my placeholder guy. At least, not that I'm aware of. Maybe subconsciously..."

"Your what?" Bodhi looks utterly confused.

I shake my head. "Never mind. It's just..." I look at him, wondering whether or not I should say the next thing. "The lady who did my hair a while back told me about this thing women my age apparently do where we put old flames on pedestals or something."

"Sounds very Olympic Games." He's smiling now.

"Men do it, too, you know."

"You think that's what I'm doing? Putting you on a pedestal?"

I shrug.

"I don't have to," Bodhi says. "You never came down from the one you were on when I first met you."

Now I can't even look him in the eye. It's too personal, this thing he's saying. Too naked.

"I know that sounds ridiculous, like you're being worshipped or something."

"It does, a little." I'm staring at the floor, considering what to do next. It's been so long since I felt the endorphin-fueled fireworks that are currently detonating in the space between my hips and heart.

"I know you don't want that," he's saying. "Hell, *I* don't want that. But what am I supposed to do, Jill? You've always been..." He reaches high above his head with one hand. "Up here. As far as I'm concerned, nobody else even comes close.

But that said, I don't want you to think that I, you know, expect anything, either." He's stammering a little now. "You have a lot on your plate, and I have so much respect—"

And that's when I take a step forward and kiss him.

Bodhi kisses back. The feel of his lips, the smell of his skin, are familiar, like an old photograph, or song, or candy that you haven't tasted since childhood. But there are unfamiliar layers now, too; maybe it really is true what they say about certain men aging like fine wine.

I don't know how much time has passed when we reach the point of escalation where we're all lips and hands and chests and bellies pressed against each other, our clothing tangled as it's removed and discarded. We stumble backward and sideways toward the futon together like some love-struck Hydra, that mythical, multi-headed beast I first learned about in Professor Xenakis's class.

At one point, poised above me, Bodhi pauses. "Did you hear that?"

"What?" I ask, pulling him down so I can find his lips again, the most feral, secret part of myself still, apparently, alive.

"Thunder snow," he murmurs as my hands travel down his back, thumbs hooking into the elastic waistband of his boxers. I raise my hips, and he helps rid me of my undergarments as well, the two of us giggling at our mutual contortions. When the last layer of clothing between us is finally gone, we find our way to a more perfect union, a completely interlocked position. It's almost overwhelming, the insistent hardness of him introducing itself into the place where there has only been my own softness for far too long.

It occurs to me that the sheepherder Cabin where we first did this decades ago, where I spotted the blue feather that's once again looming large and vivid in my imagination, is literally yards away right now. The feel of Bodhi inside me, expanding the most secret place the way he first did so long ago, brings me to the edge of a wildness that I've all but forgotten over the years. And then there is no more thought, only wave upon wave of pulsating warmth contracting and expanding, engulfing me completely as it spreads out from my center in every direction.

I wake up the next morning before it's fully light outside. Carefully extricating myself from the blanket, I slide off the futon, pull on my clothes, and tiptoe as quietly as possible across the studio floor so I won't wake him. Looking through the window, I can see fresh powder on the pine boughs outside. The storm has moved on though; the sky is a clear, cloudless blue. Moments later, I'm stirring still-glowing embers in the woodstove with an iron poker, preparing to add kindling and a wedge of aspen, when I hear Bodhi's voice behind me.

"I know you probably don't want anyone seeing it yet," he says from the futon. "It's been sitting here draped in that drop cloth every time I come in. I've been tempted to peek, but I've been good. I promise."

"It's okay," I tell him. "It's not exactly where it needs to be yet, but I think I'm ready for a critique." Putting on my shoes so my feet don't get cut by smalti shards, I walk over to the sculpture. "It probably still needs a lot of work," I say, chewing at a fingernail.

After pulling on his jeans and his shoes (but, thankfully, not his T-shirt), Bodhi comes over and circles the piece slowly. He's all business now. "I don't think so, actually," he says, squinting. "But, I mean, you're the artist."

I'm having a little trouble focusing on what he's saying, distracted as I am by the bunny trail of hair leading from his navel down to the top button of his jeans.

"Have you thought about whether it would be more suitable for an indoor or outdoor installation?"

"Huh? Oh, yeah. I have, actually. I want to see it outside. Somewhere in changing light, changing seasons. Does that make sense?"

Bodhi nods. "Go on."

"Okay," I say, taking a deep breath. "I imagine it covered with snow, dripping with rain, cradling fall leaves. Just definitely outside. Unless someone has a room in their house huge enough to house this beast. The adhesive can go either way, and it will just be stronger when it's grouted and sealed." I stop talking and shake my head. Looking down at the ground, I feel myself blushing once again; somehow, I'm managing to sound sappy *and* arrogant. "Not that anyone would actually buy it."

"Don't be so sure," Bodhi says. "I'm guessing I could call up half a dozen dealers right now who'd want it in their galleries."

"That's very kind of you to say."

"Kindness has nothing to do with it. It's good, Jill. Even in this unfinished state. And it's okay for you to acknowledge that."

"Okay, then," I say, looking him in the eye and taking another breath. "I guess I still have to practice just saying 'thank you.'"

Bodhi smiles. "You're welcome," he says, holding my gaze. "Now please tell me how it's possible to be away from art all these years without missing a beat."

"Okay, *now* you're being kind."

"Maybe a little bit. But seriously, if anything, the dormancy has served you well. I mean, let's face it: You know what you're doing, which isn't a surprise to me, of course. But, apparently, it's no big deal for you to do the hard work of pulling up this old knowledge and skill from the past. And that's no small thing. Are you documenting this process?"

The question makes me squirm. "Well, Hadley's been taking videos of me every once in a while, which seems kind of silly..."

"I think it's a good idea," he says. "Maybe just go with it. In fact, I have another idea. What if I list the piece on my company's website when it's done? See if we can get any nibbles?"

I don't say anything.

"I can maybe post a few of Hadley's video clips, too. People enjoy seeing what artists are up to, what their processes are like."

"My work is nowhere near good enough for that," I say quietly.

"It's a business proposal. How about we let the market decide? My clients know what they want. They're looking for interesting new work all the time." He pauses. "I mean, you'll have to do something for me in return, of course."

My back stiffens as Lawrence's voice from just after I gave birth to Evan reaches across the decades: *I'll get my pound of flesh.* "I'm not sure I'm at all comfortable with where this is headed," I tell Bodhi.

"Suit yourself," he says with a shrug, not reacting to the sudden chill in my voice. "I was only going to say I'd like to have a shot at listing your next piece. But if you'd rather go with someone else, I totally understand. Just bear in mind that other brokers probably won't want to list your stuff commission-free, but you do whatever works for you."

I frown at him, still suspicious. "So, you're an art dealer now?"

He shrugs and smiles, clearly hoping I'll loosen up and play along. "Sure, why not?"

"Okay," I tell him. "But why are you so interested in helping me? What have I ever done for you?"

Bodhi's smile falters. "Are you being serious? Jill, you gave me some of the happiest memories of my life. You gave me hope when I really needed it, whether that was obvious at the time or not. And I don't even care how cheesy that sounds. I was the new kid, transplanted without much warning to a strange place and a strange school where most kids had known each other since kindergarten. I've honestly been waiting half my life for a chance to repay you for that."

Silence stretches out between us for several seconds. "Some businessman you are," I finally say, taking a step toward him until we're breathing each other's air again.

Book 22: 2009

Life passes by in such an overwhelming blur. Sometimes, like now, so many feelings swirl around inside her all at once that Jillian doesn't quite know what to do with them. Crying things out used to work when she was younger, but she has to be careful about doing that now. As silly as it sounds, something tells her that once she starts she might not be able to stop.

Baking is always an option. The fall faculty banquet's coming up soon though, and she's already planning to make wine-soaked dates and a walnut cake in the not-too-distant future. Best not to overindulge beforehand.

That leaves cleaning. Fetching the broom from its hook in the garage, Jillian thinks about how everything has come down to this moment. Her only child is leaving home in less than twenty-four hours, and the idea of Evan no longer residing within the invisible bubble of protection she's painstakingly constructed during the past eighteen years, is...well, it's unthinkable, frankly.

Still, Jillian thinks as she sweeps crumbs from the corners of the kitchen floor, it's her job to help him fledge the nest. And help him she will. She has to believe that all the time spent teaching him how to iron a dress shirt, how to do a load of laundry, and how to cook a basic meal like spaghetti and meatballs will pay off once he's on his own. At times during the past year or so, Evan has seemed so ready to go, it wasn't funny. But his bravado was inconsistent; prickly and annoyed one moment, he'd soon need help with college applications or grow suddenly despondent about leaving his girlfriend.

Jillian sweeps the tidy pile of kitchen dirt into the dustpan. Between the enmeshment with Tabitha and Evan's job busing tables at a fancy restaurant in Old Town Scottsdale, he'd sometimes disappear for days. Other times, he and his friends would come in late after a party; Jillian would wake in the morning to find four or five almost-men sacked out in the living room. Right after graduation, he apparently couldn't stand the sight of Jillian and Lawrence. Then, toward the middle of summer, he wanted to be around them more. Lately, he's been shadowing Jillian when she least expects it; she'll turn around in the kitchen and almost run right into him.

Returning the broom to its hook and grabbing the mop, Jillian considers Lawrence's reaction to all of this. Men go through their own empty nest grief process, too, or so she's heard. As Evan's entered adulthood, he and his father haven't always seen eye to eye. Evan wants to major in something artistic yet practical, something like Architecture, which Lawrence sees as a lesser academic pursuit. For the past several months, Jillian has grown accustomed to bracing herself for their tense conversations at the dinner table.

After running the mop head under the kitchen faucet and wringing out the excess water, she sets to work on the freshly swept floor. Once Evan's gone, she knows it will take some time for Lawrence to get used to being the only man of the house again. She knows this the way she knew her husband was wearing a new cologne the other day when they passed each other in the hallway. The scent of lime juice drizzled over warm forest moss surprised her no less than if she'd turned to discover the back of a stranger receding into the guest room.

Mentioning the cologne would have been unthinkable, of course. It's always such a careful dance they do lately, a hesitant choreography of words and movement whenever they're in the same room together (which, admittedly, isn't often; most nights, Lawrence sleeps in the guest room or on the couch in his home office). Sometimes, she hears the notifications from his cell phone going off into the wee hours of the morning.

A sweaty strand of Jillian's hair comes loose from the barrette holding it back as she scrubs at a particularly stubborn stain on the kitchen tile. Panting a little at the effort, she tucks the strand behind her ear. They haven't been intimate in months. And it's not for lack of trying on her part, this nonexistent sex life. Lately, feeling a tad desperate, she's taken things to the next level by looking up "intimacy enhancers" online. A quick internet search yielded thousands of results—tinctures and lubricants, feathered and leathered devices, silk sashes for temporarily binding and blinding. She found something called the Honey Badger, another called the Mechanical Bull. And that's when she'd closed the browser. Thank goodness she and Lawrence don't believe in divorce; otherwise, she'd probably end up actually placing an order to save her marriage—not that it needs saving, of course. Not exactly. She's pretty sure it's common for novice empty nesters to experience bumps in the road. She makes a mental note to pick up a book about it this week, *Empty Nesting for Dummies,* or something like that. Because, more than ever now, the most important thing is her marriage to Lawrence. Longsuffering Lawrence, who has put up with her focused mothering of Evan for the past eighteen years with hardly a complaint. Jillian wrings the mop hard, several times, before returning it to the garage.

Heading for the hallway closet where they keep the vacuum cleaner, she wonders if they shouldn't think about going on a trip somewhere together, just the two of them. When she was newly pregnant, they'd talked about honeymooning in Athens, but at the last minute his teaching schedule wouldn't allow it. Then the baby came before the ink on their marriage license was even dry, and...well. Every parent knows how the rest goes.

But big deal. So she didn't have a honeymoon at nineteen. *No time like the present,* she thinks as she navigates the vacuum back and forth, and back and forth, leaving neatly symmetrical lines in the living room carpet. Jillian daydreams about what she might wear if they decided to go someplace tropical, like Hawaii. Something strapless, probably, with a revealing slit going up one leg. True, she'll be forty in a few months, but it's not like she's an unattractive woman—not as far as she knows, anyway. A little on the plain side, perhaps, but that's always been the case.

Leaving a precise, fan-shaped vacuum pattern in the carpet by the entrance to the dining room, Jillian thinks of what

Lawrence told her when they first got together, that it was important to pay attention to her appearance. Her roots need a touch-up, as do her brows and nails.

Not all of the faculty wives are beauty obsessed, of course. There are the Arts College wives, for example, with their free-flowing clothes, simple shoes, and minimal makeup. *The Patchouli Hags,* Lawrence calls them. Jillian unplugs the vacuum cord and coils it tightly in place around the neck of the appliance. She can't help but wonder how Lawrence would react if he came home one evening to find her in a pair of the old denim overalls she wore nearly every day before they met. She recalls her own disdain for makeup and fancy clothes back then, as a high school senior, when she dreamed of running away to art school with the love of her life. She gives her head a quick shake: Ruminating on the past isn't going to help anything.

Still, Jillian admits to herself as she returns the vacuum to the hall closet and grabs the blue feather duster from under the sink, sometimes things overwhelm her lately—little things, tiny ones, hardly worth mentioning. Recently, for instance, Lawrence left one of his social media accounts open on her computer, which he'd been borrowing while his own was being repaired. Not thinking anything of it, Jillian was about to open a new window when the top line of the chat conversation he'd been having caught her eye.

ProfKens: *You look so sexy in that pic.*
He typed another message below it:
ProfKens: *I'm a bad boy, aren't I?*
followed by

ProfKens: *Do you ever get tired of being so beautiful?*

The third time must have been the charm: He was rewarded with a picture of bare breasts from someone named *ClassicBooty*.

"My God," he said, clearly disgusted when Jillian confronted him that evening. "Are you going to have a nervous breakdown every time I talk to another woman?"

"I—" She couldn't say anything more. She was shaking too hard.

"Because I'm fairly sure there's a pill or something you could take." His voice was exasperation-soaked.

Having dusted the bookshelf in the living room, Jillian moves to the entry hall. A crack of monsoon thunder sends a shudder through her as she sweeps the blue feathers of the duster toward the base of the bronze eagle statue Lawrence has always prized so highly.

It's the talons that stop her in her tracks.

Book 23: 2010

Now I am making an end of my anger. It does not become me, unrelentingly to rage on.

~Homer

The bank teller, a young woman with purple nail polish, swivels the monitor toward me so I can see the error message for myself:

ACCOUNT CONTAINS INSUFFICIENT FUNDS TO COMPLETE TRANSACTION

I stare at the screen. I'd only stopped at this branch at the edge of town to withdraw a few twenties on my way to Prescott. Dad and Helen invited me down for the weekend a couple of days ago; the idea of a getaway to somewhere a few thousand feet lower and a dozen degrees warmer than Flagstaff sounded immediately appealing.

Someone in line behind me coughs.

"It's *all* gone?" I ask, incredulous. "The money I made subbing, too?"

The teller maintains a professionally bland expression despite how completely untethered I must look and sound at that moment. "There's a remaining balance of $36.84," she says, turning the screen back toward herself.

Thunderstruck, I place my hands on the counter and blow a lungful of air through my cheeks. "He can't do this," I say, my voice full of a detached sort of wonder as the teller bites her lip and gives an awkward shrug.

"You can't do this, Lawrence," I yell into my cell phone twenty minutes later. I'm pacing back and forth in the A-frame's kitchen, trying to remind myself to breathe as Hadley stands in a corner of the kitchen watching my side of the conversation unfold. "You can't just take the money I earned. It was at least three-thousand dollars."

"I'm protecting both of us," he says in the voice I used to consider patient. Now it just sounds condescending. Malevolent. "I can give you a weekly allowance until things get sorted out."

"An *allowance*?" A white-hot fireball of rage courses through me like a fast-moving kidney stone. I start to tell him what he can do with his allowance, but then I think better of it and simply hang up on him instead. Turning to Hadley, who looks like she wants to sort out Lawrence's face right about now, I let out a little laugh. "This is ridiculous," I tell her, my voice full of something like wonder. "I need to contact the school district down in the Valley and get back on their call list. I have to get a job."

"Or not," Hadley says.

We're standing in the middle of her living room, next to the Christmas tree we cut in the forest a few weeks ago. She'd had her permit since just before Thanksgiving, so we headed out to the assigned cutting area near Williams. She brought a couple of vintage plaid-patterned thermoses full of hot cider, and I steadied the tree we chose, breathing in the suddenly pine sap-drenched air as Hadley's chainsaw snarled through the trunk.

"What did you say?"

Hadley's standing very still. "I said 'or not.' As in, you don't necessarily have to get a job."

A bitter laugh escapes me. "Yeah, right. I've already been here for four months, Hads. I can't just inhabit your travel trailer indefinitely. I need to get a life. And that means I need to get a stable job, and probably a lawyer." Dropping my forehead into the crook of my thumb and index finger, I debate whether or not to call Dad and cancel the overnight trip. I'd planned to already be halfway to Prescott by now to avoid the worst of the afternoon commuter traffic. "What an idiot I was to think Lawrence and I could do any of this in a civil way."

"You know what?" Hadley says. "On second thought, let's not even think about this right now. It's all going to work out. I promise. I'm sure you'll get alimony and—"

"I don't want alimony."

"You've been married for nearly twenty years, Jill. It's not okay for you to end up with nothing."

"Twenty years," I repeat, looking off at some nonexistent horizon. "I should have left sooner. I've wasted my entire adult life. How stupid am I?"

"Hey, let's not go there again, okay? And don't be too hard on yourself. Growing a set of balls takes time."

But it's impossible for me to not go there. "What am I going to do? Where am I going to live? I mean, he can't just *do* this…can he?"

"That, my dear, would be a question for said attorney. But as far as where you're going to live, I may just have an answer for that one."

I look at her and then down at her hand, which I only now realize is holding something. It's an envelope. "What have you got there?"

"Promise you won't get mad." She looks sheepish (or expectant, or guilty—I'm not quite sure which). "There's something I've been meaning to tell you. I've been waiting for the right time, and…well, I think this might be it."

I squint at her. "What did you do?"

Hadley hands me the envelope.

"What is this?"

"It's world renowned," she says, the words tumbling out in a rush. "They do classes and workshops for poor people, rich people, kids, veterans. Just ask Gunnar."

I open the letter and read it. It's an official scholarship offer from the artist colony in Taos, the one where Gunnar had his involuntary art therapy experience.

"It's not a huge amount," Hadley continues as my eyes scan the page, "but it's enough for now. It's money you can live on while you make your amazing art. Eventually, you can get hired there to teach. You're so good at both." Her voice drops off. "You're mad, aren't you."

I look up from the letter. "I can't believe you did this behind my back without consulting me. It's like you think I'm an invalid or something."

"Jill," Hadley says after a long pause. Her voice is strangely calm now. "It's okay to let people help you sometimes. It's okay to need your friends."

"I have to get down to Prescott," I say, tossing the letter onto the kitchen table. "Helen's going to be pissed if I don't show up for dinner on time."

"We're birders now," Dad announces when he opens the door and sees me standing there on his porch with my overnight bag. A massive pair of binoculars hangs from a thick strap around his too-thin neck. He looks frailer than the last time I saw him, which was at Evan's high school graduation in June, seven months ago. It seems ridiculous to go that long without visiting, especially since Prescott is only about an hour and a half from both Phoenix and Flagstaff. But Helen, who never had kids of her own, is a total mother hen with my dad. She probably didn't want him any more involved in my drama than he had to be. Which hurts, but I also get it. I could easily resent her, and maybe I would have a year ago. But Dad adores Helen; the truth is she's just what he's needed his whole life, someone to take care of him. And I know he's done his best to be supportive of me in his own way, from afar, these past four months.

They take me to one of the lakes in the area with willow trees on one side and massive, primordial looking boulders on the other. A group of senior citizens in bright yellow kayaks glides across the surface of the water, laughing and hollering back and forth to each other.

"Oh, honey, look!" Helen whispers, grabbing Dad's arm. It takes me several seconds to see what she's pointing at.

When I do see it, I gasp. It's a bald eagle perched on a nest. Helen has already brought her binoculars to her face to get a closer look. "Here," Dad whispers, handing me his pair.

I hold them up to my eyes and start scanning the trees until I locate the raptor. She's nothing like the terrifying bronze statue outside Lawrence's office at the Scottsdale house. Instead, she looks calm but fiercely proud and protective, ever watchful, her beak slightly open as if she's panting a little or tasting the air. She looks certain of her place in the world.

That night, after I've brushed my teeth and washed my face in Dad and Helen's guest bathroom, I flip open my phone and see that I have a new voicemail. It's from Gunnar. *Hadley came by the studio,* his voice says. *She told me what was going on with you two. Look, it was my idea. The whole thing. Applying to the colony in Taos. I'm an idiot, okay? I thought you sounded, I don't know, inspired by it or something that night we spent in the studio drinking beer and definitely not having sex. So, forget about the colony. But you do know you'd be a fool to let that friendship go, right, Jill? I mean, seriously, I don't even frickin' know what you're so pissed off about at this point. I do know that it's time for you to buckle down and man up, or whatever. Hell, I don't know. Just...don't do the kind of stupid stuff I did. Don't burn all those bridges. 'Cause once you do, I'm pretty sure you're gonna find that most of them can't be rebuilt. The chasms have grown too wide, or...shit. I'm no good at this touchy-feely stuff. Just...try not to be a total asshole, okay?*

The second notification, the one that makes me sit down on the edge of the bed, is from the school district down in

Scottsdale. They have an immediate opening for office support staff at one of the middle schools, and they're wondering if I'd be interested.

Saving the message, I let out a sigh. I know what "office support staff" means at this particular school (and at pretty much all public schools in the Valley). It means filing. Answering the phone. Typing name tags for student folders on the ancient, cantankerous Selectric typewriter that seems to be a required fixture in every school's front office. Nothing exciting or inspiring—psychologically deadening, even—but it's a job I'm qualified for. It's money.

The next morning at breakfast, Dad looks at me over the top of his reading glasses as he butters an English muffin. Helen's still in their bedroom getting ready for the day. "So, what's next for you, my girl?"

My eyes tear up without warning. It's been so long since he's called me that. "I don't know exactly," I tell him. "My friends have concocted a harebrained scheme to ship me off to the mountains of New Mexico. There's apparently this crazy artists colony they think I should teach for."

His eyebrows go up. "Sounds perfect for you."

"Why? Because of the 'crazy" part?"

My father smiles, but he looks concerned, too.

"The time's not right," I tell him, my voice glum. "Maybe someday. Anyway, the school district I used to work for just called a while ago. They want to hire me."

"Is that what you want to do?"

I shrug. "It's probably what I *should* do."

"How come?"

"Because it's what I'm qualified for."

"Hmm," Dad says after a while. "Well, I don't know about that, but I do know it's about time you did something just for you."

"What do you mean?"

He hesitates for several long seconds. "You've always put other people before yourself," he says finally. "Just look at Lawrence and Evan. Hell, look how you took care of me when you were a kid."

I'm so shocked to hear him voice this thought for the first time in my entire life that I start to protest.

"Now don't argue with me," he insists. "I was a grown man, for crissakes."

I don't know what to say. I think of all the mornings I spent cooking breakfast for him as he wandered around the house in his bathrobe, both of us stricken by Mom's too-frequent absence. Something about leaping into action by making French toast or flipping eggs took away the sting of her choosing her work over us. Dad and I have never really talked openly about those days. There were always too many excuses not to, things that stole the spotlight—me going away to college, my break-up with Bodhi, the start of Dad's dating life, his marriage, my marriage, Evan's birth.

"Evan's on his way with his own life," my father continues. "And Lawrence...well, who the hell cares about him anymore? Like I said, it's time for you to put yourself first for a change."

I stare at my father in a sort of wonderment.

"The world," he says as Helen takes his plate, "won't stop spinning if you do."

When I get back to Hadley's, I decide to sneak into the Ovum to give myself a little more time to figure out what I'm going to say to her. I didn't exactly leave here on the most solid footing yesterday, but staying overnight in Prescott gave me a chance to figure out once and for all what I need to do.

My friends have been like scaffolding around me, like a sort of protective shell, for these past four months I've been on the mountain. But here's the thing: I've been living from the damaged parts of myself for practically my entire adult life, and I refuse to just keep doing that indefinitely. I have to do something useful. I have to go, even if I'm not looking forward to it. I need to figure out what it means to stand on my own. It's time to pull myself up by the bootstraps, force myself into some kind of productive forward momentum. At some point in the future, I can get back to my art. For now, there are more practical matters to attend to—legal negotiations with Lawrence, for starters, and at least one court date. After that, there will be more stuff to deal with. There always is. But for now, for this moment in my life, I have to be smart. I have to be practical. And the jobs I'm qualified for—jobs like subbing and office support—are way more plentiful down in the Valley than they are here on the mountain.

"Are you still mad?" a voice asks as I reach for the door of the Ovum. I turn to see Hadley sitting on the back porch step in her Carhartt overalls, scratching Finster the goat behind his ears with her gloved hands.

"No," I tell her, turning to walk over the snow-encrusted path to the porch. "I never really was. Taken aback, yes. But I'm not mad. It's just...There's no way I can go to that art colony, Hads."

"Why not? You were given that scholarship because your work is seriously good. And I'm pretty sure you'll be offered a teaching position before too long for the same reason."

"You do know that I got through just one year of college before dropping out, right?"

"I know that," Hadley says. "Which is why I also knew you'd never apply on your own."

"Subbing for a few months will pay almost as well," I tell her. "And I have to think long-term. I have connections down in the Valley."

"Connections, huh?"

"Yeah."

Hadley looks unimpressed. "I think you're just scared."

"Maybe. But it's not practical for me to pull up stakes and move to New Mexico. It's not a good time."

"It's never a good time. And New Mexico's right next door. You saw the part where room and board is included for the year, right?"

"But Evan, he's…"

"Evan's fine. He's a man now, Jill."

"You sound like my dad."

Hadley shrugs. "You have nothing keeping you in Arizona, nothing you need to tend to on a daily basis anymore. Except yourself, of course."

"That's harsh," I say. "It sounds so sad."

"Okay, I hear you. But if you look at it another way, it's pretty freeing, too. Right?"

"But what if…" My voice falters, and I look down.

Hadley watches me without saying anything further.

I take a deep breath, hesitant to voice the next thing. "What if I don't want freedom?"

She crosses her arms over her chest and frowns. "In that case, Jacobs, I suppose you should go rob a bank. That way, you'll be guaranteed three square meals a day *and* a place to sleep. Maybe even a spouse."

"Hads—"

"Oh, but you've already had that," she says. "Haven't you."

It's my turn to not respond.

"And was it really all that great?"

I look away from her. "Truth? It was what I knew. It was familiar."

Panting as if suddenly overheated, Hadley fans herself with one hand. "Sounds scintillating," she moans. "Seriously, stop. You're making me so hot."

My hands are on my hips now. "You realize you're being a bully, right? Why are you pushing me about this?"

"Because," Hadley says, clearly no longer joking, "I'm your best friend. And whether you like it or not, sometimes I actually know what's best for you.

Book 24: 2010

What you leave behind is not what is engraved in stone monuments, but what is woven into the lives of others.

~Pericles

"I have a buyer," Bodhi says, rushing into the studio without warning.

I've stopped by to gather up any odds and ends I might have left here. I wasn't expecting to see him until this evening. He and Gunnar are supposed to come over to the A-frame for the birthday-slash-goodbye party Hadley insists on throwing before I move down to Phoenix tomorrow. With any luck, I'll only be in the extended stay hotel for about a week as I shop for a cheap one-room apartment. Bodhi coming in so suddenly startles me; I just stand there stunned. "What did you say?"

"You told me I could list the chrysalis on my website," he answers. "So, I did. It got an offer today."

My mouth drops open. "But how? Who?"

"A physical therapy center in Denver. Chrysalis Health. The director said, and I quote, 'I can't imagine a more perfect piece for our courtyard.'"

I just stare at him in astonishment. "But don't they want to see it in person? Make sure it's not, you know, a piece of junk?"

"Nope."

"But what if they don't like it once they *do* see it in person?"

"The photos and video are high quality," he says. "And the description is thorough. Look, I've been working with these people for a long time. Trust me, it's exactly what they want."

"I hope they didn't offer too much."

"Ninety-five hundred. And it's a bargain."

"Ninety-five hundred…*dollars*?"

"Nope," he says with a wink. "M&Ms. I told them they all had to be green ones though."

I aim a playful swat at him.

"Yes, dollars. Honestly, if you were a bigger name in the art world, I could have gotten more. But that'll come."

I shake my head. "I can't believe it."

Bodhi frowns as if he hasn't heard me. "I do wonder if we should have maybe held out for a higher offer. Then again, I like the exposure this piece will get. Everyone who walks through their courtyard will see it—therapists, patients, visitors. The director is completely psyched, but of course it's your decision either way. The bigwig art brokers are going to be fighting over you in no time."

"You have a lot more confidence in me than I do," I tell him.

Bodhi puts his hands on the sides of my arms and looks into my eyes. At first, I think he's going to kiss me, and I'm suddenly not so sure that's a good idea: I know for a fact I'm falling for him again and falling hard. I also know it wouldn't be fair for him to be tied down to someone who's going to live in the Phoenix area, more than two hours away from here. I have a lot to think about. We both do. I watch his face as it comes close, but he doesn't kiss me. "I think you're forgetting something," he says instead.

Predictably, my knees feel like they're going to buckle, even now, from the proximity, heat, and beauty of him. "What's that?"

"You're forgetting that you're basically Elektra Woman and Dyna Girl rolled into one."

The second he says it, I'm back on a snowy mountain, trying to find balance on the cusp of the unknown—exhilarated and terrified about what's to come once I commit to moving forward. "Don't forget the dash of She-Ra," I whisper.

Our words are still tumbling around in my head like stones in a polishing machine the next afternoon, on my fortieth birthday, as I drive out of Flagstaff. I'm also thinking about the chocolate cake Hadley set on the kitchen table last night after Bodhi and Gunnar showed up and how the three of them sang to me before I blew out the candles.

A blue and red I-40 sign flashes by on the side of the road like some sort of greeting card from the Department of Transportation. Then the big interchange sign comes into view about half a mile up ahead. That's where I'll turn south to merge onto I-17 toward Phoenix, while I-40 continues east toward Albuquerque. The last thing Hadley said to me before I got into my car and shut the door ten minutes ago rises up in my mind: *You have until five o'clock today to tell the colony if you're coming or not. After that, they give your scholarship to someone else.*

I check the Toyota's dashboard clock: It's 3:32. I need to stop for gas. Allowing myself to slip into fantasy mode for a minute (because, really, why the hell not?), I think about the impossible possibilities. I could make the call while the tank fills. Albuquerque's an easy five-hour drive from here, depending on traffic—a straight shot. From there it's just an hour's drive into the mountains of Santa Fe and then another hour or so to Taos, the land of Georgia O'Keeffe, patroness saint of flowers and skulls, life and death. If I play my cards right, I could be at the art colony just after midnight.

A trucker passing me in the left lane taps his air horn. Flustered, I shake the fantasy from my head. I need to stop *dreamdriving*. Taos is an absurd idea—a lovely one, but absurd, nevertheless.

The interchange sign is closer now, only about a quarter of a mile away. The fingers of my left hand stretch forward to flick the turn signal upward, alerting drivers behind me that I will, indeed, be taking the off-ramp toward Phoenix. I don't signal though. Not yet.

Because what's to stop me from doing the unexpected? People have done crazier things, right? *I've* done crazier things, back when I was less afraid. Back when I was...me.

All this back and forth is ridiculous. Fantasizing is fun, but actually running off to an art colony in the mountains of New Mexico would just be...irresponsible...or something. I mean, could there *be* a more classic midlife cliché?

The fork in the road, is only about an eighth of a mile away. Ponderosa pines blur past as the speed limit drops from 75 to 65 mph. For a fleeting moment, I wonder if maybe the gods of art, of love, of life, are trying to get me to slow down, to think this through a little more.

But no.

It's high time to get my head screwed on straight and focus on the road. There will be plenty of time to figure out what I want to be when I grow up after I'm established in a secure job somewhere in Phoenix.

The interchange is only a hundred yards ahead now. My fingers reach toward the turn signal lever once again. Flicking it downward and merging into the left lane, I ignore the sign for I-17 as it flashes past in my peripheral vision.

Keeping the Toyota's nose pointed east, toward Albuquerque, I step on the gas.

About the author

Nicole McInnes is also the author of *100 Days* and *Brianna on the Brink*. In her non-writing time, she teaches writing at the MFA level and hosts The Groovy Writer podcast. Connect with her at www.nicolemcinnes.com.

If you enjoyed *The Jilliad,* please consider leaving a review.

www.ingramcontent.com/pod-product-compliance
Lightning Source LLC
LaVergne TN
LVHW041112080826
845145LV00007B/1778

* 9 7 8 1 9 5 7 0 2 7 0 1 2 *